THE
ASSET

ALSO BY MARK DAWSON

MARK DAWSON
THE
ASSET

AN ISABELLA ROSE THRILLER

THOMAS & MERCER

Published by Thomas & Mercer, Seattle
www.apub.com

Amazon, the Amazon logo, and Thomas & Mercer are trademarks of Amazon.com, Inc., or its affiliates.

ISBN-13: 9781503938199
ISBN-10: 1503938190

Cover design by Stuart Bache

Printed in the United States of America

To Mrs D, FD and SD

Prologue
London

The man they called Mohammed sat in his old Ford Transit van and watched. It was two in the morning. The empty farmhouse was set on the edge of the village, with a fifty-foot garden bordering the open fields to the rear. Mohammed had scouted the property the previous week. It was isolated and remote, half a mile from the nearest property. The owner had died six months before, and it was available at a very reasonable rate thanks to the fact that it was directly beneath a flight path of the nearby airport.

Mohammed stepped down from his van and made his way onto the short gravel drive and up to the front door. He took latex gloves, overshoes and a hairnet from his pocket and put them on. He had no intention of leaving any forensic evidence that might be used to prove he had been inside the property. His sponsor had made it very clear that this was to be a completely pristine operation, and it would be. Mohammed understood the reason for that very well. He had been scrupulously careful with what had happened at Westminster, ensuring that there were no threads that could be followed back from the bombers to him. The bomber who had failed and lost his nerve had been shot and his body had been dumped into the river. There were no loose ends there, and there would be none here.

The door was locked, but it was a simple enough thing to pick it. He went inside and waited in the hallway for a moment, just listening. There was nothing, not that he was expecting anything.

The property was modest. The door opened into a small hallway, which, in turn, offered access to a kitchen, dining room, living room and conservatory. Mohammed checked each room, ensuring that there was no one else in the house. He went back outside again, got back into his van and reversed it up the drive. There was a long transport case in the load area. It was five and a half feet long, made from aluminium and painted in forest camouflage. He pulled the case toward him, flipped it onto its side so that he could reach down for the handles and hauled it out. It was heavy. He closed and locked the doors and carried the case into the house.

Mohammed rested the case on the floor of the living room, flipped the clasps and opened it. Nestled within the embrace of hard-form internal cradles was a shoulder-mounted 9K388 Igla-S launcher with a single missile. It was a Russian surface-to-air system, designated by NATO as Grinch. Mohammed had sourced the launcher from the same contact in Chechnya who had provided the shells from which he had harvested the explosives for the Westminster operation. It, together with the shells and the fighters who had stormed the Palace of Westminster, had been smuggled into the country aboard a trawler and then driven to London. Mohammed had used the model before. He had checked this one and was confident that it would operate as he expected; he brushed his fingers against the slender missile and then closed the lid of the case.

He checked his watch: two-thirty.

A few hours to wait.

British Airways flight 117 from London to New York was in the latter stages of its departure preparations. The cabin crew ushered the last stragglers into the big Boeing 747, politely encouraging them to hurry with stowing their bags in the overhead lockers so that the jammed aisles could be cleared. The baggage handlers had finished loading the last of the aluminium luggage containers down below; they were sealing the hold doors and retracting their loading trucks away from the fuselage. The two pilots had settled into the flight deck. The scheduled departure time had already passed. They had been delayed because of the increased security around the airport.

Captain James Wilkes checked the forecast: there was localised low-level mist in the vicinity of the airport, but otherwise it promised to be a clear and smooth flight. Nice and easy.

"Walk round was good," Wilkes said. "Everything where it should be."

His senior first officer, Kaye Hosler, acknowledged that. "We have the loadsheet and performance figures. Fuelling is complete."

Hosler had loaded the pre-planned route into the aircraft's navigation database, including their initial track out of Heathrow. They had been allocated a WOBUN 3F departure. The route had been confirmed to the pilots via a digital message from air traffic control, along with their transponder squawk code: 3762. Hosler busied herself and checked the switches, setting the correct configuration for the aircraft's electrics, the auxiliary power unit, the pressurisation system and the fuel system with its multiple tanks and pumps.

The senior cabin crew member stepped onto the flight deck and confirmed that the cabin was ready for pushback. Wilkes closed and locked the flight deck door.

Hosler keyed her radio transmit button. "Heathrow ground, good morning. Speedbird 117 on gate 535, request push back."

"Speedbird 117, good morning to you. You are cleared to push and start off stand 535, face north."

Wilkes keyed the intercom and told the external ground crew below that they were ready to go. With their push and start clearance relayed to the tug driver, the brakes were released and the aircraft lurched back as the squat vehicle commenced the push back. The pilots started the engines. As the tug was driven clear, the ground handler turned and indicated by way of a hand signal that the aircraft was ready to taxi.

"Ground, Speedbird 117 request taxi," Hosler called on the radio.

"Speedbird 117, taxi via Bravo and hold short of Echo."

Wilkes released the brakes, squeezed a trickle of power with the thrust levers and commenced the taxi.

"Full flight today," Hosler said as they went through the pre-flight checks.

"Glad we're away. Security was a nightmare."

"You see the terminal?" she asked. "Chaos."

"See what was outside?" he said.

"The soldiers?"

"No, the tank! There was a bloody tank parked in the taxi rank."

They were cleared all the way to the runway holding point.

"They expect another attack. That's what they're saying. 'Keep your eyes open, report anything suspicious.' Scary."

The captain slowed as they approached Alpha 3 holding point, just short of the runway, and brought the 380-tonne jet to a gentle stop.

Hosler keyed the radio. "Tower, Speedbird 117, ready for departure."

"Speedbird 117, behind the departing Virgin 747 now on the runway, line up and wait runway 27 Right."

Wilkes looked out of the flight-deck window. It was a damp and foggy morning. He could see the office buildings and hotels along the Bath Road to the north, all of them wreathed in mist, the lights reduced to a fuzzy glow that bled through the moisture. He heard the sudden roar of engines as the Virgin 747 ahead of them powered down the runway, the jumbo streaking away. The air pressure dropped over the top of the 747's wing, and the water vapour condensed out as a cloudy mist that almost enveloped the entire aircraft.

He allowed his 747 to roll forward again.

"Speedbird 117, runway 27 Right, cleared for take-off, surface wind 220 degrees, four knots."

Wilkes lined the aircraft up on the runway centre line and, as they straightened out, he steadily advanced all four thrust levers.

"Setting thrust."

The engines grew louder and the plane picked up speed, the acceleration pressing the pilots back into their seats. Wilkes held a gentle forward pressure on the control column to keep some weight on the nose wheel and played the rudder pedals with his feet to keep the aircraft straight.

"Thrust set," called Hosler. "Eighty knots."

The aircraft continued its acceleration. Wilkes released the pressure on the control column, allowing it to find its neutral position.

"V1," Hosler reported.

One hundred and fifty-five knots. If they tried to abort the take-off now, there would be no guarantee that they could stop the aircraft before it reached the end of the runway.

The aircraft ate up tarmac, almost four thousand metres of it rapidly disappearing beneath them.

"Rotate," called Hosler.

Wilkes slowly pulled back on the control column and the nose lifted up. The nose gear cleared the runway, its wheels now spinning freely in space as the whole fuselage started to rise from the front. The tail dropped as the main undercarriage followed the nose and lifted off the tarmac.

"Positive climb," Hosler confirmed, checking the vertical speed indicator.

"Gear up," replied Wickes.

British Airways flight 117, with three hundred and thirty-three passengers, twelve flight attendants and two flight crew, was on its way.

Mohammed received a text message from an anonymous number to tell him that the jet was about to take off. He quickly prepared the Igla, opening the case and removing the launcher from the foam inserts. The Igla comprised the missile round within the launch tube, a separable grip stock and a battery unit. He inserted the coolant unit into the missile round and took the launcher outside.

A second text message arrived. The target was airborne.

He went outside. There was a table with four chairs and a barbecue covered with a green tarpaulin. The lawn hadn't been cut for several weeks, and the grass reached up to his ankles as he walked out beyond the edge of the conservatory to the three-bar fence that marked the start of the fields beyond. It was cold, with a dense mist clinging to the ground. The sky above was clear, though, with the moon still visible above the tree line on the far side of the field beyond the garden. Mohammed looked away from the moon and blinked to clear his vision, and then turned in the direction of the airport. A jet was approaching. He could see the steady navigation lights on the leading edge of each wingtip—red on the left and green on the right—and the brighter white lights on the trailing edges.

He had been provided with a dossier of information as he had prepared the operation. Chipperfield was directly beneath the flight-line of aircraft that had just taken off from Heathrow heading north. Jets passed over the village at between three and four thousand feet. The Igla had an effective ceiling of up to eleven thousand feet, so the approaching jumbo would be well within its operational parameters.

He rested the fibreglass launch tube on his right shoulder, took the grip stock in his right hand and moved his head so that his right eye was pressed to the sighting assembly. He stepped directly toward the target with his left foot and leaned very slightly in that direction. The aircraft was approaching quickly on a track that would bring it almost directly over the house. Mohammed sighted the aircraft in the range ring and tracked it.

He activated the missile. It took six seconds for the IR seeker to cool, the gyro to spin up and the electronics to activate. He tracked the jet and made continuous size estimates, using those to determine when the target was within range of the missile. He pressed and held the uncage switch to activate the seeker. The detector logic locked onto the jet's infrared source and a buzzer sounded, quickly becoming louder and steadier.

He adjusted his aim for superelevation and lead, and then held his breath for three seconds. Then he squeezed the trigger. Two seconds later, the launch rocket shot the missile out of the launch tube. The forward fins and tail fins extended, and after a short coasting period that took it over the fence and a safe distance away from the launcher, the launch engine fell away and the missile's solid rocket ignited.

The projectile curved upwards and then carved a straight path directly at the approaching jet.

The 747 was climbing through four thousand feet. Wilkes took a moment to look out his side window. He could see the low-level mist amongst the trees and the fields. England was beautiful. He was about to turn his attention back to his instruments when he saw a flash of light from the murky gloom of the country-side below them. There was a bright flare of light and then a yellow-white streak that came toward them across a fast diagonal track. It took him half a second to process what it was and then another to accept the awful prospect that it really was what he thought it was.

"Shit," he said.

"What is it?"

Wilkes tried to convince himself that he was wrong. But he wasn't wrong: the little speck was moving at a horrific speed, climbing up straight towards the 747. He snatched the control column and violently rolled it to his right, disengaging the autopilot and giving him direct control of the aircraft.

"Missile!"

The aircraft started to bank. Wilkes slammed the four thrust levers back against their idle stop position at the same time as he pushed forward on the control column, still holding in the right bank. The aircraft was big and cumbersome, slow to respond and unable to out-climb the missile; their only hope was to try to duck below it. The missile's rate of climb might mean that it would scream past and above them, unable to adjust its own trajectory quickly enough.

He stole another quick glance back over his left shoulder and through the window, hoping that maybe he had made a mistake.

He had not.

It was still there, hunting them, dropping below his line of vision as the aircraft rolled to the right. The jumbo nosed over into negative G, Wilkes becoming momentarily light in his seat but held down by his seat belts. The bank angle increased as Wilkes held the turn.

"What are you doing?" screamed Hosler. She hadn't heard him. She reached for her own control column, her natural instinct to correct Wilkes's erratic input.

The attitude indicator was showing a fifty-degree bank and the nose was dropping rapidly.

"It's a missile," he yelled. "There's a fucking missile!" His voice was almost drowned by the autopilot's warning horn and then the altimeter alert as they descended below their cleared altitude.

The jet was not built for snap manoeuvres. The engines groaned from the sudden stress as the jet bent away from its flight path.

There came a sudden explosion from behind and just below the plane.

The aircraft jolted and the noise level raced up. There was the scream of rushing air and Wilkes felt instant discomfort in his ears. The pressure hull had been breached. The vibration was violent, the whole aircraft shaking viciously. The shaking was so severe that there was no way to read the engine and flight instruments. Red warning lights blurred and flashed, accompanied by the cacophony of the engine fire bell warnings. Wilkes needed to arrest the sudden descent and pulled back.

Nothing.

"I have no control," he shouted. "Take it!"

Hosler fought her own redundant control column. More warning sirens sounded and lights flashed. The hydraulic systems were venting their fluids into the air, the pipes and lines ruptured by the peppering of shrapnel from the explosion of the missile.

There came the sound of frantic screaming from behind the cockpit door.

Wilkes yelled into the radio, "Mayday, Mayday, Mayday, Speedbird 117."

"What's happening?" Hosler shouted at him.

"Missile, I say again, missile attack!" Wilkes yelled into the radio.

He craned his neck to look back through his window. His view of the aircraft's left wing was limited, but he could see that the number one engine was engulfed in flames ferocious enough to hold their own against the slipstream. He saw the trailing streaks of smoke and pieces of debris that were breaking away from the jet. The cowlings were missing completely. The wing was badly damaged, shreds of skin flailing in the three-hundred-mile-an-hour airflow, everything disintegrating as he watched.

"Speedbird 117, Mayday acknowledged."

"Get the nose up!" Hosler cried. "Get the nose up!"

The flight controller radioed again. "Speedbird 117, you have flames—repeat, you have flames behind you."

Wilkes saw the tailplane assembly as it detached and fell away. There was nothing he could do. It was hopeless.

He looked forward again and saw the fields for the second time that morning. They filled the entire front windscreen.

Mohammed allowed himself the luxury of watching as the Igla's engine left a fiery trail across the darkened sky. The jet banked hard, but there was nowhere near enough time for it to take effective evasive action. It wouldn't have made any difference if the pilot had been given an additional ten or twenty seconds to turn away; the jumbo was big and slow, and its exhaust plumes presented the infrared seeker with a target that it couldn't possibly lose. The missile changed its course ever so slightly, a tight curl that ended when it detonated just short of the jet. The Igla was armed with a fragmentation warhead, and thousands of pieces of shrapnel were

ejected in all directions at high speed. The jet, with its flimsy fuselage and delicate engine parts, would be shredded.

He waited for another five seconds, long enough to see the
streamer of fire that ejected from the left-hand wing. The jet was
close enough, and there was enough of the dawn's light, for him
to watch as the tail assembly tore away from the main body of the
plane and plummeted to the ground. The rest of the 747, powered
by three of its four engines, flew on. But that could only be a short-
lived state of affairs.

The launcher tube was much lighter now as Mohammed lowered it from his shoulder. He went back into the living room, closed
the French doors and put the tube back into the aluminium case.
He fastened the clips to close the case, grasped the handle and
picked it up. He looked around one final time to ensure that he
hadn't left anything that could be traced back to him, and went into
the hallway.

There was a woman waiting next to the door that led to the
downstairs cloakroom.

Mohammed stopped, the heavy case dangling from his hand.

She was dressed all in black: black boots, black trousers, black
jacket.

She was holding a suppressed pistol in her right hand. It was
aimed at Mohammed.

"Who are you?"

The woman didn't answer.

Mohammed looked at the woman's face. It was blank, without
expression. He saw no empathy there. No pity. No emotion.

He saw nothing at all.

"Who are you?" he asked again.

The woman fired twice, each report muffled a little by the
suppressor. Both rounds found their marks in the centre of
Mohammed's torso. He stumbled back against the door to the living

room, bumped it open and fell down onto his backside. He let go of the case and put his gloved hand to his chest. He held it up; the blue latex was stained with red. He tried to draw breath, but he felt a sharp pain in the right-hand side of his chest. At least one of the rounds had penetrated his lung on that side. Air was rushing into the cavity and collapsing it. He was simultaneously being choked for air and bleeding out.

The woman followed him into the living room. Mohammed tried to scrabble away from her, raising his left hand and holding it up in entreaty. He looked up into the woman's face, still absent of expression, and knew that an appeal for mercy would be pointless. Mohammed had been involved in killing all of his adult life, and he recognised a killer when he saw one.

This woman, whoever she was, was a killer.

Somewhere outside but reasonably close at hand, there came the rolling boom of a huge explosion.

The woman aimed the pistol for a third time.

Mohammed closed his eyes.

The Asset's codename was Maia. Her real name didn't matter. She had several identities, assumed as easily as pulling on a fresh set of clothes at the beginning of a new day. For the months since she had been placed in London, she had lived the life of Lisa Katich, a businesswoman from Pensacola, Florida, engaged in the buying and selling of medical supplies. She rented a pleasant two-bedroom property in Pinner, a suburb in the north of London, and travelled in to her central London office every day. She conducted her business there and returned home. A dull and predictable routine. The perfect disguise.

She did not mind the drudgery. Her training, which had lasted all of her life and had been almost sadistically thorough, had included extensive modules that taught her the benefit of glacial patience. She would hold in place for as long as was required until she was reassigned or activated.

And she had been activated two days ago.

The fringe of dawn light that was visible above the tree line to the southwest had been lent an unearthly red and orange glow. Maia had heard the explosion, and she knew what it was: the main body of the stricken jet had fallen to earth and the fuel tanks had exploded. She paused at the door to the house and watched as a layer of dirty cloud filled the cold morning sky, a roiling pall of black and grey that stretched higher and higher. She estimated that the fire was five or six miles away. The area would become thick with activity as the police and military rushed in; the clean-up would have to be quick and efficient. She needed to be as far away from here as possible.

She had brought a tightly folded plastic package with her. She collected it and went into the living room. Mohammed was on his back, his sightless eyes staring up at the ceiling. Maia took the plastic bundle, unfastened the ties that held it together, and spread it out on the living room floor next to the corpse. It was a body bag made from vinyl material and with heat-sealed seams to prevent leakage. There were cleaning products inside the bag, together with towels and a mop with a folding handle. She took them all out and laid them on the floor.

Maia put her arms beneath Mohammed's shoulders and moved him until he was lying atop the splayed-open body bag. It had envelope-style heavy-duty zippers with dual pulls, and she drew them together so that the bag was sealed tight. She grabbed the padded handles and dragged the body into the hall.

A pool of blood had gathered where the body had fallen. The floor was a smooth laminate that was designed to look like wood, and Maia mopped the blood off it, rinsing the mop out in the kitchen sink. She took a bottle of Domestos Spray Bleach, sprayed the floor and then wiped it down with the towel until all traces of the blood were gone. She took the bleach and sprayed the sink, too.

She stuffed the wet mop head and towel into the body bag, opened the door and checked outside: there was still no sign of anyone. She opened up the van, transferred the body inside and then hauled it all the way to the front. Her motorcycle was parked next to the van. She stepped down, wheeled the bike to the rear doors and, with strength that would not have been credited to so slender a woman, lifted the front wheel into the van and then lifted and pushed the rest inside, too. She rested the bike on the floor and went back into the house for a final check. She stooped down to collect the brass casings that had been ejected from her pistol and put them into her pocket. She checked the living room and the garden one final time, collected the launcher and its case, switched off the lights and went back outside to the van. She slid the case inside and shut the doors.

Maia got into the driver's seat, started the engine and pulled away. The sun was up now. She could hear the sound of sirens when she wound down the window to let in some fresh air, and as she drove beneath the flyover for the M3, she saw the flashing blue lights of an emergency vehicle as it raced overhead. She followed the ramp onto the motorway and started to accelerate.

The line of trees that screened the motorway to the left petered out, and Maia was presented with a hellish vista. Large pieces of debris were scattered over the fields for hundreds of yards, some of them still burning. She saw the houses of a village perhaps half a mile away, some of the buildings on fire. Beyond that, the thunderhead of black smoke that must have marked the spot where the bulk of the jet had come down had taken on monstrous proportions, a mushroom cloud that was unfurling higher and higher into the otherwise blue sky.

She took out her burner phone and dialled her handler's number.

"It's done."

PART ONE

The Nur Mountains

Chapter One

I sabella Rose sat quietly in her seat as the engineers attempted
to fix the stricken Learjet. The lights in the cabin had gone out
soon after they had passed over the coast of Turkey. She didn't
know what the problem was, but it had caused a moment of panic.
The pilot had reported over the PA that the issue wasn't serious but
that they would have to land in Turkey. The panic dissipated, to be
replaced by consternation and impatience.

They had touched down in the early morning as dawn was just
breaking over the terminal building. Antalya had been quiet then,
with just the occasional smaller plane touching down, but now it
was five hours later and the facility was thronging with activity.
Isabella looked out the window. Nothing seemed to be taking off,
but a lot of jets were landing, jostling and nudging into position at
the terminal building.

She had held her tongue for several hours. She had tried to
speak before they had left Switzerland, and Salim al-Khawari had
told her to be silent. When she had spoken again, he had slapped
her across the face. And so she had been quiet after that and concentrated instead on taking in every last scrap of information that she
could. Her mother had taught her that it was important to always

know as much about your surroundings as possible. It was impossible to predict when your enemies might let down their guard. When that happened, she needed to know as much as she could so she could improve her odds of getting away from them.

She replayed the last few hours. The helicopter that had taken them from the al-Khawari house had headed to the east. She remembered that there was an airport at Sion, and she had not been surprised when she saw it through the window, the illuminated runway cutting through the darkened countryside like a lance. They had landed on a private apron next to a Learjet, and she had been forced to board the aircraft with the rest of the family. They had very quickly taken to the air again. She had looked down at the fast-disappearing ground and then at the stars arrayed across the porthole window, and decided that they had headed to the south.

The cabin was equipped with LCD screens fore and aft, and one of them was switched on mid-flight to show their progress. She was right: they *were* travelling to the south. Isabella had watched the tiny icon of the plane as it had then turned east and passed across the vast green swath of the continent. Her home, in Marrakech, seemed very far away from her now. Pope and Kelleher and Snow, who had been with her in Geneva, seemed very far away, too.

As they had passed over the Turkish coast and headed on towards Cyprus, Isabella had felt very alone indeed.

Beyond the information that she could assess from the map came the more intangible things. She had watched the family. Salim, the father, sat quietly at the front of the cabin. His face was a black cloud of anger and impatience, and he rebuffed all attempts at conversation.

His wife, Jasmin, seemed more angry than anything else. Isabella had looked around the cabin and, on more than one occasion, had seen the older woman staring at her with an expression that was impossible to mistake for anything other than hatred. Isabella had been disturbed by Jasmin after she had planted a data-tap in Salim's study. She had knocked the woman out and tied her up. Her anger wasn't unreasonable.

Khalil had been more difficult to read. There was shame and embarrassment and fear. He knew that he had let down his parents.

Isabella could see that all of the al-Khawaris were confused. The raid on the property that had followed Isabella's betrayal of the family had precipitated their hurried flight from the estate and the transfer to the Learjet. They were confused and frightened, and now they were on the run.

She was in a tight spot, but she consoled herself with one thing: Mr Pope would not abandon her. Whatever had happened must have been unexpected, and it had caught him off guard. But she knew that he would come after her. The plane would have been tracked and Turkey was a NATO country. He would find her himself or alert the Turkish authorities to her plight. She just had to keep her head down and be ready for the moment when it came.

Chapter Two

They were on the ground for five hours. Finally, one of the engineers climbed the steps to the cabin and looked over at Salim with a rueful cast to his face. Salim crossed the cabin so that he could talk to him. Isabella was close enough to overhear fragments of their conversation. She heard the engineer apologise and explain that the problem was electrical. They had fixed it, but there had been a crash near Heathrow and, because of that, all flights had been grounded. They were unable to take off. Salim spat an angry denunciation, but after a short consultation with his bodyguard, he turned and announced that they were going to have to deplane and continue their journey by car.

"Where are we going?"

It was the first thing that she had said for hours.

"Be quiet," Salim said.

"You need to tell me where we're going."

"I don't need to tell you a thing."

She made a show of being frightened and did as she was told. Jasmin and Khalil went first, stepping down into the bright sunlight beyond the subdued lighting of the cabin. Isabella was next, with the bodyguard close behind her. The steps led down to the asphalt strip. A silver Mercedes Viano was waiting for them twenty yards away. Jasmin and Khalil walked quickly across to the SUV and got inside. Isabella looked left and right. There was the wide expanse of the runway, with a chain-link fence just visible at the perimeter, and then a series of hangars where private planes were stored and maintained. She wondered, for a moment, whether this was her opportunity. She could run. She knew she would be able to outpace Khalil's parents. She was confident enough that she would be able to outpace him, too, assuming that he would have the presence of mind to pursue her if she ran. She had just taken a lungful of air in readiness when she felt the big paw of the bodyguard on her shoulder, the man squeezing tight.

"Don't get ideas," he said to her. "Just get into the car."

They walked on. Isabella saw that there was no driver in the car. The bodyguard split from the rest of the group and went around to the driver's side. She wondered whether that might lead to an opportunity.

Jasmin and Khalil got into the back of the SUV. Salim grabbed her around the arm, squeezed tight and hauled her to the side of the vehicle. There were two rows of seats in the back. Jasmin was sitting in the second row, on the far side of the cabin. Khalil was ahead of his mother in the first row.

Isabella stopped. She turned back to Salim. "Please," she said.

The man's face was hard and unyielding. "Get in."

Isabella started to cry. She looked down, willing the tears to come, and when they did, she looked back up at him and sobbed. "Please. I don't want to be here. I've said I'm sorry. I just want to go home."

"Get in *now*."

He turned her around and pushed her into the back of the car. The distraction paid off. He was more concerned that she should be inside than where she should be sitting, so when she took the seat next to Khalil, his father did not protest. He climbed in after her, shuffled around to sit next to his wife, and slid the door closed.

"Drive," he called out.

Isabella was next to the door. Khalil was to her right and his father was behind her. She was pleased about that. It would give her an opportunity.

The man put the car into gear and they pulled away. He turned sharply, leaving the jet behind them, and headed towards a gate in the chain-link fence.

She glanced over at Khalil. He still wouldn't hold her eye. She knew why. He had thought that she was interested in him. She had led him on expertly, playing the part with an adroitness that had surprised her. He had swallowed her deception, and now what must he have thought? That she had tricked him so that she could get into the house and ransack it? That would have made him feel stupid, and he would not have been helped by his father's tirade of abuse as they had flown away from the house. The boy was surly and aggressive toward her now, but that, she could tell, was to hide the truth of it.

He was confused. His pride was hurt.

Poor lamb. She had no pity for him. He was a spoiled, unpleasant brat, too used to flaunting his wealth and getting his own way, and now that he had been shown to be the fool that he was, he didn't like it.

A guard opened the gate in the fence and they drove through it, passing onto a narrow access road that bent around toward the terminal building and the confluence of roads beyond it. Isabella watched through the windshield, taking it all in. She was looking for Pope, half expecting to see him there. The concourse was busy, with new arrivals hauling their luggage out into the morning heat, in search of a taxi, and others barging through the crush to get inside. The crowd ebbed and flowed, bulging into the road in places, with the taxis that were waiting to pick up or set down their fares muscling through the commotion.

She looked, but she couldn't see Pope anywhere.

A taxi cut across them and forced the driver to hit the brakes. Both the Viano and the taxi came to a sudden stop. The bodyguard slammed his palm against the horn, the blare sounding loudly. Isabella had been waiting for an opening and knew that this could be it.

She felt a jolt of adrenaline and leaned forward a little.

The driver of the taxi flung open his door and stepped out. He was a big man, broad-shouldered and with a head of shoulder-length hair, and he came back to the Viano and started to shout abuse at the bodyguard. The bodyguard hit the horn again, but the taxi driver showed no sign that he was ready to move. The bodyguard cursed, unclipped his seat belt, opened the door and stepped out.

Ready.

Isabella watched through the windshield as the two men squared up. The bodyguard was bigger than the taxi driver, but the Turk did not back down. Instead, he launched into a tirade of abuse that he punctuated by spitting theatrically at the bigger man's feet. The bodyguard drew back his meaty fist and threw a big, heavy punch.

Now.

Isabella raised her arm horizontally, so that it was level with Khalil's head, and then drilled her elbow back into his face. He turned at the last minute and the impact was not quite as flush as she would have liked, but it was a sharp and unexpected blow to the cheekbone and it would have hurt.

He yelped in sudden pain, but Isabella was already moving.

She reached for the door handle and pulled it back, yanking hard on the door so that it slid back on its runners.

The heat washed into the air-conditioned cabin.

25

Isabella slid across the seat.

The crowds were dense. She only needed to get out of the SUV, step down onto the road and melt into the throng. What would the al-Khawaris do? Follow her? Cause a scene?

No.

She swung around and put her feet on the sill. She scanned her surroundings, the busy crowd and the dozens of vehicles, and, for a split second, her eyes locked on a boy who couldn't have been very much older than she was. He was brown skinned, a little taller than her, pulling a small carry-on case behind him.

She started to step down, when she felt hands on her hips. She tried to shake them off, but instead, they slithered ahead, around her waist, and locked there. She looked down, saw a pair of slender, manicured, feminine hands and realised that Jasmin had leaned over the seat and grabbed her.

"Stop her!"

Jasmin pulled her back, and Isabella felt her shoulder as it pressed between her own shoulder blades. She threw her head back, her crown crashing into something similarly hard, and the grip loosened. Isabella butted her a second time and her hands parted. She shrugged her off and turned back to the door, but before she could move, she felt strong fingers fasten around her bicep.

It was Salim. She craned her neck, looking back into the SUV. Jasmin was sprawled back on the seat, blood running down her chin from a lacerated lip. Salim was on the same side of the SUV as she was, and he had stood to reach for her left arm. She shook her arm again and he responded by digging his fingers into the joint.

She winced from the pain, tried to free herself again, but he held on. She swivelled her hips and drew back her right fist, ready to hit him, when she was jostled back down into her seat.

Khalil had roused himself from the shock of being struck, and he had shouldered his way around her so that he could reach for the door. He yanked it back, sliding the door so fast that it shut with a crash.

"Drive!"

She hadn't noticed: the bodyguard was back in the Viano again. He threw the SUV into gear and pulled out into a gap that had opened in the outside lane. Khalil pushed Isabella back into the seat, and Salim locked his arms around her shoulders and her clavicle, holding her there. She bucked, tried to free her pinioned arms, tried to butt first Khalil and then his father, but the two of them were too strong for her. She found herself panting from the effort and the desperation, the adrenaline buzzing around her veins, the energy coiled and sprung but with nowhere to go. Finally, she realised it was pointless and that the opportunity had passed, and she let the fight drain out of her.

She looked out the window. She saw the boy who had been watching her as they drove past the spot on the pavement where he was waiting. The glass was blacked out, but as Isabella gazed out at him, he seemed to be looking straight at her. The moment did not last long. The Viano found a little extra space ahead of it, and the driver accelerated hard.

The airport quickly disappeared behind them.

The moment had passed.

The opportunity was lost.

Chapter Three

Captain Michael Pope was waiting with a cup of cold coffee at the café at Geneva International Airport. He had been sitting there in the same chair for three hours. He was wearing a cap that he had purchased from a twenty-four-hour concession in the concourse, the bill pulled down and his head angled down so that most of the top half of his face was obscured. He had chosen a seat just inside the café, where he was hidden from the concourse yet still able to observe the comings and goings.

There was a screen inside the café that was tuned to a rolling news channel. Pope wasn't paying any attention to it; he was staring down into his cup of coffee as he listlessly stirred his spoon in it. He was thinking about Isabella and how it was he who was responsible for what had happened to her. He had no idea where she was, or even whether she was alive or dead. It had been his fault. His plan. His stupid, reckless plan. And she was paying the price for his recklessness.

He realised the conversation around him had quietened down. He looked up. The noise had been replaced by a stunned hush. The men and women at the tables, the staff behind the desk, they were all staring at the screen behind him. He turned to look and saw shaky footage of what was unmistakably a plane crash. The footage was being shot from behind a police cordon that had been erected at the edge of a large arable field. A trail of smoking debris could be seen all the way across the field, leading directly to what looked like a village. The houses and buildings looked as if they were half a mile away from the camera, but they were obviously on fire, smoke billowing into the air.

The ticker along the bottom of the screen announced that British Airways flight 117 from London to New York had crashed just after taking off from Heathrow.

Pope got up and went outside into the concourse. He looked at the screen that displayed information on arrivals and departures. All of the flights that were due to depart from the airport had been cancelled. Flights were still landing, and the board reported that the flight from London Heathrow had just touched down.

He watched as the passengers emerged in the arrivals hall, until he saw the man that he had been waiting to meet. Vivian Bloom was in his seventies and looked his age. His skin was leathery and heavily lined, and his eyes were rheumy behind his spectacles. He dressed badly, in the way of a man with a modest amount of capital but no taste, favouring old tweed jackets and badly fitting waistcoats. He was wearing brown cord trousers, frayed at the cuffs, with the fabric thinning in places, and comfortably inelegant shoes. The collar of his shirt was curled up like old pieces of toast, and his tie bore a stain just below its badly arranged knot.

Bloom was a legend within the service, though, and throughout the course of his distinguished career, countless individuals had been thoroughly embarrassed after mistaking his dishevelled appearance for incompetence. His time at Berlin Station during the Cold War was spoken of in hushed tones, the jousting with his Soviet adversaries demonstrating an incredible mental sharpness and a ruthlessness that had seen several enemy players removed from the field of battle by the forerunners to Group Fifteen. They called him the Reverend, on account of his previous profession as sub-rector of Lincoln College, Oxford. But there was nothing ecclesiastical about him beyond the donnish appearance. Vivian Bloom was a powerful man.

Pope crossed the concourse to him. Bloom had stopped with his back to him and was looking over at the area with the rows of benches.

"Sir," Pope said, taking Bloom by the elbow and gently impelling him onwards. "This way, please."

Bloom did as Pope asked, and they walked together through the concourse. Pope had scouted the area quickly when he had arrived, and led the way now to a restroom that was out of the way and less busy than others. The cleaner had left his cart outside the door. There was a small plastic "Do Not Use" sign hanging from the cart and Pope took it, leaving it on the floor in front of the door. He pushed the door open, waited until Bloom was inside and then followed. He checked that the room was empty and the cubicles were unoccupied. They were alone.

Bloom rearranged his glasses on his nose. "What a mess. What a fucking mess."

"I just saw it on the TV. It's not an accident?"

"Can't say for sure, but the odds are very much against it. Heathrow tower said the engine was on fire. That could be a fault, of course, but the police have had reports of something being fired from the ground."

"A missile?"

"Yes, Pope, a fucking missile." Pope had forgotten that Bloom had an unusually salty tongue; his proclivity toward profanity was at odds with his appearance and what Pope knew of his history. "We'll know for sure once they've checked the radar. Of course, we knew it would happen eventually. It's just a question of smuggling one into the country. That's not hard, and there's nothing you can do if they manage that. You can't guard a big jumbo against a missile."

"Everything is on lockdown?"

"All of Europe. Anything in the air is landing and nothing is taking off. The Americans, too, until they know it's safe. Bloody lucky I was already in the air. It won't be far short of 9/11 by the time it's done. If they did manage to shoot one down, there's nothing to say they won't do it again."

Pope exhaled. He felt as if he was at the centre of a vortex of events that was whirling faster and faster outside of his control.

"Are you all right, Control?"

"Fine, sir. Just tired."

"What about your agents?"

"I'm afraid they're dead."

"Jesus." Bloom shook his head. "What happened?"

Pope had been running the events of the last few days through his head while he had been waiting for Bloom to arrive. The operation had started inauspiciously and quickly worsened. Bloom had spoken to Pope off the record and sent him and three of his head-hunters to unravel the threads that he hoped would provide them with the identity of the jihadi plotters who were behind the attacks on Westminster. They had done that, with some success. They had collected a firebrand cleric, Alam Hussain, from his house in Manchester and delivered him to the CIA for rendition. The Americans had questioned him—half drowned him, most likely—and Hussain had admitted that his mosque had been responsible for radicalising the bombers.

And even more importantly, Hussain had admitted that Salim Hasan Mafuz Muslim al-Khawari had financed the operation.

Pope had put Salim under surveillance. They had successfully infiltrated Isabella Rose into the exclusive school where Salim's son,

Khalil, studied. She had forged a relationship with the boy and had been invited to a party at Salim's house. Once inside, she had planted the data-tap to grant the Firm's analysts access to his servers. But there had been an FBI raid on the property before Isabella could escape, and then, in the confusion that followed, Pope and his agents had come under attack. Snow and Kelleher had been killed, and he had only just managed to escape by commandeering a boat and piloting it into the middle of Lake Geneva. He had come ashore at the Hotel de la Paix. It had been late, and the shorefront was quiet. He had hurried into the streets around the Square du Mont-Blanc, found a taxi and told the driver to take him to the airport. And he had been here ever since.

Bloom rapped his knuckles against the sink when Pope had finished. "What a bloody mess," he said again.

"The FBI," Pope said. "Why were they there? And how did we not know about them?"

"Another fuck-up. I made enquiries before I left. They were interested in Salim, too. They were following another lead. We couldn't have told them about what we were doing, but we might have planned differently if we'd known they were going to be involved."

"We would have, sir. We would have aborted."

"Yes, of course. But what about the men who attacked you? Do you know who they were?"

"No," Pope said.

"You have no idea?"

"None. But they were very good."

Bloom took a paper towel from the dispenser, removed his glasses and scrupulously cleaned them. The old man's fingers were long and delicate, the tips yellowed with nicotine.

"Isabella Rose did very well," he said. "The data-tap worked perfectly. We have everything we hoped that we might get."

"Such as?"

"We were able to follow the money. That was the main thing. One hundred thousand dollars. Salim channelled it from one of his companies in the United States, moved it through Switzerland and then distributed it via a number of Western Union transfers."

"To whom?"

"Some of the locations where the money was collected are served by CCTV. The same man collected three of the transfers. We believe he is a courier."

"Do you have him?"

"Not yet, but the police have footage. He'll be ID'd today. It's just a matter of time."

"Who did the courier deliver it to?"

"We think it was most likely via a dead drop."

"So he might not know who they were?"

"No," Bloom admitted. "Probably not. But I bet Salim does."

"It would be useful if we could ask him."

"We're working on that." Bloom slid his glasses back onto his nose.

"What about Isabella?" Pope said.

"Salim took her with him," Bloom reported. "We have her on CCTV at Sion. They flew to Turkey. We have assets there, and they've confirmed that she's with him. They'll try to cross the border and get to Syria."

"I have to go and get her," Pope said. "I owe her mother. And she's just a child. I can't leave her with them."

"I thought you'd say that. Good show, Control. I'll help you."

Pope knew that Bloom would not have offered his assistance through any sense of altruism or a sense of regret over what had happened to Isabella. He did not play the game that way. The Reverend was a strategist, thinking several moves ahead, and his motives would not bear any relation to what was right, but what was best for the achievement of his objective. Perhaps there was a conjunction between what both men wanted. Perhaps Pope could advance Bloom's cause while also recovering Isabella.

"I'll need something from you, too, of course," Bloom said. "Whilst you're *in situ*, so to speak. We need to speak to Salim very badly. This morning makes it more urgent now than it was before, of course. I want undeniable confirmation that these attacks are an ISIS operation, but that doesn't really matter. We know it's them. What we really need to know is who is responsible for the plotting. There's a cell in the UK. They're still extant and the Westminster martyrdom videos threatened more of the same. They delivered on that today, and they'll keep delivering until we can get to them. We need to know who they are and where they are so that they can be prevented from doing so."

Pope listened, hearing all the old euphemisms. 'Speak.' 'Prevented.' Bloom was steeped in the curiously self-conscious language of the career spook, but Pope knew what he meant. He was talking about torture and murder.

Pope was comfortable with that under the present circumstances.

"What intelligence do we have?"

"They flew from Sion on a private jet. We thought they'd fly straight to Syria, but they didn't. They landed in Antalya five hours ago."

"Turkey? Why there? We can extradite him."

"They had an electrical failure. Akrotiri picked up the communications from the plane. They stayed on the tarmac at Antalya for hours while they tried to fix it, but they couldn't get it done. Our woman at the airport saw them disembark."

"So where are they now?"

"In transit. They were seen driving away from the airport, heading east. They're following the coastal road. Alanya, Mersin, Adana, Iskenderun. They can get into Syria from there."

"Isabella is with him?"

"She was seen."

"Why? Why don't they just get rid of her?"

"We don't know what she has told them. Perhaps they know that she is working for us. Perhaps they think she might have use to them as a bargaining chip. Or as a hostage. It's difficult to be sure. But she is with them. She was seen at the airport."

"We have to stop them. If they get into Syria, it'll be impossible to get to her."

"Not impossible, but very difficult indeed. They won't get that far. We have assets looking for them now."

"And they can stop them?"

He shook his head. "I'm afraid not. They're not those kinds of assets. Intelligence only."

"We could ask the Turks."

"Really, Control? You want to ask them?"

Pope knew that Bloom was right. "Me, then. But how can I get there in time? I'm not going to be able to fly."

"Actually, you are. I've taken the liberty of making arrangements on your behalf. I've called in a favour from the RAF. They're sending a jet for you now."

Pope remembered what Bloom had said before. "This was supposed to be off the books. I'm supposed to be suspended, sir. Has something changed?"

"Events are giving me a little more flexibility, Control. This is still deniable. The pilot doesn't know who you are or what you're going to be doing when he drops you off."

"What am I going to be doing?"

Bloom took out a passport and gave it to him. "Your cover is as a military liaison between us and the Turks. Your name is John Creasey."

Pope nodded, absorbing the new information.

"Salim can't be much farther along the road than Manavgat, and it's still eight hours to the border from there. You'll be picked up at Hatay. You should have a few hours on them."

"Equipment?"

"The local quartermaster is collecting you. You'll have everything you need. There's one thing you can take now."

He reached into his pocket and took out a small phone with a large, thick antenna. Pope recognised it: an Iridium satphone. It would have worldwide range and enough standby time to last a day and a half. Bloom put it, and a spare battery, on the edge of the sink.

"If you need me, call the number programmed into the memory. We've established a small situation room. It's staffed twenty-four seven. If I can help, I will."

Pope collected the phone and the battery and put them into his own pocket. "Thank you, sir."

"Your codename is Archangel."

"Understood. And my orders?"

"Get Salim before he leaves Turkey. If you can get the girl, too, so much the better."

Pope clenched his jaw and gave a single nod of his head. "Yes, sir."

Chapter Four

Aqil and Yasin Malik had arrived in Turkey a day earlier. They had bought a package holiday from an online travel agent. A week of sun and fun in a five-star resort in Antalya. That was how the trip had been advertised on the company's website, but that was not what they had in mind. They had checked into their hotel, left most of their luggage behind and disappeared. The MI6 agents who later inspected their room found two abandoned suitcases and a discarded beard trimmer.

Aqil and Yasin took a train to Iskenderun in eastern Turkey. The journey traced the coastline and passed towns with names that Aqil did not recognise: Alanya, Anamur, Icel, Ceyhan.

From Iskenderun, they took a taxi to Reyhanli.

The border town was little more than a ragged, bombed-out collection of shanties. They had taken a room at the Kent Hotel. It was a three-storey structure with fifteen rooms. It was filthy, with stains on the walls and carpets and a proprietor who sat at reception wearing a vest that had evidently been unwashed for weeks. He knew what they were here for as soon as Yasin started to speak. The town, and this hotel in particular, was a favourite for European jihadis making the journey to the south. The hotel was almost full. Business was good.

They had time to kill, so they toured the town. The town was a crazy mix of cultures, with shops bearing the logos of international brands standing next to rickety shacks whose owners catered to the flood of Syrian refugees who had swarmed across the border as the civil war had become increasingly bloody. The smells were overpowering: raw sewage; the sweetness of *mamuniyah*, rich with butter and ghee; sweat; fresh *ma'amoul* cookies flavoured with pistachio and walnut. They walked amid the crowd, saw men wearing Western business suits and women in niqabs. It was full of crumbling buildings and dusty streets. The refugees were everywhere. Decaying brick structures, tarps held down with rocks, tents pitched on rooftops.

Reyhanli was on a hill. They followed the street to the top until they were elevated enough to be afforded an excellent view of the Syrian landscape beyond. A few hundred yards south of the border, someone had flown the flag of the Islamic State atop a watchtower. They could see the black fabric snapping in the breeze, the flash of white betraying the *shahada* written across it. It was a potent symbol. Aqil found that he was afraid of it.

They could see the main gateway into Syria from here, too. The Bab al-Hawa Border Crossing was situated on the Syrian M45 and the Turkish D827 highways. It had the facilities to cater for plenty of traffic, but it was quiet today. A handful of lorries were waiting to cross, but Turkish border patrol were making sure that the cargos were legitimate. No oil was to come out. No arms or recruits were to go in. Yasin watched them for a moment and spat into the sand at his feet.

"That's all for show. We're not going through the front door."

Yasin had arranged to meet their handler outside a Vodafone shop. They had been there fifteen minutes before the appointed time. The man, an Arab with a wild beard and a distended belly that wobbled beneath his *dishdash,* had welcomed them with warm embraces that filled Aqil's nostrils with his foul odour. He did not give them his name and they did not ask. He took them both to a local trader who had an impressive line in second-hand military equipment. They bought hunting knives, binoculars, desert camouflage fatigues and magazine vests for carrying spare AK-47 ammunition. The man said that they would be provided with Kalashnikovs once they reached their training camp.

"We will go now," he said to them. "Collect your things. We drive."

The wide open stretch of Turkish border was rugged and uninviting. They left the city and headed due south. The desert stretched away as far as they could see, pierced by the wire-mesh border fence.

The handler took one hand off the wheel to indicate the vista with a sweep of his arm. "This is it," he said.

"This is what?"

"It is what they call the 'Gateway to Jihad.'"

"How much farther?"

"A few miles."

They left the road and took a dry, dusty track. The handler explained that it was one of the ancient smuggling routes that crisscrossed over the Turkish hills into Syria. As they drove on, the only things that demarked the border were scraps of broken barbed wire. The track led down to the Orontes River. It meandered through a valley of olive plantations, and on the other side of the water was Syria. They followed the track as it mirrored the river.

A Turkish army truck full of soldiers drove by. They ignored them. The next people they passed were men from local villages, carting oil drums and boxes of food. They were smugglers, and they were going to deliver the goods to the riverbank, where they would be taken across on rafts.

"That is for the caliphate," the man said. "We are well supplied, thanks be to Allah. And it is where you will cross. We must wait until dark."

He parked the car. Others appeared. Soon, there were another ten people waiting to cross. Aqil heard French and German, and two of them spoke English. Yasin nodded to them, shared a gruff hello, but they kept to themselves. There was an atmosphere of excitement among the men. They were all keen to get across.

The sense of anticipation was contagious, yet Aqil started to feel nervous. He had started to doubt his choice as soon as they had landed in Turkey. He did not want his brother to think he was having second thoughts, so he had managed to ignore it, distracting himself with the practicalities of getting across the country to the border. But now that they were here, he couldn't help himself.

He was thinking about his mother and father. He wondered what they would be thinking. What would they be doing? Would they have contacted the police? Probably. Yasin had explained that they would call them once they had crossed safely into the caliphate. Aqil knew that they would be relieved to hear from them, but that it would be cold comfort once they realised where they were and what they were planning on doing. He had been consumed with guilt. They had left their parents to deal with everything on their own. And when the papers found out where their sons had gone . . . how much worse would it get for them then? One twin was a failed suicide bomber, murdered and dumped in the river. The surviving twin, together with their eldest son, had travelled to Syria to fight for the most hated—the most reviled—organisation in the world.

The sun dipped beneath the horizon. It very quickly grew cold, and Aqil was pleased that he had listened to his brother and packed a fleece in his travel bag. He pulled it on.

The raft came back across the water again. It was a ramshackle vessel, a square of wood fashioned from logs that had been lashed together, a metal fence providing something for them to lean against so that the passengers did not fall over the edge. It was pulled across the river by a man wearing a Barcelona top with "MESSI" on the back.

"Everybody on."

The men waded out into the shallows and were pulled up by the man with the Messi shirt. Aqil shuffled to the back, letting the others go before him.

Yasin was alongside him. "Are you sure you really want this, little brother?"

He swallowed, but his throat was suddenly dry. "No," he said.

"We have to decide now."

"What are you going to do?"

Yasin's self-confidence and certainty were suddenly missing.

"Come on," the man with the Barcelona shirt said. "Get on."

Yasin turned back to his brother. "Yes," he said, although there was no conviction in his voice. He tried again. "Yes. I'm going. There's nothing for us at home."

They were the last to embark. "Last chance," the handler said. "If you want to go, you get on the raft now."

"Give us a moment," Yasin said. He turned to his brother.

Aqil swallowed again. He closed his eyes and remembered his brother's body laid out in the front room, the *kafan* parted to show his face and the ugly wound that brutalised it. He blinked hard, trying to shift the image, but he could still see it. He knew that he would always be able to see it for as long as he lived. Aamir had made a mistake, but his brother had refused to compound it. He had not detonated his vest. He had tried to do the right thing. He had been vulnerable, and he had been killed anyway. Aqil knew that the security services were responsible, and he felt a tremor of anger. It made his mind up for him.

"I'm sure," he said, his voice cracking. "Let's go."

They boarded. The raft was overbalanced and it pitched to one side, water sloshing over it and soaking their feet. The handler rearranged them so that their weight was distributed more evenly, and then he stepped down, his robe floating on the water. The man in the Barcelona top started to haul the rope, passing it hand over hand, and the raft jerked out into the current.

"Congratulations, boys," the handler said, his voice carrying out over the water. "You're nearly there. That land, Syria, is where God's judgment will come to pass. Praise be to Allah."

Chapter Five

There was an observation window in the departures lounge, and Pope had been staring out onto the runway when he saw his ride make its approach. A series of other, larger jets had landed, but this was obviously nothing like them. He recognised it as soon as it was close enough to pick out the detail: the engine intake mounted at the bottom of the fuselage, the foreplanes mounted before the main wing, the delta mainplane and the tall and sharply swept tail. It was a Typhoon FGR4, the larger bubble cockpit and the deeper upper fuselage distinguishing it as the two-seat version. The jet glided down to the runway, its bright landing lights glaring out from underneath the mainplane. It touched down and taxied toward the terminal building. Bloom had explained that a member of the airport security staff would escort him down to the runway after the jet had been refuelled.

Pope sat down, took out the satellite phone and switched it on. He dialled Rachel. Even though she had grown used to extended periods of time when he was out of contact with her, he always tried to let her know before he went dark.

The call connected.

"It's me."

"Michael! Are you all right?"

"I'm fine."

"You can't say where you are?"

"I can't say."

"You sound tired."

"I am. I've been up all night. But I'm fine. I just wanted to let you know that I'm going to be out of contact for a while."

"Do you know for how long?"

"Three, four days. I'll be back as soon as I can."

"Have you seen the news? You know what's happened?"

"Yes."

"It's horrible. They're saying it was a missile. Can you believe that? They can shoot jets down now."

She spoke about what was being said about the attack, but Pope was only half listening to her. Something—the sound of her voice, perhaps, or the sound of his daughters' laughter just audible in the background—coalesced the nascent thoughts that he had been considering without even really being aware of them. He had wanted to tell Rachel that he was going to be incommunicado, but that wasn't the real reason for the call. He was frightened, and he wanted to tell her that now was the time to put into action the contingency that they had first discussed years earlier. He had just joined Group Fifteen, and it had seemed prudent then. They had never had to take the next step, but something was nagging at him, worrying him, and he wanted to be sure that they were safe.

Pope interrupted her. "When's Flora's recital?"

It was true that his daughter played the violin, but there was no recital. That simple sentence, those three precise words, that was their own private code. Pope knew that it was very likely that there was a permanent tap on his home number, and knowing that, it was wise to obfuscate. This was the first time that he had invoked their secret protocol, but what had happened to him in Geneva made him nervous that he was only glimpsing the edges of a larger, and more dangerous, situation.

Rachel was not expecting to hear it, and she stumbled over her response. "It's—it's—"

"It's all right," Pope said, trying to reassure her without giving himself away. "I just couldn't remember what day it was."

"Monday," she said, confirming that she understood what he had said to her. "It's Monday. Will you be back for it?"

"I'll do my best."

There was silence, and Pope could easily visualise his wife gripping the telephone a little tighter, her face a little paler. As soon as they finished the call, she would need to start planning. The Popes had an apartment in Montepulciano; that was the hideout that they had selected. She would need to pack the things that she and the girls would need, get them ready and go. They had spoken about the plan on many occasions: how she would drive to Felixstowe and take the car on the ferry, rather than flying; how she would confiscate the girls' cellphones in order to remove the temptation that they might use them and give away their position; how they would all lay up in the apartment until Pope could get to them.

He felt awful. He wanted to tell Rachel more about what he was about to do, but that was impossible. He wanted to tell her that it would all be fine, but that would alert anyone who might be eavesdropping to the secret context that lay beneath their domestic platitudes. "Is everything else okay?"

"We miss you."

"I miss you, too. Tell the girls I love them."

"I will. Any message for me?"

"I love you, too."

"Love you. Be careful."

"I always am."

They said goodbye and he ended the call. Pope hoped that he had done the right thing. He thought that he had.

But the thought of his daughters had made him think about Isabella and what had happened to her. It was impossible not to feel responsible. Pope had known her extraordinary mother, of course, and the girl had inherited the same steely demeanour. It was a mask that she wore very well, but it was just a mask; Pope knew that she was just a fifteen-year-old girl behind it. He had doubted his own decision to involve her as soon as he had recommended it to Bloom, but they had no other recourse, and the country had been threatened with further attacks. More people would die unless they discovered the terrorist cell that was responsible. Isabella was their best chance of doing that quickly.

Did that mean that the risk of involving her was justified?

He had finally decided that it was, but that was before.

Now he was starting to doubt himself again.

He put the phone away and looked up at the television screen again. A piece of recorded VT was playing. A group of men, all dressed in obviously expensive suits, were arranged around a large conference room table. There were flags at the head of the table: the red and white of the Lebanon and the red, white and black tricolour of Egypt. The camera focussed on one man. He held a pen, and with a theatrical grin, he looked into the lens. He put the pen to the paper with a flourish and made to sign his name. Flashbulbs popped, throwing bright white light over his face, and he grinned again.

Pope recognised him even before the rolling ticker at the bottom of the screen named him.

"Salim Hasan Mafuz Muslim al-Khawari Named as Suspect in London Attacks"

Bloom had said that this would happen. They wanted Salim's name out there so that the conversation could be shaped according to the narrative that they had chosen. There would be a briefing, and his links with ISIS would be revealed. It didn't make any difference to Pope. It wouldn't make his task any more difficult. Al-Khawari already knew that he was a wanted man. The FBI had made that abundantly clear when they assaulted his compound.

"Excuse me, sir."

It was a man in a suit. Airport security? Swiss intelligence? Pope didn't know.

"Yes?" he said, standing.

"They are ready for you," he said.

Chapter Six

There were around fifteen hundred nautical miles between Geneva and Hatay Airport in the southeast of Turkey. The normal flight time for a commercial jet would have been around four hours. The Typhoon, though, was a little faster than that. The pilot took them up to forty thousand feet and then went supersonic, maintaining Mach 1.5 for almost the entire duration of the seventy-minute flight. They passed through a heavy bank of cloud and then emerged into the brightness of the morning, the sky a bright blue and the cloud below a perfect white. The cloud dispersed as they crossed over the Dalmatian Coast, and Pope looked out from the bubble cockpit as Bosnia, Serbia, Bulgaria and then Turkey rushed below them.

"This is pretty weird," the pilot said, his voice playing out through the speakers in Pope's helmet. "We're the only ones up here."

The pilot started a gentle descent, and after five minutes, the long strip of runway at Hatay became clearer through the haze on the ground. It was a small regional airport that served domestic flights, and Pope saw that all of its jets had been pushed back to the terminal building on the taxiway. Nothing was moving.

The pilot lowered the Typhoon's undercarriage and dropped into a gentle glide path to bring them down.

Pope was greeted by a man and a woman who introduced themselves as members of airport security. Pope doubted that; they looked very much like spooks to him.

He made his way quickly through the requirements of immigration. He stopped in the arrivals lounge and realised that he was hungry. There was a café there and he picked up breakfast—Turkish sourdough bread, beef sausage and "fruit juice" that turned out to be powdered and almost undrinkable—and then took it with him as he made his way out into the busy throng of the arrivals hall. A path had been formed between two rows of temporary barriers, and on each side of the rails a line of taxi drivers held out their signs. Pope saw a woman holding a placard upon which had been written, in untidy script, his *nom de guerre*: "Mr Creasey".

He went over to the woman. She was middle-aged, a blowsy blonde with too much make-up and clothes that were a touch too young for her. She had a wary expression on her face as she regarded the travellers who were making their way through the building. Pope knew that it was very unlikely that she had been provided with a photograph or any other details save that he was male.

"I'm Creasey," he said.

She regarded him critically. "Mr Creasey from London?"

"No," he said, recognising one of the exchanges that Group Fifteen agents used to identify themselves with the functionaries that were embedded around the world. "From Birmingham."

"Very good, Mr Creasey. This way, please. We need to hurry."

She led the way through the terminal to a multi-storey parking lot. Pope assessed her a little more. He had no way of knowing, but the chances were that she was a local who had been recruited by the embassy years previously. She would have been thoroughly vetted and given a series of tasks to demonstrate that she was reliable and trustworthy. Then she would have been promoted to the position of quartermaster for this part of the world. It was the same with all of the embedded assets that provided the on-the-ground assistance to the Group. The Israelis had a similar set-up for the Mossad. Those agents were called *sayanim*, men and women who lived unassuming lives and were activated only when they were needed. The Mossad relied upon the sense of loyalty to Israel as the motivation for the *sayanim*. Group Fifteen was far grubbier. It paid for the loyalty of its helpers or, if the situation permitted it, threatened them with the release of unsavoury information. There was no guessing the motivation of this particular agent.

Her car was parked on the second floor, and they took the elevator in silence. She led the way through the dimly lit space to a Renault Espace and indicated that Pope should get in. She got into the driver's side and started the engine.

"We must hurry," she said as she pulled out.

"Do you know where they are?"

"They were seen at Kuzuculu," she said. "Fifteen minutes ago."

"How far away is that?"

"Twenty-two miles to the north. Thirty minutes by car, depending on the traffic."

"Which way will they go?"

"The border with Syria is porous. It is hard to say."

"Your best guess?"

"They had a choice at Kuzuculu. They could have taken the 214 east and crossed the border near Kilis or they could have gone south and crossed at Reyhanli. They went south. Reyhanli is still the most popular crossing point. I think it will be there."

"So they're heading toward us?"

"Yes. I suggest we drive to Belen. The E91 meets the E98 there. If I were in their shoes, I would follow that and then go over the border in the back country. It is very easy to get across. From there, they will head east, probably to Raqqa."

"We need to make sure they don't get that far," Pope said.

Chapter Seven

The district of Belen comprised the small town of the same name together with a cluster of villages that gathered around it on the slopes of the Nur Mountains. The area was within the outcrop of Turkish territory that was pressed between the Mediterranean to the west and the shoulder of Syria to the east.

The quartermaster drove quickly as they left the airport, and Pope watched through the windows as the terrain climbed on either side.

"This area," Pope said. "Tell me about it."

"We will reach the Belen Pass in ten minutes. It's the only way across the mountains between Iskenderun and Antakya. It is the main route between Anatolia and the Middle East. They call it the Syrian Gates. If they keep coming south, they have to come this way. The kids who have crossed into Syria to join the jihad, many of them come this way." She pointed to the glovebox. "There's a map in there."

Pope opened the glovebox and took out the map. He unfolded it and pinpointed their location. They were on the D817, heading south. The O-53 was the main route, bypassing Iskenderun. Salim's vehicle would most likely have followed it rather than the slower coastal road. The two roads merged to the northwest of Belen and became the E91.

The mountains continued to climb on either side of them. The terrain became less dusty and sandy and more rocky, and Pope had to swallow to equalise the pressure in his ears. The roads were in excellent condition, recently paved, and that was good; the route swung left and right as it traced the easiest path up the mountains, with a number of vicious switchbacks with increasingly steep drops on the other side of the guard rails. The mountains climbed higher on either side of the pass, with low cloud obscuring the summits.

Pope looked behind him to where two large suitcases and a backpack had been left on the back seat. "Is that the gear?"

"Yes," she said. "In the back, too."

He unclipped his seat belt and clambered into the rear of the cabin. The suitcases were locked, but the quartermaster handed him two small keys, and when he tried them, the locks opened so that he could push back the lids. The cases held a generous supply of firearms and other ordnance.

Pope selected the items he would need. He took an M4A1 assault rifle and a Beretta M9 semiautomatic 9mm pistol. He added a set of binoculars.

"What's in the backpack?"

"A general load-out," she said. "Grenades, GPS, rations."

Pope didn't think that he would need it, and he didn't want to encumber himself.

He took a tactical jacket and an ammo belt and collected seven 5.56mm magazines for his primary weapon and five magazines for his side arm. That made for fourteen magazines in total, given the two that were already in the weapons.

"Where do you want to stop?" she asked him.

He didn't know the area and there was not going to be sufficient time to reconnoitre it properly. He studied the map. He didn't want them to get beyond Belen. There was another town, Hallibey, and then Cankaya, Kirikhan and Akpinar. If he allowed them to get that far, they would be within five clicks of the border. He had no idea, nor could he guess, where they would try to cross. It made much sounder tactical sense to intercept them before they had additional options to make things more uncertain.

This stretch of road would likely be as good as any other. They were on a reasonably long straight preceded by a sharp left-hander and then an equally challenging right as the road swung around to continue the climb up the flank of the mountain. There was a parking spot three hundred feet ahead, and Pope pointed to it. "There."

The quartermaster began to slow.

Pope collected the shoulder holster and put it on. He took the M9 and pushed it into the holster, leaving the retention strip unclasped. He grabbed the M4, checked the safety and slung it over his shoulder.

The Espace pulled over and came to a stop.

Pope told the woman what he wanted her to do. He opened the door, slid down to the ground and moved briskly away from the car. The parking spot was hemmed in by a slope on three sides. Pope clambered up it, forcing his way through the sparse vegetation until he stopped and looked back. He was thirty feet above the roof of the car. The road was laid out before him, several hundred feet of it, with wide run-offs to either side. There was no drop until it began the right-hand turn that was another fifty feet up the road. It offered a reasonably safe position for what Pope intended to do.

Chapter Eight

I sabella looked out the window of the car. She knew that they were still in Turkey and that they were headed south, but she didn't recognise any of the names of the towns and villages through which they had passed.

Karsi.

Karayilan.

Azganlik.

Sariseki.

She hadn't heard of any of them before.

Every fresh mile that they travelled made her doubt just a little more. Where was Pope? Perhaps he had been prevented from following her by the accident that had closed European airspace, but if that was true, why had he not contacted the Turkish authorities? Where were the roadblocks? Where were the police? Where were the attempts to stop them? She glanced back frequently through the rear window, but she didn't think that they were even being followed.

Was she wrong about Pope?

Had he abandoned her?

Isabella flexed her legs to try to bring a little life back to them. They had been travelling for hours. They had stopped twice. The first time had been in Mersin, to refuel the Viano. The second time had been at an empty truck stop outside Kuzuculu, to allow them all to use the bathroom. Isabella had been primed for an opportunity to escape on both occasions, but the driver had a handgun and he had kept it pressed tight to her ribs until they were moving again. Jasmin had used the bathroom at the truck stop before her and had confirmed that it was empty; they had only allowed her to go inside once they were sure that there was no chance that anyone else would try to go inside. Her attempt to get away had set them all on edge, and if they had once thought that they could take their eyes off her for a moment, they did not think that now.

The road that they were following was obviously a well-used route. The traffic had been dense around the westbound turn-off that was marked for Iskenderun, but as they continued to the south, it had thinned out again. Now there were just a handful of other vehicles on the road. The landscape was rockier and the road had started to ascend. She wished that she knew where she was.

She looked at the others. Jasmin was asleep and Salim was speaking to someone on his cellphone. He was talking in Arabic. Isabella had taught herself the language and understood it well enough. There was no reason why Salim would suspect that she could translate most of what he said; that was useful, because he was not as guarded as he might otherwise have been. He told whoever was on the other end of the line that they were in Turkey, and that they were going to cross the border at Yayladagi. Isabella didn't recognise the name. Salim listened for a moment and then said that they would follow the coast road to Tartus and then cross the border at Al-Hamidiyah. She didn't recognise those names either.

Isabella turned to Khalil. The boy was staring sullenly out the window.

"Where are we going?" she said.

He looked over at her with distaste. A bruise had formed on his face from where she had elbowed him. She had noticed that he occasionally reached up to prod at it; it must have been painful.

"Come on," she said. "You can tell me that."

"Home."

"Where is that?"

"Somewhere we will be safe."

"Where? Syria?"

"Syria? Are you mad?"

"Where, then?"

"Beirut. My father is an influential man. The government will protect us."

"Shut up, Khalil!" Salim barked out from behind them. "Don't talk to her."

Isabella turned. Salim had finished his call and was glaring at her.

"You don't need me," she said. "Whatever it is you're running from, you're safe now. Let me go."

"Be quiet," he said sternly.

"Why do you still need me?"

"I won't tell you again. Don't make me gag you."

She clenched her fists in frustration, but she didn't push her luck. She turned back to the front and glanced across at Khalil. He gave her a look of withering contempt and turned his head away to look through the window again.

They continued to the south. As they swung around, following a sharp hairpin that climbed suddenly, she could see the road behind them. She saw another car, the first that she had seen for several miles. It was a reasonable distance behind them, but it was moving quickly, much faster than they were. The road straightened out again and Isabella lost sight of the car.

Chapter Nine

Pope lay prone in the sparse vegetation, pressed flat to the ground with stones and rocks sharp against his belly. It was uncomfortable, but he ignored it. He was happy with his position. It offered a clear view of the entire stretch of road. He was elevated above the asphalt by thirty-five feet, and the slope that led down to it was steep, but not so steep that it would be too difficult to negotiate quickly when he needed to move. There was enough brush and scrub that he would be difficult to spot from the road. The sun was behind him, meaning that there would be no telltale reflection against the lens of his sight or his binoculars. He collected them and put them to his eyes. The road was empty in both directions. The only noise was the harsh cawing of a buzzard as it circled high overhead in search of carrion.

A vehicle negotiated the sharp bend at the start of the straight to the north of Pope's position.

It was an SUV.

The quartermaster had described the vehicle that Salim had been travelling in: a silver Mercedes Viano.

He took the glasses and focussed on the vehicle.

A silver Viano.

He held the glasses steady and focussed on the registration plate. 38 VU 055.

It matched the registration of the vehicle that had been observed earlier.

It was possible that they had changed vehicles, but it seemed unlikely. This was the same car as the one that had been spotted, following the same route that they had predicted for it.

Pope saw the shape of the driver, his details obscured through the darkened glass and the glare of the sun as it shone down upon it. He couldn't see into the cabin, but he didn't need convincing. This was it. Isabella was inside that car.

He put the glasses beside him and lowered his face to the M4, pressing his eye against the sight and nudging the weapon so that the car filled the reticule. He slid his index finger through the guard, feeling the trigger against the pad of his finger. He pulled a little, feeling the trigger give, knowing he needed just a few extra ounces of pressure to send the first rounds down range.

He slid the reticule across the windshield until the driver filled it. He aimed down a bit, allowing a little for the closing speed of the SUV and the gentle breeze that was blowing toward it.

He started to squeeze.

Another car turned the corner.

Shit.

He saw it coming, glimpsed it through the scope. A Mitsubishi Grandis.

Shit.

The SUV was approaching.

He couldn't delay too long.

The first option was to continue with his plan, take the shot to disable the Viano and then mount his attack. There would be witnesses, though. Whoever was in the Mitsubishi would see the Viano leave the road. They might stop and help. They would complicate matters.

The second option? Let al-Khawari progress and make an alternative plan to stop him.

He discounted the second option immediately. Salim would be ahead of him, and the longer he was allowed to progress to the south, the more locations he would have to cross the border into Syria. The more difficult it would be for Pope to stop him. The closer he would be to reinforcements.

No.

Pope knew that he had to act now.

Chapter Ten

The car that Isabella had seen closed on them quickly. Isabella could see that their driver was concerned. She saw him looking in the rear-view mirror, his eyes flicking up, back down to the road ahead, back up to the mirror again.

"Sir," he said, "I think someone is following us."

Salim turned around and looked through the wide rear windows of the Viano.

"For how long?"

"I saw them just outside Iskenderun," the driver said. "They started to close a minute ago."

"What do you think?"

"I don't know, sir."

"The Americans?"

"It's possible."

"Can we outrun them?"

The driver looked over at the satnav that was stuck to the inside of the window. He tapped the screen to scroll out and looked at the map. "We're a long way from Antakya. If we could get to one of the towns—Kurtlusoguksu, maybe—then we'd have a chance. But, out here, with no one around, nowhere to lose them, I don't know."

Isabella was watching the man when she saw the movement of another car farther down the road to the south, in the direction that they were travelling.

The driver swore.

The second car had pulled out of a blind turning and reversed right across the road. It couldn't have been an accident; the road passed through two shoulders of rock at that point, narrowing significantly, and the car had stopped in the middle. It did not completely block the way ahead, but it would make it more difficult to pass through.

"It's an ambush," Salim said.

The driver gripped the wheel.

"Don't stop. Do you understand? Do *not* stop."

"No, sir. I can get through there."

"Give me your weapon."

The driver took his right hand off the wheel and reached into his jacket. He collected his pistol and, with his attention on the road ahead, he handed it back to Salim.

Isabella knew this was the chance that she had been waiting for. She seized the man's wrist with both of her hands and yanked down. His arm was halfway into the rear of the cabin, his elbow above the top of his chair. She pulled down again, as hard as she could, the man's elbow bending the wrong way. She heard the pop as the tendons in his elbow hyperextended, and with a groan of pain, he loosened his grip on the pistol.

It was a Beretta M9.

Isabella reached for it.

Khalil pushed across her, trying to pin her back against her seat. The gun fell into the footwell between the seats.

Salim shouted, "Stop her!"

The driver, his right arm disabled, lost control of the vehicle. The wheels turned sharply to the right, the rubber screeched horribly and with dreadful inevitability, the vehicle tipped over on its side and slammed down hard onto the road.

———

Pope settled back down again, squeezed the buttstock into the cleft between his shoulder and neck, and corrected his aim. The quartermaster had blocked the road as best she could, but the Viano kept coming. There was enough space for the people carrier to negotiate the narrow pass, but it would be tight and it would have to slow.

It would be an excellent moment for Pope to take his shot.

He saw a blur of movement from the driver's side of the cabin, saw the nose of the Viano jerk to the right, and then watched with horror as the vehicle overbalanced and crashed down onto its left-hand side. It had been travelling quickly, and the momentum was not immediately arrested. The car slid down the road, its roof and hood all that Pope could see. Sparks gushed out from beneath the bodywork as the metal scraped against the pitted surface of the road.

The Mitsubishi was accelerating and catching the Viano quickly from the rear.

Pope moved away from the scope and raised his binoculars for a wider view.

The Viano's momentum was finally scraped away and it came to rest.

Pope's heart raced. The Grandis stopped fifteen feet away from the Viano. There was a brief pause, just a couple of seconds, and then the doors opened and four men disembarked.

They were wearing desert combat fatigues with black balaclavas over their heads.

They were all armed.

———

Isabella would have been thrown from the SUV were it not for the seat belt around her waist. The fabric bit sharply into the skin, holding her roughly in place, and she anchored herself a little more by throwing her hands forward and pressing against the forward seats.

The Beretta was gone. She caught a glimpse of something flying up at the newly upended ceiling, saw it bounce, then lost it. It could be anywhere now. Khalil was above her, his own belt holding him in place, his shoulder pressed against hers and his right arm diagonally across her chest. The driver was struggling to free himself. The windshield had shattered as the frame buckled during the flip, and the man was trying to crawl out onto the road.

Isabella shrugged her shoulder and managed to free herself from beneath Khalil's weight. He was dazed. She reached down for the belt clip and released it. She tried to orientate herself. She was on the side of the Viano that was leaning against the road. The windows had smashed, the glass scattered liberally all about. Khalil was moaning, but he was awake and didn't look as if he had been badly hurt. She pushed away from the seat and righted herself, her feet finding the surface of the road through the newly empty window frames.

This was her chance.

She had to get out.

She turned. Jasmin al-Khawari looked drunk. She was covered with pieces of broken glass, and her head lolled between her shoulders. Her husband, though, seemed unhurt. He unfastened his seat belt and squeezed himself between the two rows of chairs so that he, too, was upright. He blocked the way to the rear exit.

"You little bitch . . ."

Isabella turned and moved ahead, scrambling across the driver's seat to the windshield. She would get out the same way as the driver. She clambered ahead before Salim could get to her, and as she reached out for the dash, she saw the glitter of something metallic below her.

The Beretta.

She grabbed for it, her fingers brushing against the butt, coaxing it within reach. She got enough of it, pulled it into her grip and slid her finger inside the guard. She got her feet onto the armrest of the driver's seat, then the central console, and pushed up until she could get her body out the window without cutting herself on the shards of glass that remained in the frame, standing out like snaggled teeth.

She scrambled clear and assessed left and right. Ahead of her, to the south, the car that had moved to block the road was still there. She could see the figure of a woman inside it. Salim's driver was to her right, standing at the side of the road. His hands were raised. Isabella thought that was odd. She raised the pistol, aiming it at him, and then saw the movement from her right.

She turned.

The car that had been behind them was parked. Four men, dressed in desert fatigues with balaclavas over their heads, were approaching. They were all armed with Kalashnikovs. One of them ran on toward the blocking car ahead. The rifles of the remaining three were aimed at the driver, and as Isabella emerged, two turned their weapons onto her.

"Drop it!"

She did as she was told.

Chapter Eleven

P ope knew that the quartermaster was doomed. The front
of the Espace was too close to the shoulder of rock, and
the quartermaster would need to reverse before she had the
clearance to turn the car to the south and drive away. The four men
with Kalashnikovs looked as if they were well drilled. Three of them
trained their weapons on Salim's overturned Viano, but the fourth
man hurried to the south, passing the Viano and breaking into a
sprint as the quartermaster threw the car into reverse.

The man stopped when he was thirty feet away and raised the
muzzle of his rifle.

The quartermaster had panicked, crashing the rear of the car
into the outcrop behind it. The gearbox protested as she tried to
force it into first, and then the engine screamed as she fed in the revs
whilst it was still in neutral.

Pope pressed the scope to his eye and drew a bead on the
man with the Kalashnikov. He started to squeeze the trigger, then
stopped. He couldn't. If he fired, he would give away his position.
He was outgunned. He couldn't miss his target from this range, but
that would leave three tangos remaining.

And Isabella was probably in the overturned car.

The quartermaster was finished, and there was nothing he could do about it.

He closed his eyes as the Kalashnikov barked. He heard the sound of breaking glass, of bullets thudding into metal, and then the firing stopped. He opened his eyes and assessed through the scope of his rifle. The Espace had been riddled with rounds. The quartermaster was slumped forward across the wheel. The driver-side window was blown out, and a large bloom of red had splashed across the window on the other side of the compartment. The shooter, his rifle still shouldered, went forward to check that the threat was neutralised.

Pope felt an itch in his trigger finger, ignored it and turned back to the overturned SUV.

The SUV had turned as it slid to a halt, and the angle at which it had come to rest hid anything or anyone who might be on the other side of it.

Pope was blinded.

"Salim Al-Khawari," a man called. "Get out of the car."

Isabella stood with her arms raised above her head. She had dropped the pistol; it was on the ground a few feet away. She had made sure that she didn't toss it so far away that it couldn't be easily retrieved, but the men were too well organised to be fooled by such an elementary move. The fact that she had emerged with a weapon seemed to accord her special status. One of the men—tall and thin, with the smoothest dark brown skin—separated from the trio and approached. He flicked the muzzle of the rifle, indicating that she should step away. She did as she was told.

"Naughty," the man said, shaking his head. He spoke with an English accent. He crouched down, the rifle held with his right hand as he collected the Beretta with his left. He stood, pushed the pistol into the waistband of his combat trousers and stepped back again. "What are you doing with that, then?"

She ignored him.

"Get out now!"

Isabella turned her head as she heard the sound of someone clambering out of the car behind her. It was Salim. He had his hands raised. Khalil was next, carefully pulling his mother out after him.

"Mr al-Khawari," the man said.

"Who are you?"

"My name is Usman."

"What is this?"

"You are coming with us."

"Where?"

The man pointed to the east. "To the caliphate, of course."

"No," Salim said. "I'm not. I'm going home. To the Lebanon."

Usman's English was formal, without much in the way of inflection. "I am afraid that you are not the one giving orders here. You will do as we tell you, or there will be consequences for you and your family."

Salim started to speak, but the man cut him off.

"Who is this?" He was pointing his AK-47 at the driver.

"My chauffeur," he said.

The man pulled the trigger and a quick burst of gunfire spat out, cutting the driver right across the midriff. Jasmin screamed as squibs of blood splashed out, the driver hopelessly trying to staunch the sudden outflow of blood as he dropped to his knees and then toppled onto his side.

The man turned the Kalashnikov onto Isabella.

"And her?"

"She has nothing to do with us."

"So I should shoot her, Mr al-Khawari?"

"Do what you want."

Chapter Twelve

The passengers from the overturned SUV had been ushered away from the vehicle such that Pope could now see them. He recognised Salim and Jasmin al-Khawari and their brattish son, Khalil.

And he recognised Isabella.

One of the group of men who had intercepted the car looked to be interrogating Salim. Pope was too far off to pick up the details of the conversation, but the tone was evident.

The man was confident.

Salim was frightened.

The man who had shot up the Espace was searching it.

Pope adjusted the aim of the carbine so that he could quickly cover any of the protagonists should they make a move that might cause an immediate threat to Isabella. He had aimed the sights on the man who had been talking to Salim, and watched as the man swivelled so that he faced the driver and pulled the trigger.

He saw the driver fall dead and heard Jasmin al-Khawari scream.

The man turned the Kalashnikov onto Isabella.

Pope took aim at him and prepared to fire. He would take him out and then try to take out another. After that, he didn't know what he would do. But he was not prepared to wait and do nothing.

The man with the rifle continued to speak to Salim. Pope held him in tight focus and started to squeeze the trigger.

The man lowered the rifle.

Pope relaxed his finger.

The man who had been searching the Espace emerged and looked up at the cliffs on the opposite side of the road. He was looking for anyone else who might have been in the SUV. Pope quickly pulled the rifle back and pressed himself down.

He could still watch the road through a cleft in the rocks. One of the others went forward and took Isabella by the arm, dragging her to the Mitsubishi. Salim, Jasmin and Khalil followed. They all got into the back of the Grandis. It was a seven-seat vehicle and it would have been cramped for all eight of them, but the doors were slammed shut and the people carrier pulled away. It rumbled to the south, squeezed past the bullet-riddled Espace and passed out of view.

Pope approached the overturned Mercedes. He got right up close. The interior of the vehicle was a mess. The windows had smashed and fragments had been thrown all the way to the back of the cabin, a fine dusting of shards that glittered in the sunlight. There was little in the way of luggage. The al-Khawaris had been forced to leave Switzerland quickly, and they had not had the opportunity to pack. There was an empty Coke bottle, and the remains of a half-eaten sandwich had been scattered across one of the bench seats. The sat-nav unit that must have been attached to the glass had fallen against the door. Pope jammed the muzzle of his M4A1 into the empty window, using it to brush out the remaining jagged shards, and then reached in and collected the unit.

He glanced at it. The route was still displayed, a green line that tracked through the mountains. Something about it looked awry. He tapped on the screen to zoom out, pulling back until the scale revealed the entirety of the route. It started from Antalya, as he had expected, the green line following the Turkish coast to Mersin, Adana and Iskenderun. But instead of turning east toward Syria, the route continued south. It passed through Antakya and kept going, crossing the Syrian border at Yayladagi and continuing into the shoulder of territory that was squeezed between the sea to the west and the Islamic State to the east. It did not deviate. The route continued south, pressed up against the coast, before it crossed the border into the Lebanon near Talkalakh.

The Lebanon? Why were they going there? Their intelligence was that Salim would flee to Raqqa.

Pope put the satnav in his pocket and went to the Espace.

The quartermaster was slumped to the side, her clothes soaked in blood. They had riddled her body with bullets; at least she would have died quickly. The vehicle had been badly damaged. Both offside tyres had been punctured, and a jagged stitching of bullet holes picked a path to the fuel tank. Diesel was running out of the holes. The vehicle wasn't going anywhere.

Pope opened the rear door and hauled out the backpack. He opened the ruck and examined the contents. The man who had searched the car had not taken any of them out. There were three pairs of flex cuffs, six flashbangs, a thermite grenade, a Penflare gun and flares, a CamelBak water carrier, and a pistol belt with an escape and evasion kit. His plan did not call for all of the additional equipment, but the need to be prepared for all eventualities had been drilled into him, so he packed it all back inside. He took a claymore mine, sliding the small grey-green plastic carrying case into the pack. He added white phosphorous grenades in case he needed to lay down a smokescreen, and paused as he saw a disposable 66mm rocket. It was an American-made M72 LAW, intended to be deployed against tanks and light armour, consisting of two tubes that were pulled apart when it was readied for firing; the rocket was inside the second tube. Pope estimated that he was already committed to hauling 110 or 120 pounds, and the 66 would add another 5.

What the hell, he concluded. In for a penny. He fastened the launcher to the backpack, hauled the pack onto the road, and propped it against the car.

He heard the sound of an engine approaching. He ducked behind the chassis of the Espace, popping out quickly to glance at the motorbike that was speeding down the straight toward him. The driver would see the wreckage. Would they stop? Pope couldn't predict it, but he wasn't prepared to take the chance. He waited, and then, as the bike was fifty feet away, he swung out from behind the wing, raised the rifle and aimed down the road.

The bike was a blue Suzuki Bandit. The rider, a man, had started to slow as he drew closer to the stricken SUV. Now, with Pope directly ahead and with a high-powered firearm aimed at him, he had two choices: swerve and try to accelerate away, or stop. Pope fired a warning shot just to the right of the Bandit, and the driver made up his mind. The bike's tyres squealed as the rider squeezed the brakes, the bike coming to rest when it was still twenty feet away. The rider put down the kickstand and dismounted, his hands raised above his head as he backed away from Pope's determined approach. The man dared not turn his back to him, but as soon as he had put thirty feet between them, he spun and sprinted away back down the road in the direction from which he had arrived.

Pope grabbed his backpack and mounted the bike. The keys were in the ignition and the engine was still running. He settled the straps of the pack so that it was as evenly balanced as he could manage, slung the rifle over his shoulder and gunned the engine. The bike leapt forward, and Pope began his pursuit.

Chapter Thirteen

Isabella sat quietly in the back of the people carrier. The Grandis was not a particularly new or powerful vehicle. The Viano would, in all likelihood, have been able to outrun it. She had made that possibility moot when she had caused the Mercedes to crash, and she wondered whether that might be something that she would come to regret. Out of the frying pan and into the fire. There was nothing to do about it now, though, so she dismissed the thought. This was not a time to be occupied by distractions. She needed to be vigilant and alert. To begin with, she needed to work out what was happening to her.

The car was musty. It had seven seats, and it was cramped. One of the men was driving, leaving Usman to sit in the passenger seat next to him. He had drawn a pistol from a shoulder holster and was aiming it back into the cabin at them. He held the gun with the kind of casual confidence that Isabella had seen in Michael Pope and her mother. He had already demonstrated that he was ruthless, with the murder of Salim's driver. This was not a moment to push her luck. She would try to build an understanding of the new situation first.

The al-Khawaris were quiet, too. Khalil looked ill. She realised, with a moment of empathy that she quickly and easily dismissed, that he would have been frightened, too. He was immature, little more than a boy, and he had led a cosseted and spoilt life. What had happened to him over the course of the last day and a half would have been enough to frighten anyone in his situation. He had been there, on the road next to her, when their driver had been killed. He had turned away and vomited, retching up his dinner on the margin of the road.

Jasmin looked bilious, too, and her face bore the unmistakeable signs of fright.

"The car that was blocking the road," Usman said. "What was that about?"

"I don't know," Salim said. "I've never seen it before."

"There was a backpack inside, with military equipment in it. Do you know why that might be?"

"No," he said. "I've no idea."

Salim had composed himself. He, too, had been cowed into timid silence by the display on the road, but as Isabella looked back at him now, she saw that he had settled himself enough that he could start to try to assess the situation into which he and his family had fallen. Whatever this was, it had taken him by surprise.

She thought about what Usman had just said. There had been weapons inside the car. What if there had been a passenger? She hadn't seen anybody else, but what if there had been? What if it had been Pope?

Pope rode fast.

The vehicle carrying Isabella had about a ten-minute head start. Assuming the car was travelling at sixty, and that the road was straight and that there was no traffic, he guessed that it would be around ten miles down the road. But the road was winding, clambering through the mountain pass via a series of hairpin bends and switchbacks. Forty miles an hour might be the best average speed that they could manage, with the result that they might only be four or five miles ahead of him. He thought he might be able to reel that in.

The E91 continued to the southeast, passing through Halilbey and Kici. Pope rode as quickly as he dared. The road was in good condition, mostly three lanes across and demarked by a series of white posts along each side. The terrain climbed to the left of the bike and descended on the right, the slope occasionally dropping away in vertiginous plunges that would certainly have been fatal if he misjudged the corners. The vehicle that he was pursuing was large and would have limited manoeuvrability. The Suzuki was powerful and nimble, and as Pope leaned through the corners and powered down the straights, he was confident that he would be able to close on them. He pushed the bike up to 120 before he felt the need to pull back. He took one particularly vicious left-hander too fast, and had to let most of the throttle out and lean all the way down as the bike edged out too close to the side of the road and the drop beyond. The rear wheel chewed through the loose gravel before he was able to point it back in the right direction, gunning the engine again and quickly returning to his previous pace. He looked down at the fuel gauge as he raced down toward Halilbey. He guessed it was a seventeen-litre or four-gallon tank, and the needle showed that it was still half full. Fuel wouldn't be a problem.

Halilbey was a small town, a series of buildings gathered around the road, and Pope raced through it at eighty miles an hour. He had expected to have closed on them by now, and he was beginning to wonder whether they might have turned off the road. He didn't think it was likely—he had seen no obvious turnings, and the Grandis wasn't built for off-roading—but it was beginning to reach the point where it would have been impossible for them to stay ahead of him.

He was about to slow down and refer to the satnav in his pocket when he saw them.

The road had descended a little and reached a roundabout. The E91 continued on a southeasterly route. It merged with the D825, a similar road that headed to the northeast and the southwest. Pope had just negotiated a very sharp hairpin when he saw the vehicle a half mile ahead. The road to the southwest lead to Antakya. The town of Kirikhan was six miles to the northwest, and it was in that direction that the Grandis turned.

Pope reduced his speed. It would be difficult to lose them now. There was the one SUV, and the road was otherwise almost empty. But that cut both ways. It would be a simple enough thing for them to notice that he was following them. He still had no idea what had just happened in the mountains. He had no idea who the masked men who had intercepted Salim's vehicle were, nor what their motive was. And most importantly, he had not decided what was the best course of action. There were four of them, all armed with Kalashnikovs. He was very well armed, too, but he was at a loss as to how he could stop them on his own, especially without putting Isabella at risk.

Until he had worked that out, he would follow them.

⌣

They drove on throughout the afternoon and into the evening.

Isabella had been watching Salim for the last few miles. He had been silent, but it was obvious that he had been quietly ruminating about their predicament. When he finally spoke, his face was clouded with anger. "What is this about?"

"Quiet."

"You have abducted my family. I want to know why. What have I done?"

Usman said nothing, but he raised his pistol so Salim could see it more clearly.

"At least tell me who you are?"

The man smiled and shook his head.

"You're with ISIS?"

"No more questions," the man said.

Isabella watched him. He was very calm, with a wry upturn at the corners of his mouth as if he was perpetually on the cusp of laughter. He spoke occasionally with the driver. Isabella was close enough to hear the odd word over the noise of the engine, and he spoke with a strong London accent. The driver, on the other hand, had a singsong drawl that she thought was Scandinavian. The two of them made for an odd couple. The other two men had been quiet.

"Please," Salim said. "Where are we going?"

"I said no more questions. You are not in control now, Mr al-Khawari. You're my prisoner and you'll do whatever I tell you to do. If you do not, there will be consequences for you and your family." He raised the pistol and tapped the index finger of his left hand on the barrel. "The caliph only told me to collect you. Your wife and son are still alive because I'm a considerate man. But don't test my patience."

Isabella looked back at Salim and willed him to be silent. She had no doubt that the man meant what he said. She had no doubt either that she was of even less value to him than Khalil and Jasmin were. If demonstrations of violence were required, she knew that the first would be directed at her.

Salim looked as if he was about to retort, but, thankfully, the threat finally seemed to register. He bit his lip, his teeth pressing down enough that the flesh whitened, and turned away, looking out into the looming darkness. Isabella noticed that his hand snaked out across his lap to his wife's hand, clasping them both together.

Pope followed. He stayed a minimum of a half mile behind them, driving without lights as dusk fell. He saw the glow of the brake lights as the Grandis slowed and pulled off the road. The terrain had continued to be rugged, but now the mountains of the Belen Pass had been replaced by a series of gentler hills. The road had continued to wend its way down the slopes, and now, ten miles from Syria, it had passed into a thickly wooded area. Pope had expected them to continue and then take one of the tracks and trails that would lead to the porous border; the sight of them slowing and drawing to a halt was a surprise. He killed the engine and brought the bike to rest.

He took out the satphone that Bloom had given him, activated it, waited for it to acquire a lock on the satellite and then called the number that had been stored in the memory.

The call connected. "This is Archangel."

"Copy that, Archangel." Pope recognised Bloom's withered voice. "Where are you?"

"North of Akpinar."

"Still in Turkey?"

"Yes."

He told Bloom about the attack in the Belen Pass, about how Salim and his party had been abducted by the four masked men. He explained that the quartermaster had been killed, and that he was in pursuit.

"Do you know who they are?"

"I don't."

"ISIS?"

"Seems most likely. But that doesn't make any sense. Why would ISIS capture Salim if he was running to them anyway?"

"I don't know."

"I found a satnav in Salim's car. They were heading south, not east. Their route would have taken them through Turkey, right through Syria and then into the Lebanon. They were avoiding ISIS. They were headed for Beirut."

"That doesn't make sense."

"No, sir. It doesn't." Pope squeezed the phone between his chin and shoulder as he scanned down into the valley with the binoculars; the car was still parked. "The jet—do you think they could have been headed for Beirut before it turned back?"

"It's possible. We assumed they were going to Raqqa. The military airbase at Tabaqa seemed likely."

"But they weren't. If they were going to Raqqa, why didn't they drive straight there? And why were they attacked?"

"I can't answer that." There was a pause on the line and then a burst of static before Bloom spoke again. "What do you propose?"

"My options are limited. I'm outnumbered. I could attack them, but I can't guarantee I can get Isabella out."

"Don't be sentimental, Archangel. Your orders are clear. You're there for Salim."

"I know that, sir, but not at Isabella's expense." Bloom started to speak, but Pope forestalled him. "I'm going to follow them. If I think I have an opportunity to attack when I get to her, I'll take it."

"And Salim?"

"I'll kill them all."

"And if you can't get to her?"

"I'll cross that bridge when I come to it."

Chapter Fourteen

Pope heard the helicopter before he saw it. It was the end of
dusk, the light quickly fading, and the sound of the engine
rumbled through the valley. It was coming from the east,
from the Syrian border. The sound was familiar. He stayed down
low, took out his binoculars and scanned the landscape until he
saw it. It was a UH-60 Black Hawk, the workhorse chopper used
by the American military. It was coming in fast and low, cutting
through the valley at no more than fifty feet above the ground.

He pushed the bike into the trees at the side of the road, took
off his backpack and rested it against a trunk, and then unslung his
M4A1. He hurried forward on foot. There was a quarter of a mile
between him and them. He followed the road, staying close to the
margin of trees, sheltering in the deeper gloom that could be found
there. He collected his phone from his pocket, and as he ran, he
dialled Bloom's number again.

"It's Archangel."

"Report."

He spoke between breaths. "We have a problem."

"Go on."

"They've got a helicopter. They're going to exfiltrate them by air."

"Where are you now?"

"I'm closing on it. Do you have any reconnaissance assets in the vicinity?"

"We're off the books. You're not even supposed to be there."

"I realise that, sir. But if I can't stop it, you need to know where they're going. What if you said this information was provided by a British intelligence asset in Turkey? And that you needed to track it?"

"Hypothetically? Perhaps."

Pope ran harder, struggling to find the breath to carry on the conversation. "I'm going to try to stop it. Make sure it's tracked. I'll let you know what happens."

Pope reached the turning that the Grandis had taken. It was a pitted and potholed track that led through a fringe of wood to the clearing that Pope had seen from his vantage point farther up the slope. He sprinted hard, the noise of the chopper still echoing around the valley. He reached the edge of the clearing and stayed low, hiding behind the trees and brush.

The chopper was coming down. It descended into a storm of downdraft, the wash throwing out a vortex of dust and small pieces of debris. It touched down with its tail facing in Pope's direction. If it had been the other way around, with the cabin facing toward him, he might have been presented with a shot to take out the pilot. That would have been the cleanest way to prevent the bird from taking off again, but it was facing away from him, and he didn't think that he would be able to remain unseen if he tried to skirt the undergrowth so that he could open up an angle. He could try to put a few rounds into the rotor assembly, but there was no guarantee that it would work, and he would immediately reveal that he was there.

Isabella and the others watched through the dirty windshield of the Grandis as the helicopter descended. It touched down ten metres away from them, the downdraft sending a blizzard of tiny debris to ricochet off the glass and ping off the bodywork. Isabella looked back at the al-Khawaris. They were all aghast as the next stage of their abduction was revealed to them.

"Out," the man with the London accent said, opening the door and climbing out of the people carrier.

Isabella was taken by the arm and dragged outside by the driver of the Grandis. She was hauled across the clearing to the open door of the helicopter. Khalil came next, with Salim and Jasmin behind them. One of the other men was behind them, marshalling them with his Kalashnikov. The other two had gone to the edge of the clearing.

Isabella was pumped full of adrenaline.

She was still uncertain as to what had happened to her, but she knew one thing for sure.

She did not want to get into that helicopter.

There were only two guards with them now. The moment would pass, the chance gone as soon as the other two returned, but, for now, it was an opportunity.

She planted her feet and struggled to free her arm. She wanted the man to be irritated with her, to get in close. He pulled harder. He was bigger and stronger than she was, but she knew how to make herself a dead weight.

"Don't make me hit you," he said, raising his voice above the roar of the turbine.

She kept struggling. "Let me go!"

Isabella heard the sound of laughter behind her. "You having trouble, Mehdi?"

"Come *on*," the man said firmly.

"She's half your size. Pick her up!"

The man stopped trying to drag her. Instead, he turned and grabbed her with both hands on her shoulders. He forced her around so that they were facing each other, and then released his right hand and drew it back, ready to strike her across the face. Isabella was ready for that. She moved quickly and with purpose, taking a step with her left foot so that the distance between them was halved, and then, before he could do anything to defend himself, she brought up her right knee into his crotch. The blow landed flush, the bone of her knee sinking into the man's groin. He gasped with the shock of the sudden pain and dropped to his knees. Isabella saw his face as he slumped down; it was almost comical, his eyes bulging and his mouth hanging open.

Isabella tried to run. She managed a step before she felt a firm grip around her ankle. There came a yank and her leg was pulled from beneath her. She slammed down onto the dirt, the breath knocked out of her. She craned her neck around and looked back, saw that the man the others had called Mehdi had managed to reach out and snag her ankle. She tried to kick her way free. She couldn't do it. Mehdi was strong and his grip was tight. The others were laughing at the show, deriding him for being given the run around by a *girl*, and now he was angry, too.

She managed to scramble to her knees, but Mehdi pulled her leg from underneath her and she landed face first in the dust again. He stood. Isabella could see what was about to happen and was able to draw up her knees and protect her kidneys with her arms. He kicked her, hard, making her breath spurt out.

When she raised her head, she was looking down the barrel of the Kalashnikov.

Chapter Fifteen

P ope dropped to one knee and raised the M4A1 rifle. He pressed the stock to his shoulder, held the foregrip loosely and put his eye to the sight. He reconnoitred. Isabella was fifty yards away, between him and the helicopter. Salim, his wife and his son were behind her. Isabella and Salim were each next to a guard. The two others had moved from the edge of the clearing to the rear of the procession, their AKs carried in loosely cradled grips that would make them easy to bring up and fire.

Pope assessed the four guards. It was obvious that one of them was senior to the others. He stayed close to Salim, and it seemed that he was the man giving the others their orders. The remaining three men certainly deferred to him. He was older, and he had the bearing of a soldier. He wore a pair of desert boots, while the others wore trainers. He was cautious, whereas the attitude and posture of the others looked a little frivolous to Pope's eye.

Isabella started to struggle and the others laughed as their companion was unable to drag her ahead. The fourth man did not share in their boisterousness, regarding the scene with a cool eye.

The other men looked comfortable with their weapons, but that did not mean that they were seasoned. It was possible that they had been soldiers, but he didn't think so. They carried their weapons a little too nonchalantly. They were a little too relaxed. No, he thought. The first man was in charge, and he had been given the other three to help him make the excursion into Turkish territory. The other boys were civilian recruits, wannabe jihadis who had answered the call to join the caliphate.

That was useful information.

Pope knew what he would do. The leader would be his first target. He was fifty feet away from him. Not an easy shot, by any means, but Pope would have been able to put a round through the middle of a playing card with the M4 from this distance. The man was a large and inviting target. Pope was confident that he could take another of the guards down before he would face any return fire. There would be confusion as soon as he pulled the trigger. Their leader would be the first to die, and without his guidance, Pope anticipated that they would fall apart. There would be wild return fire, and they would waste their clips going full auto with no target in sight.

Pope would wait in cover and pick them off.

It would take four shots.

The only question would be whether he fired a fifth at Salim.

He pressed his cheek against the stock and aimed the sight into the body mass of the man next to Salim. No point in making it more difficult with a head shot. A round to the gut would be fine for now. It would put the target down, and Pope would be able to clean up when he was closer.

He curled his finger around the trigger and started to squeeze.

There came a howl of pain.

He pulled away from the sight and widened his focus so that he could take it all in.

The guard who had been with Isabella was on his knees. He was the one who had screamed out. Isabella must have struck him. He had managed to grab her around the ankle and he was holding on tight. She pulled as hard as she could, but it was a wasted effort. The man yanked back, pulling her leg out from beneath her and dropping her to the ground. He heard the other men call out abuse and laugh at the man's misfortune. Pope put his eye back to the sight and swivelled the barrel so that he could focus on Isabella.

He saw Isabella draw her knees up to try to protect herself.

Pope saw the man kick her, hard enough so that she was raised up a little from the ground. He saw her look up.

He saw the man take his Kalashnikov and aim it down at her.

Pope put his eye back to the sight and changed his aim. He exhaled, emptying his lungs, and reached for the trigger.

Isabella was looking up at the man when she heard the crack of the gunshot. It came a fraction of a second before the man was struck, a splash of blood escaping from a freshly dug hole in his gut. He folded over himself and then dropped to his knees like a puppet whose strings had been cut.

Isabella was looking around the clearing, trying to work out what had happened and who had fired the shot, when she saw a flash of light from the gloomy spaces between the trunks of the trees that hemmed them in. The sound of the shot echoed, just like the first, and she heard the sound of something falling to the ground behind her.

She turned. Usman was on his back, his hands pressed around his middle. She saw blood between his fingers.

"Run!"

She heard the shout and thought she recognised the voice.

"Run, Isabella!"

Pope?

Had he come for her?

If it was Pope, and if he spoke again, then she didn't hear him. The deafening clatter of automatic gunfire swamped everything. The two men who had not been shot fired wildly. She had no idea whether they had seen the muzzle flash from Pope's gun, but they were spraying enough rounds to make him stay in cover.

The Kalashnikovs were horribly loud, but even they were subsumed by what came next. The helicopter was equipped with a big 7.62mm machine gun in its open door. It fired, making a thunderous noise that sounded like the tearing of the sky. Whoever was firing the weapon must have seen the flash of Pope's weapon, for the tracer lanced into the woods and then the big rounds followed, pulverising the trees.

Isabella pressed herself to the ground, covering her head with her arms.

"Get up."

She felt a firm pressure on her shoulder.

"Get into the helicopter."

She looked up and saw a man she did not recognise. He must have been on the helicopter. He was older, in his forties, and there was a cruelty in his face that suggested that she would be wise to do as she was told. She was pulled to her feet and then manhandled to the open door. She stepped onto the sill and allowed herself to be pushed inside.

The engine cycled up, the rotors started to turn and yet more noise poured down on them. It was hopelessly disorientating. Isabella concentrated on her breathing, on staying as calm as she could. There was no reason for her to be taken with the others. They might conclude that she was more trouble than she was worth, put a bullet in her and push her out the open door. She stood a better chance of staying alive if they forgot that she was there.

Jasmin and Khalil clambered aboard, their eyes wide with terror. Salim followed.

The machine gun was fed by a belt of ammunition and it was still firing. The man using it was not as indiscriminate as the others. He was laying down covering fire, regular bursts that preserved his ammunition yet made it impossible for Pope, or whoever it was who had fired on the party, to risk another shot. The man who had collected her from the ground, and the two jihadis who had survived the attack, pulled themselves aboard.

"Take off!"

Pope lay flat on the ground as the big rounds from the machine gun rendered the trunks of the trees around him into chippings. He had taken out two of the men, and were it not for the escalation that the M60D had provided, he would have been able to put down the other two. But now he was trapped. The rifle was laid out on the ground ahead of him. He put his eye to the sight and drew a bead on the gunner inside the cabin. He was about to fire when the Black Hawk's engines whined and the chopper lifted off.

The Black Hawk rotated away from him, meaning that the M60D could no longer pin him down. Pope rose from his cover, shouldered the M4 and fired a burst at the Black Hawk. It was a large target and he was still relatively close; he couldn't miss. His rounds sparked off the fuselage, but the chopper continued regardless. Pope watched as it lifted higher into the air. The pilot dipped the nose and it gathered speed, the rotors clattering as it drew farther and farther away.

Pope took out his satphone and called Bloom again.

"It's Archangel."

"Report."

"They're airborne. It's a UH-60 Black Hawk. They're heading east into Syria."

"A Black Hawk?"

"Definitely."

"There was a rumour that the Iraqis lost a squadron at Mosul. It's not impossible that ISIS have pilots. Fuck. What happened?"

"I took out two of them, but I was outgunned."

"And Salim?"

"He's on board. The others, too."

"Unhurt?"

"I think so."

"Dammit, Pope. We need him dead."

The Black Hawk gained altitude, following the line of a small hill, passed over the crest and disappeared on the other side.

"Pope?"

"I've lost my visual. Please tell me you have it."

There was a pause, and perhaps the suggestion of a whispered conversation that Pope could not distinguish. Bloom came back on the line. "Yes. We have it."

Pope didn't need to know how. He just needed to know that they knew where Isabella was, where she was going.

"Track it. Tell me where they go."

Pope heard a cough from the clearing. One of the men he had shot was still alive.

"What are you going to do?"

"They're heading east. I'm going to go after it."

"Good luck, Archangel."

"Pope out."

Chapter Sixteen

The flight was far from comfortable. The cabin was equipped with only three seats—just simple strips of fabric webbing that were suspended between metal joists—and those were taken by their captors. Isabella and the others were forced to sit on the floor with their backs against the fuselage. The big engine was terribly loud and they had nothing to protect their ears. It was hot, too, and the temperature was slowly ticking up the longer they were aloft. Isabella felt the sweat on her brow and the drips that ran down her back.

The others were suffering, too. Salim and Khalil stared at their feet, saying nothing. Jasmin looked bilious, and it was no surprise to Isabella when she bent to one side and vomited. The man who had been manning the machine gun had pulled the door closed as soon as they had taken to the air, so the acrid stench of the vomit had nowhere to go. The heat inside the cabin made it worse, and soon Isabella was struggling to manage her own queasiness.

There had been no conversation. The al-Khawaris had learned that it was pointless as they had been driven through the mountains, and nothing had changed now. If anything, the man who had assumed command since Usman's death was even more severe.

Isabella watched him. He had taken one of the seats in the cabin, anchoring himself against the occasional sway of the chopper. He watched them with a vigilance that she hadn't seen in any of the others. He had a pistol in a holster that was fastened to his belt, his right hand resting on the butt. He looked grizzled, more seasoned than the rest, with a beard that reached halfway down his chest.

There came a shout from the cockpit, and the man unclipped his belts and went forward. Isabella watched: the pilot turned to the man, presenting his face in profile, lit up by the greenish glow of the instrumentation. She saw from his expression and the way that he punctuated his sentences with short little jabs of his hand that he was concerned about something. The noise in the cabin was too loud for her to hear what was being said.

The man came back again.

"We've come from Raqqa," he said. "We were going to return there, but it appears that whoever was shooting at us has punctured the fuel tank. We need to land now."

"Where?" Salim said.

"Al-Bab," the man said. "We will continue to Raqqa by road."

The man went over to the door. He unlatched it and pushed it back, allowing a gust of warm air to blow around the cabin. Isabella looked outside. To begin with, they were too high to see anything other than the night sky, but as the pilot banked to port, the angle changed and she could see a city beneath them. It was set out across a flat expanse of desert, fringed on all sides by the encroaching sand. To the west were the foothills of a small mountain range, and to the south she could see the banks of a river. The city itself was composed of low buildings, few of them more than six storeys tall, with trees fringing the streets. There was little evidence of life. She could see only a few vehicles, the lights tracking around wide roads.

They flew on for another five minutes, gradually descending until they were over an empty, sandy plain. It looked like a makeshift military facility, with a broad expanse of asphalt laid down in the centre and a collection of hangars and other buildings. The pilot flared the nose of the Black Hawk to bleed away what was left of their speed and reduce their altitude, bringing them down to rest on the apron. The engine cycled down and the noise gradually dissipated.

There was a line of vehicles against a wire-mesh fence. Isabella saw technicals, pickup trucks that had been fitted with anti-aircraft guns, but it was an old yellow bus that rolled out of the queue and rumbled toward the landing strip.

The man unclipped himself from his seat and turned to address his captives.

"If you do as I say, you will not be harmed."

"Where are we going?"

"You will be kept overnight. Tomorrow, we talk."

Chapter Seventeen

Pope came out from the underbrush. The two men he had shot were separated by a distance of twenty feet. One of them was face down and unmoving; he certainly looked as if he was dead, but Pope wasn't in the business of taking chances. He took out his pistol and fired a single round into the man's body. He didn't move. He was dead.

The second man was still groaning. Pope trained the pistol on him as he approached. His AK had been discarded a safe distance from his body, but there was a chance that he might have a pistol that Pope hadn't seen. The man was wearing the same sand-coloured combats with part of a black balaclava visible from where it had been stuffed into a pocket.

The man raised himself up onto his elbows and started to drag himself toward the Kalashnikov. Pope intercepted him long before he could get to it, and with the gun aimed down, he inserted the tip of his boot underneath the man's body and flipped him onto his back.

The man looked up at him fearfully. Pope frisked him. He was unarmed.

Pope holstered his pistol, took out his knife and crouched down next to the man. He laid the edge of the knife across the man's throat.

"You speak English?"

"Yes," the man said, his larynx bobbing up and down as he swallowed. "I am English."

"Really?"

"London."

"Isn't that fortunate? My Arabic is a little rusty. What's your name?"

His larynx went up and down again, his whiskers catching against the sharp edge. "Usman," he said. "Who are you?"

"There's the thing," Pope said. "I'm going to be honest with you, Usman. I've had a pretty shitty couple of days. Two of my friends were killed, I've been shot at more times than I care to remember and now I've lost the girl I came here to find. All in all, I'm not in a very good mood. So, in answer to your question, I'm bad news."

He pulled the knife away, changed his grip so that his fist was around the hilt with the blade pointing straight down, and stabbed the man in the fleshy part of his thigh.

Pope let the man scream.

"What's going on, Usman?"

All the blood had drained from Usman's face and his skin was slathered with feverish sweat. He gritted his teeth, either unable or unwilling to answer.

"Let me put it another way. Why are you interested in Salim al-Khawari?"

He gasped the words. "I don't know."

"Speculate."

"I don't—"

Pope twisted the hilt, the blade rotating and tearing through flesh and muscle, widening the wound.

"Speculate, Usman. Have a guess."

"We were told to come and get him over the border."

"And his family?"

"All of them."

"The girl?"

"We didn't . . . didn't know about her."

"So why did you take her?"

"She was there. I don't make the decisions."

"Just following orders?"

Usman managed a nod, relieved, perhaps, that they could finally share some common ground.

Pope drew the blade out of the man's thigh and put the edge against his throat. He pushed down and then slashed up, the blade slicing into the skin and then the trachea, severing it. Usman put his hands to his neck as blood rushed out of the newly opened incision, running between his fingers and down the sides of his throat and then onto the sandy ground of the clearing.

Pope wiped the knife on Usman's fatigues.

He stood, sheathed the blade, collected his rifle and started the walk back to his bike.

Chapter Eighteen

The bus took Isabella and the al-Khawaris through the streets of al-Bab. The buildings on either side of the road were in a poor state of repair. They drove by several large craters, the apartment blocks slowly collapsing into the spaces where their neighbours had once stood. Whole neighbourhoods had been levelled by enormous explosions. Twisted metal rods poked out of blocks of concrete that had been cleaved in two. Souks and mosques were reduced to rubble, chunks of debris littered the roads and clouds of thick dust hung in the air. They drove through public parks with no trees, everything chopped down for firewood. They passed the hulks of burnt-out vehicles, men and women queuing at bread lines, and long queues of traffic around the fuel stations that still had fuel to sell.

Isabella had read a lot of books during her childhood. They were her main escape from the misery of her life. One of her foster parents had a library of classical literature, and she had taken books from it and read them when she was alone at night. Dante was in the collection, and this scene, she thought, looked very much like he described hell.

The man with the beard pointed to one large building that had been partially flattened. "That used to be a school," he said. "The regime sent a helicopter with a barrel bomb. Dozens of children were killed. Now the Russians come during the day and the Americans come at night."

The bus drove on. They passed beneath large black flags, the fabric ruffled by the night's listless breeze. They passed a row of parked busses waiting to collect passengers. Men in dun-coloured military fatigues manned checkpoints, AK-47s slung across their backs. Young boys in Western football shirts played amid the rubble and debris of demolished buildings. There were enormous billboards on the other side of the street. The first had a picture of an abaya, together with Arabic script. Isabella could translate most of it. The poster set out 'Sharia stipulations for abaya.' The garments had to be made from dense material, there were to be no big brand names and the robe must not 'resemble the attire of unbelievers.'

The man noticed that Isabella was looking at the billboards. He gestured to the second one. "It says, 'We want nothing other than God's law among us,'" he said. Isabella nodded, not letting on that she had been able to read it for herself.

The driver continued to the north. And then, as they waited to turn into a quieter street, Isabella heard the rumble of a louder, more powerful engine. A tank crawled by in the opposite direction, half a dozen bearded jihadis with AK-47s hanging onto the hull.

Finally, the bus came to rest, the brakes hissing. Isabella looked out the window. They had travelled into a ruined industrial zone, the factories and warehouses on either side of them wrecked by fires and explosions. Rubble had been piled up and left, and the wrecks of burnt-out cars and trucks were all around. They had stopped before one building that was more whole than its neighbours. It had not been left unscathed—part of the building had collapsed in on itself, and the courtyard that separated it from the road was littered with debris—but the majority of the structure was whole.

The district did not appear to be far from the northern edge of the city, and the sky looked wide and inviting beyond the broken buildings. The sky in the other direction, to the south, was polluted with columns of thick black smoke that rose lazily into the air. It was an apocalyptic vista.

The bearded man stood up and turned back to address them.

"You will be staying here," he announced, pointing out the window to the building. "It is not to the standard that you expect, no doubt, but I make no apology about that. There are guards inside and outside. Do not do anything stupid. They have orders to shoot you."

Salim stood, too. "This is unacceptable."

Isabella turned her head and watched him. Salim was precariously balanced between fearfulness and indignation. He had been like that all the way throughout their journey, but now it appeared that he had found a little courage. Either that, she thought, or he was just desperate to do *something*.

The man ignored him and descended the steps.

"Don't turn your back on me. Don't you know who I am?"

The man stopped. He turned back, an amused smile playing at the edges of his mouth. "Do I know who you are?" He stepped back toward Salim again. "Yes, I do. I know that you are the man the Americans and the British are saying funded the bombing at Westminster. The man who, they say, paid for the missile that downed the British Airways flight this morning."

Salim's jaw dropped open. "What?"

"They have broadcast evidence that says you are connected with us."

"That's not true," he said.

"Which part?"

"None of it. I had nothing to do with the bombs or the plane, and I have nothing to do with you."

"Yes, Salim, we *know* you have nothing to do with the caliphate. We know of you, of course. We have researched you. Your involvement with the sheik, for example. We know about that. And you say that you had nothing to do with the bombs. That may be so. But the Imperialists have evidence that suggests you did fund the operation. Emails. Bank transfers. And they have emails from you to representatives of the caliphate that talk of a common cause. We know that these emails are false. We have never communicated with you. The question we have—the question you are going to have to help me understand—is why those emails exist and how they came to be in the possession of our enemies."

"Isn't it obvious? I've been set up."

"Perhaps. But perhaps you are an agent provocateur. Perhaps you have worked with them and running to Beirut was part of the deception, what they would expect you to do. Or perhaps you are a stooge, as you say. It is impossible for us to say without discussing it with you. The details will become clear."

"I'm telling you the truth."

"You would say that, though, wouldn't you? We will need rather more certainty than just taking your word for it. Everything will become clear when you are interrogated. Now—please go inside. I will see you all tomorrow."

⌣

They were met by four armed guards as they disembarked from the bus. These men were dressed in black robes over jeans and trainers, and they each sported AK-47s. The men led them inside, two at the back and two in front. Isabella paid close attention. They looked young, one of them particularly so; he was trying and failing to grow a beard like the ones sported by the three other men. The two in front were talking in a guttural language that she didn't recognise: Russian, perhaps. The guards' weapons did not look to be well cared for. The AK was impossibly rugged and reliable and would fire regardless, but that wasn't what she focussed upon. If they did not maintain their weapons, it suggested that they were either lazy or badly trained, or both. It was possible that their laxity would extend to their guard duties.

One of the guards behind Isabella jabbed her in the back with the muzzle of his rifle, and she made a show of her compliance, obediently scurrying ahead. But she still observed. There was a narrow corridor with two doors to the left and right and a set of double doors straight ahead. One of the guards parted the doors and ushered them through into the factory's main space. Isabella looked around. There were exposed girders in the roof, rows of pillars, windows in which every single pane of glass had been shattered and, overhead, a metallic hook for an indoor crane that would once have moved on runners. The factory must have once been dedicated to some sort of manufacturing; there were the hulks of lathes and milling machines and other machine tools that had been left to rust, their purpose impossible to discern.

They were shepherded to the back of the space. This was where the cells had been constructed. A row of small cubicles had been built out of bricks and breeze blocks, each cell fitted with a thick metal door. The row had been finished with a concrete slab that provided a ceiling; the warehouse space continued for another ten metres overhead. There was a single light that had been attached to the wall, its glow necessary to illuminate the dim space, although it was barely bright enough to do that properly. It did cast a faint glow over a wooden chair that had been fitted with belts that were intended, no doubt, to restrain prisoners during interrogations.

They were marched up to the cells. Salim and Khalil were taken away first. Jasmin reacted badly, becoming almost hysterical as she realised what was happening. She clutched Salim's arm, but they were forced apart before her husband and son were marched to the cells on the far left of the row.

Jasmin slumped down to her knees and started to sob.

Isabella watched it all dispassionately. She needed to be aware of everything that was happening. The reactions of the people around her, the surroundings she found herself in—everything. There would be a moment when another chance to escape would be presented, and she knew that she would need to be ready to take it. And, too, she knew that she needed to maintain the pretence that she had worked so hard to maintain. She didn't know how much the guards would know of what had happened before: how she had disabled the driver on the mountain road, or how she had almost escaped before they were transferred to the helicopter. Perhaps they wouldn't be told, and perhaps they would form an impression based on the evidence before them: she was a young girl, still wearing the pretty dress that she had sported to a party a thousand miles and a different world away. She was frightened, confused and fearful of what the future might hold for her. The fact that her training was at the forefront of her mind, and that she was a coiled spring ready to seize the smallest chance, she buried deep. It served her nothing to reveal anything beyond her disguise.

One of the guards opened a third cell and returned for Jasmin. She wouldn't stand when he told her to get up, so he dragged her across the room, deposited her in the cell and shut the door.

Isabella was next. Her cell was to be next to Jasmin's. The guard opened it and gestured that she should go inside. She walked forward. The cell was tiny, no more than the span of her arms from side to side and seven or eight feet deep. There was a thin mattress that was spotted with brown stains and an empty plastic bottle. Nothing else.

Isabella was shoved the rest of the way inside. She pretended to trip over the edge of the mattress and sprawled over it, turning back just as the door was slammed closed. She heard the key turn in the lock.

It was almost completely dark inside the cell. She reached out with both hands to touch the walls so that she could orient herself, and then stood. There was a tiny sliver of light around the top of the cell, where the concrete slab had been lowered onto the bricks. It was eight feet to the ceiling, but it wouldn't have made any difference if it had been lower; it would have been impossibly heavy for Isabella to move.

She heard the sound of laughter and retreating footsteps as the guards walked away.

———

Isabella stayed awake for two hours to get an idea of the functioning of the prison. She listened for the guards and tried to gauge the pattern of their patrols. She concluded, in the end, that there was no pattern. They were disorganised and haphazard and not particularly well trained. That all being said, the cells had been well constructed, and Isabella concluded that it would be difficult to break out of them without help.

She was tired, and she needed sleep. There would be a chance to escape, and she didn't want to waste it because she had no energy. She lay down on the thin mattress, ignoring the stains that she had seen while the door had been open, and closed her eyes. She could hear gentle sobs from the cell to her right. She thought that it was Jasmin, but Jasmin was next to her and this sounded farther away.

It must have been Salim.

Chapter Nineteen

The motorbike lost power suddenly and without warning. Pope heard the sound of a sharp snap and felt a painful sting as something whipped against his left leg. He applied the brakes and came to a stop at the side of the road.

Pope was not a mechanic, but it was simple enough to diagnose the fault. The chain had snapped in half, part of it draping down onto the sandy road. He had been fortunate. It would have been easy enough for the snapped chain to have bound and locked the drivetrain, or the broken end to have whipped back into his leg with enough force to sever a tendon. As it was, the only damage to his calf was a painful welt that was already beginning to discolour with a fresh bruise. He prodded and poked at the chain, but he knew that there was nothing he could do. There was no repair that he could make out here, with no spare parts and no tools. The bike was a write-off.

He cursed his misfortune. He was going to need to find alternative transport.

He took his binoculars out of his backpack and scanned the surroundings. The desert stretched away in all directions, a bland

and generally featureless expanse composed of blacks and greys, gradually disappearing into the encroaching darkness. There was a large butte perhaps twenty miles to the east, the road swerving around it and continuing through the wide basin over which the mountain presided. The road continued, marked by vivid yellow stripes that warned against straying onto the verge and the dotted white central line. Electricity pylons accompanied the road in both directions, the fizz and pop that Pope could hear suggesting that they were still functional.

Pope looked back to the west. He had crossed the border twenty minutes earlier, and he had been travelling at around fifty miles an hour. That meant that he was around sixteen miles inside the border.

There was no sign of traffic in either direction.

He had two options.

He could retrace his steps and cross back into Turkey. It would be safer, it would be easier there to secure more suitable transport, and it would give him the opportunity to plan for a second incursion with the benefit of greater preparedness. Pope dismissed it at once. It would take time to do that, perhaps a day or even two days before he would be ready to return. Isabella might not have the time to permit him that luxury.

The only other option was to continue onward. He had no interest in trekking through the desert during the heat of the day, but it would be cool now, and he had the benefit of the darkness to help him avoid detection. There was no sign of habitation on the road ahead, but he knew that there were towns within reach.

He went back to the bike and rolled it off the road, pushing it into a ditch and arranging it so that it was lying flat and impossible to see from a passing car. He put the binoculars back into his backpack, replaced it on his back and scrambled back up to the road. He would travel across the smooth surface rather than the more rugged terrain for as long as he had enough time to hide if he saw a vehicle.

Pope checked left and right again. He was alone, with just the calling of a nightjar high overhead to keep him company.

He set off to the east.

Chapter Twenty

They were woken at dawn.

There was a slat at the bottom of the cell door that Isabella had not noticed. One of the guards opened it and pushed in a bowl of rice and beans, a spoon and a cup of water.

"Eat," he said through the door. "We go soon."

The man left the slat open so that she had a little light. Isabella looked down at the bowl. It looked barely edible, but she hadn't eaten since lunch on the day that she had been abducted. She tried to remember how long ago that was. Thirty-six hours? She would have to eat to try to maintain her strength; she intended to escape, and, if she could carry that off, there was no way of knowing how long it would be before she was able to find food again. She took the spoon and shovelled the rice into her mouth, washing it down with glugs of the tepid water that she hoped might disguise its foulness, but in reality just substituted one unpleasant taste for another.

Isabella heard the guards return half an hour later, and as she listened, trying to anticipate what might happen next, she heard the sound of cell doors to her right being opened. She counted three doors, and then her own was unlocked. Shafts of sunlight filtered down from the holes in the ceiling and through the broken windows, casting their light over the idle machinery, the debris that littered the spaces between them, and the coating of sand and grit that had fallen over everything.

Salim and Khalil were already halfway across the factory floor, two guards behind urging them toward the corridor and the exit. Jasmin was outside her cell, a woman standing next to her with her hand on Jasmin's arm. One of the guards had stayed with them, his AK trained on them with lazy technique.

"This is Aabidah," the man said, indicating the woman. "She is from the al-Khansaa brigade. You know who they are?"

"No," Isabella said.

"They are our moral police. They raise awareness of our religion among women and punish those who do not abide by the law. You will do what she says."

Jasmin shook her head. "No. I want to be with my husband and my son. Where are they taking them?"

"You will do what she says," the man said, his voice becoming more forceful. "No argument. Okay?"

Jasmin looked as if she was going to resist, and Isabella could see from the attitude of the man that he would not stand for her disobedience. They would use force if they needed to, and Isabella was concerned that rough treatment could very easily be extended to her, too. She had no interest in taking a beating for no reason. She turned to Jasmin and took her gently by the elbow.

"That's okay," she said. "We'll do what she says."

Jasmin turned to look at her, the expression on her face suggesting that she didn't know how to respond to Isabella's intervention, but she did not demur. She gave a nod, her eyes rimmed red from crying.

The woman gestured down to the bag at her feet. "Your new clothes are inside," she said.

Isabella crouched down and unzipped the bag. She took out two double-layered niqabs, two loose abayas and two pairs of gloves. Isabella had lived in Morocco long enough to have become familiar with Arabic dress, but Marrakech was a cosmopolitan city and attitudes were relaxed. The full-face niqab was not common, and certainly not as thick as this one. These items were more conservative than any she had ever seen before.

The woman turned and said something to the man that Isabella didn't catch. He grunted a response, turned and walked to the other side of the room. They were left with Aabidah. Isabella felt her fists clench, an almost subconscious reaction, as she reassessed the situation. Was this the chance she had been waiting for? There was nothing in the room that she could use as a weapon, but she was confident that she could disable the woman with no difficulty. Aabidah was encumbered with her own abaya and veil and would not be able to react quickly enough to stop Isabella from disabling her. But what would she do after that? The man was on the other side of the room. He had an automatic rifle. She would have to get by him in order to get outside. The other guards had gone in that direction. Even if she was able to take the guard out and get outside, what would she do then? She didn't know where she was.

No. This wasn't the opportunity. She held up the abaya. Her dress would make her hopelessly conspicuous. The abaya and the niqab would offer her anonymity. She would stand a better chance of getting away if she was wearing the clothes that they wanted her to wear. It made better sense to be compliant, at least for now.

There would be another chance.

"That dress," the woman said distastefully. "Remove it."

Isabella pretended that she didn't know what she was supposed to do with the clothes, and Aabidah helped her. She removed the dirty party dress and accepted a pair of plain denim jeans, a white T-shirt and a pair of second-hand trainers. The abaya was loose, much more voluminous than any she had seen before and, she suspected, designed to eliminate the smallest possibility that it might reveal the outline of the wearer's body. The double veil was stifling and uncomfortable, reflecting her breath back against her face. The gloves, too, were made from a fabric that was not best suited to the temperature inside the room. When she had finished dressing, she felt different. Isabella was not concerned with appearance. Vanity was a weakness that her mother had scoured out of her.

Aabidah adjusted the fall of the garment and, satisfied, gave a nod. "You must wear this always. If you go outside without it, the *hisbah* will punish you. Always black. Always thick, always baggy. It must not attract attention. No decoration, no perfume. Everything must be covered."

Jasmin dressed, too, and when they were both done, the woman called out to the guard and he returned to escort them out of the room and into the corridor beyond. The daylight was bright, and Isabella was glad of the shield across her eyes. She could see through the gauze strip that covered the eye slit, and outside she noticed the same yellow bus that had brought them here yesterday.

They were hustled outside. The guard went first, opening the door and admitting the noise of the bus's engine and a waft of stifling, dry heat.

Salim and Khalil were at the front of the bus. Jasmin sat next to her husband, and Isabella, who was going to sit beyond Khalil, was pushed so that she fell down onto the bench next to him.

The guards boarded and the driver closed the doors and pulled away.

"You're dead," Khalil said to Isabella as they bounced across the road. "At least we are Muslim. You're a *keffir*. They'll kill you."

A huge curtain of pitch-black smoke billowed into the air on the other side of town. It was wide, at least a mile across, and as it drifted up, it cowled the sun. One of the guards pointed to the smoke and told the man next to him that it was from a pipeline that had been destroyed by Russian jets.

The bus drew to a stop and the guards indicated that the four of them should disembark. Salim and Jasmin went first, then Khalil, then Isabella. They were outside a building that had obviously once been a hotel. It was set back from the road and surrounded by gardens that had not been tended for many months. Weeds had been allowed to grow tall and unkempt, and lawns that might once have been green had been flattened under the brutal hand of the sun. Late-model cars lined the roads, and two fighters in fatigues transported blankets and other belongings from the trunk of a Nissan. A sign above the door read "Karnak" and as they were hurried inside the reception, Isabella saw a wall that had been decorated in an array of crazy colours; parched potted plants; and a counter that was no longer used, relegated to holding stacks of paper and folders.

They were led through the reception to a flight of stairs. They climbed the stairs, emerging on an outside pathway that overlooked a pleasant garden, and continued along the pathway until they came to a door. One of the guards knocked on the door and, at a command from inside, opened it. They went inside.

It was a pleasant room, clean and tidy and with decent furnishings. There was a wide desk facing them and, behind it, the man who had been on the helicopter yesterday.

He smiled warmly at them all. He was dressed in a loose black robe, and his greying beard reached down to the surface of the desk. She remembered the promise of cruelty in his face and the way his black eyes glittered.

"My name is Abu Abdul al-Fatma. I will be in charge of you during your stay with us in Raqqa. I am sure I need not explain this, but you are deep within the caliphate. I hope that you can understand this fact. You will not be able to get away from us, and no one will be able to find you here and help you escape. Accepting that to be the case will make things easier for you. Can we all agree on that?"

No one spoke. Abu frowned.

"Mr al-Khawari," he said, "please—I need to know that you understand your situation."

Salim nodded. "I understand."

"That is good. I would like us to proceed on as friendly a basis as possible under the circumstances. As I say, I will be responsible for you now. It might be helpful for you to know a little about me, yes?"

He paused to take a sip from a glass of water and then gestured to the jug and the other glasses. Jasmin nodded her thanks and poured out water for herself, her husband and Khalil; she ignored Isabella. If Abu noticed the snub, he did not acknowledge it. Isabella was thirsty and didn't know when she would next be offered something to drink. She took a glass, filled it and drank it down before anyone could stop her.

Abu continued. "I was a lieutenant colonel in the Istikhbarat, Saddam's military intelligence unit. I was also a Special Forces officer in the Special Republican Guard. The invasion changed everything. I was decommissioned after the U.S. arrived, and I joined Sunni insurgents to fight back. I was captured and spent time in Camp Bucca, where I met the other men who are leading the caliphate. When the opportunity to establish our new state presented itself, I made sure that I was involved, and now I have a senior position. I oversee the governors in the various cities and regions of Syria that we control. Al-Bab, where you are now, is one of those cities."

Isabella filled her glass again. Jasmin turned to glare at her but said nothing. Isabella ignored her.

"That is me, then," Abu said. "I know something of you, of course. The al-Khawari name is well known, and I recognise your wife and your son." He turned to Isabella. "But I do not know you."

Isabella sipped the water, buying a little time to compose herself and consider what she should say. She knew that she had to stay within the bounds of the false identity that Pope and the others had created for her. "My name is Daisy," she said.

"And why are you here, Daisy?"

She knew that Daisy would be frightened, reluctant to speak, afraid of the man who was smiling at her from behind the polished desk. She forced herself to swallow and, when she spoke again, it was in a quiet and timorous voice. "I don't know. I shouldn't be here. I don't understand what's happened to me. I just want to go home."

Abu turned to Salim. "What can you tell me?"

"I—"

Jasmin interrupted, speaking over her husband. "She is a thief! She was in our house, trying to steal from us."

"She is more than a thief," Salim said.

"How so?"

"What you said yesterday—about what they are saying about me. The evidence they say they have. None of it is true. The evidence—it must have been planted in my house. And she was in my house."

"Daisy?"

114

"I was there for his party," she said, pointing at Khalil. "I'm just at school with him. I shouldn't be here."

"So why is she here, Salim?"

"It must have been her," Salim said, his anger getting the better of him. "She planted it. She was in my study, with my computer. She did something."

Abu stood and held up his hands. "Calm down, Mr al-Khawari. We will get to the bottom of everything." He poured himself a glass of water and drank it; Isabella noticed how the dampness darkened his whiskers around his mouth. "Now—I understand that what has happened to you must be disconcerting. I doubt that you have had the opportunity to have any of your questions answered, and I will be happy to put that right. But before then, I must ask you another. Would you like to tell me what happened as we boarded the helicopter? There was an attack. Who was it?"

"I do not know," Salim said.

"Please think about your answer, Mr al-Khawari. If we are going to work together, it is important that we get off on the right foot. Trying to mislead me would not be a profitable way to start our relationship. Let me ask you again. Who was it who attacked us?"

"I swear it. I do not know."

"I wondered whether you might have been able to call on security."

"No. It was nothing to do with me. The only security I had was my driver, and your men shot him."

"Then humour me. Speculate."

Abu spoke in a gentle tone, with a ready smile, but there was glittering steel in his eyes, and when he smiled, he revealed a mouthful of shockingly white teeth. Isabella thought he looked predatory. It was obvious that she wasn't the only one who felt that, because Salim looked as if he was about to panic.

"I do not know," he repeated, and then, as Abu curled his fingers to indicate that he should expound further, he said, "Something happened on the road, the Belen Pass, at the same time as your men stopped us. There was a car across the road. It was trying to block us. Someone else was trying to get to us. Your men shot at the car and killed the driver. Maybe you should ask—"

"I have spoken to them," Abu interrupted, his tone still urbane and friendly. "There was a woman in the car. We have her identification papers, and it says that she has a mundane job in Ankara. We believe that her papers are fake. There were weapons in her car. A lot of weapons. What do you think about that?"

"I don't know. It's nothing to do with me. Why would I attack my own vehicle?"

"Yes," Abu said. "I can see that. It does seem unusual. Let me ask another question, then. Who might have wanted to stop you?"

"Tell him about what happened at the house," Jasmin urged. She pointed to Isabella. "Tell him about this little bitch."

Salim scowled, irritated with his wife's intervention. "The FBI stormed my house. I do not know why. We found this girl in my study, like I said. She had attacked my wife. She knocked her unconscious and tied her up."

"Is that true, Daisy?"

"She attacked me. I hit her and she fell and banged her head. I panicked."

"This all sounds rather far-fetched," Abu said. He turned back to Salim. "I want to be honest with you, Mr al-Khawari. I will share what I know and I hope that you, in turn, will share what you know."

"Of course," Salim said. "Anything."

"That is good." Abu took an iPad from the desk and pressed the button to wake it. He swiped the screen until he had what he wanted, and then he reached over the desk and handed it to Salim.

Isabella could see the screen over his shoulder. It was the front page of the BBC News website. The headline was "Swiss Police Seize House of Alleged ISIS Financier."

"This is ridiculous," Salim said. "I have no relationship with—"

Abu interrupted. "We have established that. Keep reading, please."

Salim looked back down at the screen.

"No, Mr al-Khawari. Read it aloud, please. I would like everyone to hear."

Salim paused, then started to read. "'International police have issued a warrant for the arrest of the suspected chief financier of ISIS on suspicion of channelling money from Switzerland to the terrorist group's operatives worldwide, including the London cell that orchestrated the Westminster attacks in the UK.'"

"This is preposterous."

"Keep reading."

"'Police attended the Geneva property of Salim al-Khawari, but were unable to arrest him. Reports suggest that a gun battle took place and that Mr al-Khawari was able to escape by helicopter to nearby Sion airport, where he left the country aboard his private jet. Mr al-Khawari's whereabouts are presently unknown, although a police source suggested that it was likely that he would flee to parts of Syria that were controlled by the terror group.'"

"At least your location is accurate," Abu said with another of his unsettling smiles. "The rest, though?"

"Lies."

"Hmmm." Abu took the iPad and sat down again. "Let me tell you something else. We believe that the Western media will soon be reporting that the authorities have excellent evidence that demonstrates that you funded the bombing of Flight 117. Financial proof that ties your money to the purchase of the missile system that shot it down, proof that would be difficult to fabricate. They will also say that there is further proof that makes it clear that you are connected with us, and that the attacks were in our name. Of course, Mr al-Khawari, we admire the blessed soldiers who carried out those attacks. The crusaders in the United Kingdom have been attacking our people for many months. I praise Allah that its citizens are now paying for that policy with their blood, but although we would be happy to claim the credit for the attack, we cannot. Because we had no connection to the operation. We do not know the martyrs who carried it out; they have never visited the caliphate; they have never trained in one of our camps. They simply have no connection to us. It seems to me that a connection has been engineered that would implicate us. Western public opinion has been less martial since the debacles of Afghanistan, Iraq and Libya. It seems to me that the Western public is being given a reason to support a more substantial campaign against the caliphate. And we would welcome that. The Prophet predicted that the Day of Judgment will come after the Muslims defeat the crusaders at Dabiq. The Muslims will then proceed to conquer Constantinople. The apocalypse is coming, Salim, and we anticipate it eagerly."

Abu stood again and came out from behind the desk so that he was standing before them.

"It is my job to understand our enemy, Mr al-Khawari. And it seems to me that there are two possibilities when it comes to you: either you are working for the crusaders, or you have been used by them. I am going to find out which of those possibilities is correct. One way or another, I will find out."

Chapter Twenty-One

Pope had walked through the night. He decided that he would find somewhere to hide out of sight when the sun came up. He was tired, and he knew that his success in finding Isabella was dependent on him looking after himself. More than that, he was much more likely to be discovered by an enemy patrol if he tried to continue during daylight. He would find a shelter where he could get a little sleep. He would call Bloom for an update and then continue again once the sun had gone down.

It was just before dawn when Pope saw the wrecked convoy. The road had crested a shallow hill, and the vista beyond was wide and generous, visibility improved by the brightening sky. The road continued through a valley formed by the ridge that he had just surmounted and another ridge, a little taller, two or three miles away. The road arrowed down the slope, across the valley and then up the opposite bank. The convoy was in the middle of the valley. Pope counted eight vehicles on the road. He put the binoculars to his eyes and observed them. The convoy had been composed of military and civilian vehicles. He recognised two T-72 tanks, a BMP-1 and a Type 63 armoured personnel carrier, a large truck and three cars.

They had all been destroyed in an air strike. The tanks were blackened shells, both sets of tracks still intact but the hulls peeled open by the missiles or bombs that must have struck them from above. The other vehicles were similarly wrecked, panels thrown aside and charred debris tossed for metres in all directions. Despite the damage, they remained in formation, neatly arranged, pointing to the east, deeper into Syria. It must have been an ISIS convoy, and it had been attacked by bombers. It reminded Pope of Highway 80, the road between Kuwait and Iraq that had been the scene of a massacre as fleeing soldiers had been targeted by coalition aircraft. This was on a much smaller scale, but the overwhelming impression was the same: this had been a turkey shoot.

He glassed the rest of the valley and saw a building to the south of the convoy. He focussed the glasses and examined it more carefully. It was derelict, the sand blown up against the brickwork so that it looked as if the building were being swallowed. The roof had been peeled away in parts, and it didn't look as if there was any glass left in the window frames. Despite all that, Pope thought it looked perfect. He would shelter there.

Pope started down the shallow slope to the vehicles. They were a mile away, and he made good progress. He kept his eyes on them, but there was no sign of life. No wildlife either, as if the birds knew that the carrion was long since gone, or perhaps they were too frightened to alight on the crisped wreckage. The vehicle at the rear of the convoy was one of the T-72s. Pope approached it, his weapon ready, but there was nothing there. The turret had been pierced by the explosion, the jagged edges opening out like the petals of a charred metallic flower. The barrel had been flattened at the mantlet so that the muzzle had carved out a furrow in the road before the tank's momentum had been arrested. Pope reached out and rapped his knuckles against the hull; when he looked down at his fingers, they were blackened with ash.

He walked on, passing the burnt-out cars and the troop carriers and then the second tank at the front of the convoy. The sun was cresting the next hill now, the brightness reaching up into the gloom. Pope felt the day's first warmth on his face. He left the road, crossed the sandy verge and then started out across the scrubby desert to the house. He estimated that it was half a mile from the road. He would be in shelter within ten minutes.

Pope had only been walking for a handful of seconds when he stopped. He thought that he had heard something. He looked to the east. Plumes of dust announced the approach of vehicles. Pope saw the twin fingers of sand that resolved from out of the murky blur where the desert met the awakening sky. He stopped, pressed the rubber cups of the binoculars to his eyes and adjusted the focusing knob.

Two vehicles, black dots at this range, solid objects that were descending the road on the opposite ridge, standing out against the beginning of the desert haze.

He adjusted the binoculars again and brought the vehicles into sharper focus: two pickups, perhaps Toyota Hiluxes, with machine guns fitted on the flatbeds. Technicals. The retrofitted vehicles were favoured by insurgents here and all around the world.

He hadn't seen them because their approach had been hidden by the hump of the hill; now that they had crested it, they had taken him by surprise. He knew how far it was from the ridge to his position: no more than two miles. He was between the road and the derelict house, a moving figure against the blankness of the sand; they must have seen him already. His assumption was confirmed as he heard the sound of a horn, still distant but audible across the wide-open space. The second technical sounded its own horn in answer, and then both vehicles increased their pace.

It was inevitable: there was going to be an engagement. They would want to know who he was, walking alone through the desert, and Pope would not be able to answer their questions. They would arrest him or shoot him.

Pope cursed himself for not staying with the convoy; he could have hidden in one of the vehicles and been perfectly safe there. He discarded the recrimination—it wouldn't serve him—and made a tactical assessment. The ruined house was still the better part of half a mile away. The technicals would be able to cross the desert faster than he could run across it. He wouldn't be able to get to it before they did. They would catch him out in the open, with nowhere to take cover. The big 7.62mm machine guns would pick him off.

The alternative was to retrace his steps to the road.

Pope moved quickly. He sprinted as fast as he could, the heavy backpack thudding against his back, his bruised calf stinging with every footfall and push-off, and his thighs burning from the effort of bearing the weight on the give of the sand. He was still two hundred yards from the convoy when he heard the first sound of firing. He glanced to his right and saw the tracer lancing out from the first technical. It was still too far away for a hit to be very likely, but Pope knew that this wasn't an attempt to hit him. It was a warning shot. They wanted him to stop.

He didn't. He ran harder. The machine gun fired again, and the desert twenty feet ahead of him was kicked up into a storm of sand and rock as the rounds landed. It was a little too close for comfort, but still Pope did not stop.

He reached the road and was able to pick up his pace, putting the hulk of the leading tank between himself and the two vehicles. At least he had a moment of cover now, a pause while he was safe and out of sight. He sprinted farther along the road, passing deeper into the shattered convoy, giving them more vehicles to search before they reached him. He hurried by the personnel carriers and the civilian vehicles until he arrived at the second tank. It was in better condition than the one at the front of the queue.

He unslung his backpack and propped it against the hull. He checked his M4 and ascertained that the spare magazines were properly arranged in the pouches of his tactical jacket so that he could reload as quickly as possible. He took his grenades and stuffed them into another pouch. Only when he was satisfied that he was ready to defend himself did he take the satphone from his pack, power it up and call in.

"This is Archangel. I need to speak to Bloom."

"Copy that, Archangel. Please hold."

He glanced around the hull of the tank and saw the nearest technical; it was half a mile away and closing rapidly.

"Quick," Pope said.

"Archangel, I have Bloom. Patching now."

Pope took a moment to take the phone from his ear and check his coordinates on the phone's integral GPS tracker.

Bloom's voice was reedy and distorted by static, but the anxiety was obvious. "This is Bloom. What is it?"

"I've been compromised. Two vehicles, multiple tangos. I need immediate backup."

"Location?"

"I'm at GPS coordinates thirty-six, twenty-seven point one two eight four and thirty-six, thirty-seven point three six two zero." He repeated it. "Do you have it?"

"Affirmative."

"Be quick. I'm under fire."

"Hold your position."

Pope risked another glance around the side of the hull and quickly wished that he hadn't. The first technical had pulled off the road so that it could open up a wide angle of fire for the machine gun. They had seen where he was sheltering. Pope heard the chug-chug-chug and scrambled out of the way as the large-calibre rounds rang off the hull. The noise was deafening, ear-splitting clangs that echoed out over the empty desert.

"Don't hang about," Pope shouted into the handset, then clipped it to his belt.

Pope was trapped.

He grasped his rifle, shuffled to his right and risked a glimpse around the other side of the hull. The second Land Cruiser was rolling off the road, too, opening up an angle to direct fire from the opposite position. They were going to cover him from the left and the right. He saw three men in the back of the truck, each of them wearing the green camouflage uniforms that the insurgents described as Afghani robes. The familiar black flag flew from a radio antenna atop the truck.

Pope shouldered the rifle, took aim and loosed off a quick semi-automatic burst. The sound of the rounds clattered across the sand, and the driver of the technical slammed on the brakes as two rounds thumped into the wing and the passenger's door.

The soldier operating the machine gun turned it in Pope's direction and opened fire. Pope swung back into cover as the big rounds chewed into the asphalt, sending jagged chunks to ricochet off the hull of the tank.

Pope heard the sound of an engine and, his weapon ready to fire again, risked a second glance at the first technical. It was moving, bouncing over the undulating terrain, passing out of range of Pope's rifle and then turning to continue to the west. They were flanking him. The soldier behind the machine gun swivelled the barrel in his direction and opened fire again. His shots landed short, his aim thrown off by the bouncing of the Land Cruiser as it crashed through a dip. Sprays of sand and stones pattered against the tank and against Pope's face as he turned away.

He couldn't stay where he was. They had already compromised his position and he didn't have long before he was flanked. He hooked his arm through the straps of his backpack, reached up and rested his rifle on the hull of the tank, and then vaulted up after it, his boots finding purchase on the side skirt so that he could clamber up onto the engine compartment. The cupola had been badly damaged by the explosion, and the commander hatch had been blown clear to expose the darkened interior of the tank below. Pope took the backpack and lowered it inside, then followed it into the darkness.

Chapter Twenty-Two

The interior of the tank was dark. The rent where the commander's hatch had once been admitted a little of the dawn's light, but it was quickly swallowed and wasn't strong enough to reach into the deepest corners of the vehicle. It was foul-smelling, too, with the faintest suggestion of cooked meat. Pope knew what it was, and his fears were realised as he tried to find a foothold that would allow him to look up out of the opened turret. His boot landed on something softer than the metal of the hull, and, as he pushed away from it, something was dislodged and fell out of the loader's chair. Pope glanced down and saw a body, still intact, within the shaft of light that arrowed down; the flames that had engulfed the interior of the tank had incinerated the corpse, rendering him into crumbling ash and blackened bone.

Pope had no time to consider the soldier's fate, or the luxury of treating his body with respect. He placed his boot on the man's shoulder and used it to boost himself up just enough to look out. The technical that had flanked him was fifty yards away. The second Land Cruiser had closed to the same range, the tank equidistant between the two of them.

The phone's speaker hissed. "Archangel, this is Bloom."

"Copy that. Archangel here."

"Help is inbound."

"Copy that."

"I'm going to patch you through to the operator. In the event that they say anything, you are a UK special forces soldier, code-named Archangel. You have been conducting forward reconnaissance inside the border and you've identified viable targets. Have you got that?"

"Yes, sir."

"Patching you through now."

There was a moment of static and then the sound of button inputs as Pope was patched into an open communications loop. The static was obliterated by the deafening ringing of large-calibre rounds as they ricocheted against the tank's armour. He flinched involuntarily. He knew that he didn't have long. Once they realised that it was just him, and that he was outgunned, they would formulate a plan to take him out. A grenade through the opening at the top of the tank, perhaps. There was very little that Pope could do about it.

"Archangel, this is Bam Bam. Please copy."

Pope spoke quietly and confidently. "This is Archangel. I copy you loud and clear."

"Understand you've got eyes on two hostile vehicles?"

"Affirmative."

"We're coming in from your twelve. Confirm targets are at your previously advised coordinates."

"Confirmed. Two pickups, technicals, 7.62mm machine guns mounted to the flatbeds." He recited the coordinates again. "I'm between them. There's a convoy of ruined vehicles. I'm in the last tank on the eastern edge of the convoy."

Pope clambered up again and peeked out. He looked to the sky and scanned for any sign of an aircraft. He couldn't see anything.

Pope heard a voice shouting to him. One of the men had dismounted from the technical to the north of his position. He was calling out in Arabic.

"Stand by, Archangel. This is Bam Bam to JAG25. I am now tracking two vehicles."

The man next to the technical had a scarf wrapped around his face, leaving just his eyes uncovered. He saw Pope and made a gesture that he should come out of the tank. Pope brought the rifle up and fired a burst in the man's direction. The rounds fell short, but they had the desired effect. The man scurried behind the Land Cruiser.

"Copy that, Bam Bam." It was a new voice; Pope guessed, from his call sign, that it was an attack controller. Both the operator and the attack controller spoke in broad American accents.

The technicals opened fire, both of them, and Pope ducked down just below the lip of the hull. The rounds thundered as they crashed into the armour.

The phone's speaker came to life again: "Two vehicles moving predominantly westbound in the desert. We have our eyes on."

"Verify the missile is on the left, correct? Confirm that one is coded. Skynet is saying it's on the right."

"Confirm it's on the left, JAG25, and we are coded and set to fire. Understand we are clear to engage?"

"Roger that."

"Spinning missiles up now. Keep your head down, Archangel. I'll call back with the BDA."

If it was a Reaper, it would most likely be carrying four Hellfire missiles or two missiles and two five-hundred-pound bombs. Either way, the insurgents in those two technicals were about to get a very unpleasant surprise. Pope could see the sky through the opening in the hull and saw two streaks of light high in the air over the mountains to the north of his position. Missiles, then. The Hellfires could be fired from five miles distant, before the men on the ground would even have heard the approach of the drone.

Pope watched as the missiles arrowed down, dark spots propelled by bright tails of flame, and put his head up to watch as the first vehicle was consumed by a sudden, vivid explosion. The noise of the detonation rolled over the landscape. It was joined a moment later by a second blast as the technical to Pope's six was also struck.

The explosion resounded against the ridge of the valley, the faint echo rolling back down to the convoy. It faded out and it was almost quiet until Pope detected the sound of fire and then the drone of a turboprop overhead.

"This is Archangel," Pope called in. "Two direct hits."

The coordinator said, "Confirm BDA, Bam Bam."

Pope knew what that meant: the Reaper was going to overfly and evaluate the damage. He glassed the landscape again, and this time he saw the drone. It was flying at a thousand feet, the details of the fuselage slowly coalescing out of the haze. He heard the buzz of the turboprop more clearly now and watched as it angled directly between the two smoking pyres that were all that was left of the vehicles and the men who had been inside them.

"Battle damage assessment," the operator reported. "I've got two wrecks. Direct hit on both tangos. No movement. We got them. You need anything else, Archangel?"

"Can you see anything else? Any other vehicles in the area?"

"Negative, Archangel. You're clear for five miles in all directions. You're on your own."

"Copy that, Bam Bam. Thanks for the helping hand."

"Ten-four, Archangel. Happy trails. Bam Bam out."

The drone angled slowly to the east, starting a turn that would take it more deeply into Syria and then back to the north. Its course sent it directly overhead, close enough for Pope to see the two empty hard points beneath both wings. It was, he thought, disconcerting to remember that there was no pilot aboard the drone, and that it was being commanded by an operator at Creech Air Force base, near Las Vegas, more than seven thousand miles away.

Technology, Pope thought as he came out from cover and hoisted his pack onto his shoulders. *What a world we're living in.*

He knew that he couldn't stay in the area. The Reaper operator had confirmed that he was alone, but he wasn't prepared to gamble that that state of affairs would remain unchanged. The technicals might have been in contact with a command post. Even if they were not, the longer they were out in the desert without arriving at their destination, the greater the chance that someone would realise that something was amiss. And it was obvious that this road was a main route between Aleppo and the Turkish border. The area was contested by the insurgents and the Syrian regime. Another patrol would eventually be drawn in to investigate the twin pyres on either side of the road. The columns of smoke that were rising from the flames would be visible for miles.

He had to get as far away from the road as possible. He checked that he had all of his equipment and lowered his backpack to the surface of the road. He slid down the hull after it, slung it onto his back and set off.

Chapter Twenty-Three

Pope determined to put himself out of sight of the road as quickly as he could. He walked for thirty minutes until he found a wadi, a dry watercourse that followed a meandering route along the floor of the valley from west to east. The bank of the wadi sloped down for two metres, enough for Pope to feel comfortable that he would be invisible to passing traffic. He took out his Magellan GPS and checked his location, and then followed the watercourse to the east.

Pope walked for another hour, occasionally clambering up the bank of the wadi to check his surroundings. He travelled for four miles, observing as the landscape gradually changed. The browns and yellows of the desert were replaced by browns and greens as he made his way into an area that had been irrigated. There were grasses and small trees and then, when he checked again, he saw that he was on the fringe of a large olive grove. There were hundreds of trees to the east, set out in careful lines, with man-made water channels dividing the land into neat parcels. A little water was now evident in the bottom of the wadi, and as Pope continued to the east, there was more. The irrigation channels emptied into it, contributing to a small stream that ran down the centre of the rocky gully. Pope passed into an area where the trees were more plentiful, a curtain of greenery that was pushed all the way up to the water bank.

Pope checked the time: it was eight in the morning. He was starting to feel tired, but much more than that, he wanted to get inside and out of sight.

He scrambled up the loose shale until he was at the edge of the wadi. There were tall grasses here and then trees. He was inside the grove now. The landscape was flat for five or six acres until a steep hill; there were several within reasonably close range. Three hundred feet to the north Pope saw exactly what he was looking for: a large brick building with a corrugated metal roof. It had three wide windows and an opening that offered a way inside. There was nothing to suggest that anyone else was nearby. He clambered out of the wadi, readied his rifle and made his way north to the building. The only noise he could hear was the hungry calling of an eagle high overhead. He moved more carefully as he neared the building, but there was nothing to suggest that it was occupied. He reached the door and paused, listening intently. Still nothing.

He went inside.

It was a storage building. There was a small tractor, a selection of tools and, in a shaded area, large wooden boxes with overripe olives rotting inside them. Pope took off his backpack, rechecked the interior and then went back outside to satisfy himself, finally, that the building was suitable. He took out his water bottle and slaked his thirst. The interior was cool and, save the smell of the rotting olives, perfect for his purposes. Indeed, he thought, the fact that the olives had been allowed to go off suggested that the farm was not being properly tended. Perhaps something had happened to the farmer. The area was contested by several rival factions, and it was not impossible that the war had intervened and disturbed the harvest. While unfortunate for the farmer, it would suit Pope.

He took out the satphone, powered it up and called London.

"This is Archangel. I need to speak to Bloom."

"Hold, please."

Pope sat down, using an empty box as a chair, and gazed out of one of the wide windows. The sun was climbing in the sky now, and the heat was ticking up. The sky was blue, powdered with small clouds, and it promised to be a hot day. He was pleased to be inside the coolness of the storage building.

"Archangel?"

"Yes, sir."

"What's your status?"

"I'm fine. Thanks for the assistance."

"Where are you?"

"I'm in country," he said. "In shelter. I'll start out again when it's dark."

"Do you have transport?"

"No, sir. That's my first objective tonight. What about the helicopter? Where did they go?"

"Yes, I have intel on that. We tracked them to al-Bab."

That was unusual. "Not Raqqa?"

"No. We were surprised too."

"I got some rounds off," Pope said. "Maybe the chopper was damaged."

"Maybe. We've tasked a satellite now, so we have real-time surveillance. They've been taken to a building to the north of the city. I can't say for sure, but we believe that they're still there. We think it's likely that they'll be moved. They hold all of the territory east of al-Bab. They could follow Route Four to Lake Assad and be in Raqqa in time for dinner."

"Let's hope they wait," Pope said. "Do you have anyone on the ground?"

"Of course. Local sources. We're trying to find out more. How far are you from there?"

Al-Bab was seventeen miles from Aleppo. It was close. "One hundred klicks," Pope said. "If I can find transport and I can stay out of trouble, I should be able to reach it tonight."

"Understood. Do you need anything else?"

"No, sir."

"Check in again when you stop. You need to keep me up to date."

"Copy that."

"Good luck, Archangel."

He powered down the phone and put it in his backpack. He was tired, and when he considered it, he remembered that he hadn't slept for two days. He pulled the empty crates away from the wall and stacked them one atop the other until he had created a wall behind which he would be able to lie down. If someone came into the building while he was asleep, he wouldn't be immediately visible. He hid the backpack behind the crates and then lay down beside it. He took out his pistol, put it in his hand and rested his head against the crook of his arm. He was asleep within five minutes.

Chapter Twenty-Four

I t was dusk when Pope awoke. He had woken twice throughout the course of the day, but after having satisfied himself that he was still alone, he had gone back to sleep. He had slept for eleven hours in total and felt completely refreshed. He put the pistol back into its holster and took another drink from his canteen. It was already half empty. He remembered the irrigation channels outside. He collected his rifle and, pausing in the doorway, confirmed again that he was alone. As he looked out into the neatly arranged rows of olive trees, he heard the sound of a jet engine high overhead. He glanced up and saw the unmistakeable shapes of two American F-22 Raptors flying in close formation. The jets screamed overhead and disappeared over the hilltops to the north, heading back to Turkey. Pope watched them go. He felt alone and vulnerable.

He made his way to the nearest irrigation channel, refilled the canteen with muddy water and dropped in a purification tablet. He went back to the hut, collected his backpack and took out one of his Meal Ready to Eat pouches and a flameless heater to warm it up. The heater contained finely powdered magnesium alloyed with a small amount of iron, and Pope activated it by opening it and filling it with water. He left the heater to warm and took out his Magellan. He noted his coordinates and then checked them off on his paper map. He was three miles to the southwest of Termanin. He unfolded the map fully and looked at the scale of the journey before him. Al-Bab was around fifty-five miles from his position. To get there, he was going to have to skirt around Aleppo. There was an orbital road that ran around it, and the quickest way would be to follow it around in a clockwise direction and then pick up Route 212 and head northeast. The alternative was to run to the south, circle the city and take Route Four. Aleppo was still held by the government and promised to be safer than going cross-country. It would also be more heavily defended, with checkpoints where his lack of a credible story might mean that he could come unstuck. He might be better to go cross-country and follow one of the minor roads—better described as tracks—that ran to the towns of Anadan, Hraytan and Hazwan.

The heater was warm now. He collected it and dropped the MRE inside.

Of course, Pope knew that his route was determined by his ability to find transport. There was another way. He traced his finger in a straight line from where he was to where he wanted to go. There was a distance of thirty-four miles between Termanin and al-Bab as the crow flew. He knew that he would be able to manage a consistent pace of four miles an hour if he walked. It would take him between eight and nine hours, perhaps ten or eleven if the conditions required more stealth. It was just after six now. The sun would rise at around five tomorrow morning. He had eleven hours. It was possible to pull it off, and the more he considered it, the more it promised to be the safest and most reliable way to get to Isabella's position.

He took out the first MRE and replaced it with a second. The first contained chilli with beans. He tore the packet open and, using the spoon attachment on his multi-purpose eating utensil, scooped it from the packet and put it into his mouth. The meals were far from haute cuisine, but Pope had always, rather perversely, enjoyed them. He finished quickly, took the meatloaf with gravy from the heater, and ate that, too. Each MRE contained around twelve hundred calories. He wouldn't stop for another meal until he reached his destination. That would have to be enough.

Pope collected his trash, went outside and dug a hole. He relieved himself in the hole, dropped in the empty MRE packets and the spent heater and filled in the hole. It was getting dark by the time he was satisfied he had left no trace that he had been here. Dark enough to start out, in any event. He collected his backpack and worked his arms into the straps, settling the pack on his back until it was comfortable so that the chance of developing sores was minimised. He fetched his rifle, checked that it was made ready and started to walk.

Chapter Twenty-Five

P ope walked through the plantation to the northeast. It was uninhabited. He passed storehouses and a building that had once been a house, but there was no one here now. He passed a water tower, a plump bulb that sat atop four tall concrete struts, and used the water to top up his flask. The land was still tended and irrigated, and the olives were being harvested, but the farmer had moved somewhere else. Perhaps he had decided that it was unsafe.

The sky was perfectly clear, and without any light to pollute the clarity of the view, he could see the millions of stars scattered overhead. It was beautiful, but also very isolating, and Pope felt alone. It was also very dark, despite the starlight, and Pope moved a little more carefully to begin with so that his eyes were able to adjust to the conditions. He knew that it would take half an hour for his night vision to establish itself, and he didn't want to run into anything because he hadn't been able to see it until it was too late. The ground was bleak and open, with little to distinguish it. The surface underfoot was a mixture of loose sand and stones set upon a hard granite bedrock that occasionally revealed itself in sharp outcrops that cut jagged shapes in the distance.

He moved at a cautious pace, pausing regularly to listen to the noises around him. The temperature quickly dropped several degrees, and as he reached the boundary of the olive grove, it was cold enough for him to see his breath before his face. His pack was heavy and he was working hard enough to draw a sweat; the moisture was quickly cold on his skin and he started to shiver. He ignored the compulsion to hurry. He knew that he had enough time to reach his destination, and even if he did not, he would be able to find somewhere suitable to lay up and wait for the following night. Hurrying would do him no favours. Movement and noise were two of the easiest ways to give yourself away, and a slow onward patrol would minimise those risks while increasing the chances that he would see a threat before he was compromised by it. There was also the more practical reason for caution: the desert was treacherous underfoot, and he would be no good to anyone if he tripped and sprained an ankle.

He headed northeast. The terrain was flat and barren, as featureless as the surface of the moon. It was difficult to find suitable waypoints to navigate with, so Pope was left with no choice but to take out his Magellan to find his position and then cross-check with his map. It wasn't ideal: the display produced a glow of artificial light that would be visible for some distance, and every time he looked down at it—even when he squinted—his eyes were temporarily a little less effective in the dark. Better that, though, than getting lost.

He crossed a dusty track after the first two miles, pausing within the cover of a clutch of scrubby brush until he was sure that the way ahead was clear. It took him another fifteen minutes to cover the next two miles that brought him to the first major road. It was Route 62, the two-lane highway that ran between Termanin and Aleppo. Both cities were held by the government, and Pope knew that although the various forces ranged against the regime would make incursions here, it was still likely to be reasonably secure. Nevertheless, he did not want to be found. The terrain was flat, with occasional outcrops of rock amid the seemingly limitless sand. The highway was in terrible condition. Sand had blown across it, slowly reclaiming it for the desert, and there was the wreck of a civilian vehicle two hundred yards to the east. Just ahead of him was a road sign painted in blue, with white text that stood out even in the darkness. The destination indicated by an arrow, written in Arabic and English, was Aleppo.

Pope dropped to a crouch and used his binoculars to observe the approach in both directions. He couldn't see anything that gave him any reason for concern. He moved forward, stepping carefully, with his eyes to the ground. IEDs and mines were a possibility. He hurried across the pitted asphalt, across the narrow rocky verge and then onto the sand again. He continued to the northeast.

Chapter Twenty-Six

Pope walked on. He made regular stops for rest and to check his position and was pleased with the pace he was keeping and the progress he was making. He decided that he had enough time to make a short detour to the north so that he crossed Route 214, one of the main arteries that fed into Aleppo, two miles farther up the road than the crossing he would have made if he had continued on his previous path. The city was one of the regime's redoubts, and he knew that it would be populous, meaning a greater likelihood of his running into a patrol. He boxed around the hamlets of Babis and Anadan and reached the highway south of Bayanoun. He saw two cars, one coming from the south and the other from the north. He took off his backpack and dropped to his belly, pressing himself behind a large boulder as the cars crossed and went on their ways. He waited there for another minute until the lights of both cars had disappeared, listening to the barking of a dog from somewhere to the north, and then collected his gear. He swallowed a mouthful of water from his canteen to wash the dust out of his mouth and throat and then crossed the highway. He cut back onto a bearing that led to the northeast once more.

Once he was away from the more immediate risk of detection upon the road, he allowed his thoughts to wander back to the events of the last few days. He thought of Snow and Kelleher and the ambush outside Geneva that had left them dead and had almost accounted for him, too. Their assailants had been professional and utterly ruthless. He had no idea who they were, how they had known to target them or, indeed, *why* they had been targeted. Was it something to do with al-Khawari? Or was it something else, the revealing of another layer that was, as yet, hidden to him? There was no way for him to know.

———

Pope saw al-Bab just as the sun was beginning to modulate the darkness on the horizon to a gentle mauve. He had climbed a reasonably steep hill, and as he crested it, the town was laid out below him. It was a large sprawl of over sixty thousand people, yet there were only a few lights that prickled against the cowled gloom. The electricity supply to most of Syria was intermittent, and Pope guessed that it was switched off at night so that it could be conserved for the day. He saw the shape of tower blocks, some of them abbreviated where they had been demolished by bombs, a confused grid of streets with gaps where buildings had been flattened. He saw the onion-shaped cupola of a mosque and sharply pointed minarets.

The slope that led down from the hill to the town was heavily wooded with an orchard of almond trees. They had been planted closely together, in uniform lines, and Pope assessed that they would provide a reasonable level of cover within which he would be able to hide. The orchard would be the extent of his progress today; he was a mile from the first buildings and he only had another fifteen minutes or so before the sun came up. He didn't have time to make it down the slope, cover the approach and then find somewhere to hide. Pope turned back and looked across the crest of the hill. The ground behind him was barren and sparse. He had been anxious as he had surmounted and then descended it, and now that anxiety was sharpened. There was nowhere for him to hide back there. He gave thought to going back the way he had arrived and finding a spot to lay up, but he hadn't seen anything that had offered an obvious spot for miles.

The first rays of the sun's light arrowed up from beneath the horizon, turning the blacks to greys. The light bleached out the darkness and opened up more of the terrain for inspection. Pope took his binoculars and scanned ahead of him more carefully. Route 212 led into the southern districts of the town, passing two hundred metres away from the foot of the hill. As he followed the road with the glasses, he saw a small building and a collection of vehicles. He focussed on it more closely. The building was a small shack. There was light emanating from an open door, and as Pope watched, a shadow passed across an open window. There was a pickup truck parked next to the shack, with a machine gun in the flatbed. He focussed on the road itself. A large concrete block had been placed in the centre of the highway. The top half had been painted white and the bottom half was painted red, and it had been draped with a large black flag with a white circle and white calligraphy. A single man stood in front of the block; he was toting a large rifle and his face was covered with a chequered *keffiyeh*. Beyond the concrete block was an armoured Humvee. It was parked across the road at such an angle that anyone who wanted to pass into or out of the city would have to slalom around it and then the block before proceeding. The black flag was flying from the radio mast and there were two other men, their faces similarly covered, also toting large rifles.

It was a checkpoint.

Pope had the beginning of an idea.

He collected his backpack and set off carefully down the slope, very conscious now that a fall and an injury would be a catastrophe. The descent was steeper than it looked, and the footing was treacherous, with whole stretches that were little more than scree. Pope dug his boot into the scree to slow his momentum and a tiny avalanche of stones tumbled ahead of him, a soft susurration that nevertheless sounded terribly loud. He continued down, aiming for the spots where the bedrock jutted out and offered more secure footholds, and eventually made it to the first rows of almond trees. He was sweating and out of breath, and he crouched down with his weapon aimed ahead of him and acclimatised himself again. A few dislodged pebbles continued to trickle down the slope, rattling as they did so, but there was no indication that he had been seen or heard.

He was close to the guard hut now, but the trees were planted close together and there was a lot of scrub that had grown up between the trunks. Pope was well concealed here. He wouldn't be able to sleep, but he was happy that it would be safe to hunker down and wait until nightfall. He would use the time to plan exactly how to make his attack.

Chapter Twenty-Seven

The optimal times of day to make an assault were just before sunup and just after sundown. Pope had kept a close watch on the comings and goings at the checkpoint all day. The soldiers had an impressive aura with their black flags, the sinister uniforms and their ostentatious weaponry, but they were lazy and unprofessional. There were four of them at the checkpoint at any one time, two manning the blockade and two in the hut. The checkpoint itself was well designed. It would be difficult to bypass it without coming under sustained fire, and the additional concrete blocks that Pope had noticed as he closed on it would have made it very difficult for a suicide bomber to drive within range before he could be shot. But that was the extent of the cautious planning. If Pope had been the officer in charge, he would have tasked the two unoccupied men in the hut with burning down the trees that were much too close to the building. They had been planted close together, and, having been left untended, vines had been allowed to wind their way between the trunks until an almost impenetrable curtain had grown. There was a cleared border of ten metres between the trees and the hut, but to leave no more than that was sloppy. It was obvious that the soldiers considered that their main threat would approach along the road, most likely from the south. But that was short-sighted. Pope had been able to creep right up to the margin and assess the soldiers from close range.

A technical had been parked next to the guardhouse. It was a Ford Ranger with a .50-calibre machine gun mounted in the back. This one, though, had been adapted even more thoroughly than was usual. It had been fitted with crude armour: a large plate had been welded to the front of the vehicle and there was a steel box in the truck bed to protect the gunner. The vehicle was sunk down on its suspension from all the additional weight.

Pope glanced up at the horizon. The sun was dipping down. Dusk was falling.

Dusk became night.

Pope took his chance.

He left his backpack in the orchard, taking only his rifle, two extra magazines, his knife and his silenced handgun. He reached down into the dirt, took a handful and scrubbed it across his face, darkening his skin, and then used his knife to slice an opening in the curtain of vines. He slipped through, and staying low to the ground, he approached the hut. The guards on the checkpoint were looking north and south, and once he had passed across the first three metres, he was shielded by the concrete block and the Humvee.

He reached the hut. It was little more than a shed formed by planks of wood and shingles for a roof. It was not substantial, and the light from inside leaked out between the gaps in the planks. One of the gaps was wider than the others, and Pope was able to kneel down, press his face to the panels that had been baked in the sun all day and look inside. The two guards who were off duty were inside. One of them was sitting on a chair, his legs resting on a table and his hands crossed over his chest. The other was on the floor, lying on a bedroll, his knees pushed up to his chest in the foetal position.

Pope waited and listened. He heard the sound of heavy breathing. Both men were asleep. He heard the sound of an engine, and as he peeked around the edge of the building to check, he saw a car approaching from the south. It couldn't have been better timing. The two guards came to attention, their rifles raised, and signalled for the car to stop. Their attention was distracted, and not willing to squander such a fortuitous advantage, Pope crept around the hut, following it in a clockwise direction so that it would provide additional cover to obscure him from the road. The door was open. The guard by the Humvee would have been able to see him, but he was out of sight now, dealing with the car.

Pope carefully moved inside.

The interior was lit by a hurricane lamp. The men had eaten, and their dirty plates and utensils had been left on the desk. Their AK-47s were propped in the corner of the small room, and there was a shortwave radio next to the recumbent guard's crossed feet. Pope reached down to his scabbard and took out his knife. He addressed the man in the chair first of all: he was young, with a straggled beard and a scar on his cheek. Pope laid the edge of the knife to his throat and sliced from left to right, hard and fast. The man's eyes opened, bulging with terror, but Pope had cut through his trachea, so the only noise he could make was a strangled gasp. Pope had wrapped an arm around his legs and held him steady as he tried to kick, the only noise coming from the clatter of the chair legs as he jerked forward and back. His strength drained away quickly and he fell still.

The guard on the floor had not even stirred. Pope knelt down and straddled him, pinning his arms, and as he woke, Pope sliced his throat, too. The guard jerked like a beached fish as he gasped for a breath of air that would never come, and then he, too, lay still.

Pope wiped the knife on the robe of the dead man and waited, listening.

He heard the sound of a car driving away, and when that had passed out of earshot, a jovial conversation from the two guards outside.

Pope gathered his rifle and went to the open doorway. The sentries were talking together, next to one another. There was waist-high cover on the ground outside, and that meant that a prone shooting position was impractical, so Pope lowered himself to a kneeling position. His right knee was at the rear, and he laid it against the ground. His left leg supported the elbow of his left, forward arm. Pope rested his elbow on the quadriceps, knowing from hours of range shooting that to rest it on his kneecap would cause him to wobble.

There were twenty metres between him and the nearest of the two sentries. They were both toting assault rifles, but they were relaxed and at ease. They were unprofessional and unaware of the danger they were in. The two men were still close, but he knew that the second shot would be the more challenging of the two. He heard the sound of laughter and watched as one of the two men clapped the other on the shoulder and then started to move away. Pope centred the first man in the reticle of the sight. He drew in a breath and then exhaled, emptying his lungs, and put the pad of his index finger against the trigger. He squeezed, feeling the give of the smooth mechanism, feeling the pressure, and then pulling back through it.

The rifle barked, the report echoing out into the desert.

The first sentry fell.

Pope aimed again as quickly as he could manage without sacrificing accuracy. The second sentry had had his back turned as the first man had fallen, but he had heard the crack of the rifle, and when he spun around, he saw that his comrade was sprawled out on the road. Pope ensured that the mass of the man's body was square in the sight and fired again. The rifle boomed, seemingly louder this time, the echo rolling back from the hills behind the sentry hut.

The second sentry dropped.

Pope stood and, with the butt of the rifle pressed into his shoulder and the muzzle aimed ahead, he came away from the hut and crossed the scrub to the margin of the road. He checked north and south. The road was empty, with no vehicles approaching. The sentry had dragged himself across the dusty asphalt to the block with the black flag wrapped around it. He had left a trail of blood across the sand. Pope approached, covering him with the rifle. The sentry had pulled his headscarf away from his head, and Pope saw a young man's face. He had white skin and wide, frightened eyes. His weapon was on the ground beside him, but there was no prospect of him threatening Pope with it. He had been gut shot, his stomach perforated, and as Pope watched, his breathing slowed and then stopped.

Pope went back into the hut. There was a bundle of clothes that had been left on the floor. Pope sheathed his knife and rifled through them. There was a black robe and a black and white chequered headscarf. He took the robe and put it over his head, arranging it so that it fell neatly, obscuring the bulk of his tactical jacket with the ammunition and grenades. He collected the scarf and wound it around his head, leaving a strip clear for his eyes and nostrils.

He collected his backpack from the almond tree where he had left it and hauled it, and his weapons, to the armoured Ford Ranger. The keys were in the ignition; he supposed that the guards did not expect to have someone attempt to steal their wheels. He hid his pack in the back of the cabin, started the engine and drove into town.

PART TWO

Al-Bab

Chapter Twenty-Eight

Aqil stopped for a moment to take a breath. It was unbearably hot and he was gasping and covered in sweat.

"Why are you stopping?" the instructor yelled at him. "Move! Run!"

He started again, closing the distance to the others and then matching their pace. He was wearing the same outfit as the others: blue and black camouflage fatigues, sand-coloured desert boots and a yellow headscarf that covered his head save for a narrow slit that allowed him to look out. The recruits looked almost identical, and their trainer—an ex-soldier from Saddam's Republican Guard— ran them through an exercise regime that required them to match each other precisely. They had been instructed to complete the three-mile run through the desert in less than an hour. Aqil was reasonably fit, but the sun was brutal and his uniform wasn't built with running in mind. He had blisters on his feet, and two of the toenails on his right foot had turned black.

They completed the course, and after just a ten-minute interval so that they could take on fluids from a table laden with plastic bottles of water, the instructor moved on to a session dealing with hand-to-hand combat. They were given knives and taught how to use them, including a five-minute break during which the Iraqi described the most efficient way to decapitate a hostage. It wasn't like films, the man said, not like how the crusaders portrayed it. It wasn't a single swipe and it was done. You had to pull them back by the hair, expose the throat and then hack all the way through until you were through the windpipe, and the rest almost fell off.

They worked hard for another fifty minutes before they were allowed to take a proper break to eat. Aqil tugged the scarf down a little to let some fresh air flow around his face and so that he could take a drink from a pitcher of water that had been left at the side of the dusty square where the training took place.

This was their third day at the camp. They had arrived at the Omar oilfield at noon on the day that they had crossed the border. He had seen a map. It was to the south of the city of Deir ez-Zur, two hundred and fifty miles from the place from which they had been collected. It should have been a six-hour drive, but it had taken twice that because the driver had followed a route that took them away from areas of the country that were still held by the government.

Aqil had looked out the window for almost the entire duration of the journey. They passed through towns and villages that had been razed to the ground, left as smouldering piles of wood and rubble. Hungry children stared at their bus with empty eyes. Every additional ten minutes had moved Aqil another mile from Turkey and the chance to rectify the mistake that he was certain that they had made.

Their first evening had been spent in individual interviews with the instructors who ran the camp. Aqil had faced a barrage of questions—Where was he from? Why had he come to the caliphate?—and then followed an intensive session where he was expected to demonstrate his religious piety. They had asked him about his feelings toward the Nusayri regime and the Free Syrian Army and all the other groups that were contesting the embattled country. They asked him whether he accepted the strict

Salafist tenets that governed the group. Aqil had been frightened and did not know what would happen to him if he failed their tests. Would they return him to the border? Would they shoot him? He had answered with as much conviction as he could muster, hoping that they would not see through his lies.

It appeared that they had not. The new recruits had been gathered together and told that they would receive one month's training before they were sent to fight. The instructor had explained that they would receive a mixture of military and political tuition delivered by a cadre of five instructors. There would be lessons in Arabic and religious instruction. After they graduated, they would remain under supervision and could be expelled or punished if they did not maintain their standards. The instructor had taken special care to explain that the punishment would be severe, and that it would include being lashed if the recruits expressed reservations at being at the camp or questioned any of the teachings.

They had been assigned a bed in a building that had once accommodated the workers at the oilfield. Aqil and Yasin had succeeded in taking cots next to one another, and the murmured late-night conversations that the proximity allowed had been the only thing that Aqil had been able to find to take his mind off what had happened to him.

Things were beginning to settle into a pattern now. The morning started at six with an hour of religious instruction delivered by a *sharii*, a young cleric who had recently been recruited to the organisation in order to make up for the lack of imams. The lessons focussed on three main subjects: *tawhid*, or the requirement for monotheism; *bida'a*, or the forbidding of any deviation in religious matters; and *wala wal baraa*, or loyalty to Islam and disloyalty to anything that was considered un-Islamic. They were given a simple breakfast of hummus, sliced cucumber and sheep's milk yoghurt, and then the physical training began.

Aqil hated it. He existed in a state of perpetual terror and regret. He was scared that his fear and self-loathing for allowing himself to be brought here would be obvious, and even though it was always unpleasantly hot, he looked forward to when he was able to pull on the headscarf or balaclava that he had been given. It hid his face, and his hot tears were absorbed into the fabric before they could be seen.

Chapter Twenty-Nine

Yasin found him and they ate together.

"You okay?" Yasin asked him.

"What do you think?"

"You've got to keep that to yourself," he urged. "If they see what you think about it, it won't go well for you. For both of us."

"What about you?" Aqil asked his brother. "You all right?"

"The sooner we get out of here, the better."

They had spoken for an hour last night. They had conversed in low whispers, for fear of being eavesdropped upon by any of the zealous recruits who slept in the hut with them, and Aqil had confessed to his brother how he was feeling. Yasin had said that he felt the same way. Aqil had been flooded with relief. Yasin had admitted that he had made a terrible mistake and said that he would fix it. He would get them out of the country. Maybe they would be able to return to Turkey and pick up as if nothing had happened. Aqil doubted that—he expected that it would have been easy enough for the government to work out where they had gone—but he didn't care. He didn't care if he was prosecuted. He didn't care if he was given a prison sentence. He just wanted to get away.

"What are we going to do?" Aqil asked his brother.

"We have to wait for the right time. We can't just walk off into the desert, can we?"

Yasin looked over Aqil's shoulder, and his face changed. Aqil turned and saw their instructor jogging over to them.

"You two," the man said, pointing at them.

"What?"

"Come here. There's someone who wants to talk to you."

Aqil turned to Yasin. "It's all right," the older boy said. "Come on."

The instructor sent them over to the main accommodation area. There was a car parked there. Most of the vehicles at the camp were utilitarian pickups and four-by-fours, but this was a dusty but reasonably new Mercedes. There was a man leaning against the car. The brothers went over to him. His eyes were hidden behind a pair of dark glasses.

"Hello," Yasin said timorously. "Did you want to speak to us?"

"Do you know who I am?"

"No," Yasin said. "Sorry—I don't."

"My name is Abu Buhar. I'm in charge of the camps in this province. What are your names?"

"Yasin Malik."

"And him?"

"That's my brother, Aqil."

"English, yes?"

"Yes."

"Good. I have something for you both. It is important. You will go now to al-Bab. Infidels have been delivered to the caliphate, Allah be praised, and they are English. We need English-speaking guards to watch over them. You and your brother will do it."

Aqil noticed the confusion in his brother's face, but Yasin mastered it quickly. "No problem. When do we go?"

"Now. The bus is waiting."

There were twenty of them, and they were to be transferred from the camp to al-Bab aboard a bus that had seen much better times. The windshield was held together by a lattice of tape, and the aluminium flanks were studded with bullet holes. The front of the bus was decorated with a number of red and blue lights, a traditional Syrian flourish, and a cheerful scene had been painted above the window. The bus was a strange sight, both colourful and decrepit; Aqil had little confidence that it would manage ten miles across this terrain, let alone the distance between the camp and al-Bab.

Aqil and Yasin waited in line as the men were embarked. The others were graduating from the camp and being sent to the various front lines where the caliphate was contesting its enemies. There were men of several different nationalities, and there was talking and laughter between them and a palpable sense of anticipation. Yasin climbed aboard first and Aqil followed, grabbing the handrails and heaving himself up. The entrance was a third of the way down the vehicle; there were double seats on either side of a narrow aisle, and the driver was already in place, a fat man wearing a *keffiyeh* in Palestinian black and white. Yasin took an empty seat halfway down the bus and Aqil slid in next to him. The seats were as uncomfortable as they looked, with no padding and with sharp edges where the vinyl had been sliced with a knife. Aqil looked up and saw that the air vents had all been torn out of their housings, the wires that would once have served overhead reading lights now hanging loose.

The engine rumbled to life and the doors were closed. The bus rolled out.

Chapter Thirty

The journey took five hours. They drove northwest through the regime's stronghold in Raqqa, crossing the Euphrates River at the northern boundary of Lake Assad, and then continued to Manbij before they turned west for the final run along the highway to al-Bab. The route took them through small villages and hamlets where frightened-looking children would stare at them from the open windows of their fallen-down hovels.

Eventually, they crested a hill and saw a town spread out in the valley ahead. The road descended into a wide depression, the buildings arranged around a river. Aqil looked out and tried to assess how large the town was. It was difficult to say. It was evident, even from this vantage point, that some of the buildings had been destroyed. He saw a spiral of smoke rising up from the far side of the town, and some of the buildings that he could see through the haze ahead of them had been flattened.

"Al-Bab," called the driver.

"Look at it," Yasin said. "It's a war zone."

Aqil stared at the grim panorama and felt a fresh twist of anxiety in his stomach.

Yasin reached across and took his brother by the wrist. "We just stay together," he said. "Okay?"

"Okay," Aqil said.

Yasin lowered his voice. "And we look for a chance to get out. We're north. I saw a sign for Aleppo, and we're farther up than that now. There's only thirty miles from Aleppo to Turkey. Maybe this isn't so bad. Maybe this is lucky."

The roads, which had been potholed and unreliable, now became a little more passable as they followed the road down into the bowl of the depression. The driver slowed as they approached a line of vehicles that had been left in the middle of the road. There were four cars, and each had been burnt out so that all that was left was a blackened frame. The driver turned the wheel and directed the bus onto the rough desert, the suspension squeaking in protest as they rumbled slowly by the devastated convoy. The atmosphere became subdued as the men and boys gazed out at the wreckage, each of them in no doubt as to what had happened here.

The driver called out again, his sentences full of aggressive confidence.

"What did he say?" Yasin said to the man on the other side of the aisle from him.

"He said not to worry. He said this is the work of the infidels, but that we are too strong to be dissuaded by their drones and planes. They are cowards," the man went on with animation. "They should send their soldiers. That is what we want. The final battle between the crusaders and the believers. The end of the world."

Yasin swallowed, his larynx bobbing up and down, but he didn't answer.

They rolled to a halt at a checkpoint next to an orchard of almond trees. Security seemed to be particularly tight, with half a dozen heavily armed men stationed there. One of them gestured impatiently that the driver should open the door, and when he did, the guard climbed aboard and walked down the aisle. He smelt strongly of sweat, and he made a show of the big pistol that he held in his right fist. He spoke in harshly accented Arabic, and one of the men behind Aqil and Yasin answered nervously. The jihadi laughed and Aqil heard the sound of him hawking up a mouthful of phlegm and spitting it out. He dared not turn, and froze as the man stalked back down the bus and disembarked.

The bus pulled around the obstacles in the road and continued into al-Bab.

The bus stopped in the town's central square. It was surrounded on all sides by one- and two-storey buildings, with several roads leading into it. A wooden platform had been erected in the middle of the square, and on it three wooden crosses had been put up. The bodies of three men had been nailed to the crosses, and around their necks, notices in Arabic had been hung to announce their crimes. Aqil and Yasin disembarked from the bus and stared at the grisly sight.

One of the other men noticed that they were slack-jawed. "Can you read Arabic?"

"No," Yasin said.

The man pointed at the three dead men one at a time. "'Apostasy.' 'Cursing Islam.' 'Spying for infidel interests.'"

He clapped Aqil on the back, laughed and set off with the others for another bus that would take them to the front. The bus driver saw them dawdling and pointed to a car that was slowing to a halt next to the bus.

"They take you to English prisoners," he said.

The car was driven by another fighter. It had been a taxi once, and a scratched Perspex screen separated the driver from his passengers. The brothers slid inside. Aqil forced himself to look away from the three dead men as the car reversed and set off.

"We shouldn't be here," he said again quietly. "What were we thinking?"

Yasin hushed him, then said, "We need to be careful. You know what happens if they find out you want to leave? Back there—that's what happens."

"So what do we do?"

"We keep our heads down. Let's see where we're going. Maybe we've got lucky. We're just guards. Maybe they don't watch us the same way they watch the others. We wait, see what it's like and then work out how to get away."

They were driven to the north of the city. The prison was located within an area that had obviously been an industrial quarter before the war. There were factories and warehouses that had since been destroyed. The driver was forced to skirt piles of rubble that had spilled into the road, and they bounced through several shallow craters where the asphalt had been torn up.

They stopped outside a building that had escaped at least some of the damage that had been wrought on its neighbours. There was a wooden sign outside it, the stencilled letters bleached by the sun, but a drawing of a table and chairs suggested that the factory had once produced furniture.

"Out," the driver said curtly.

They stepped out. The sun was burning hot and low in the sky; Aqil shielded his eyes with his hand.

"Remember," Yasin said. "Do as they say. Okay?"

They walked into the open space that preceded the factory. There was a guardhouse, a wooden shack that offered shelter to a single guard with an AK-47. The guard, a man who was no older than the two of them, told them to wait, went inside and fetched a second man. He was older, with a thick grey beard and a face that had been rendered leathery by the sun.

"You from the oilfield?"

"Yes," Yasin said.

"English, yes?"

"That's right."

"Names?"

"Yasin and Aqil," he said, indicating first himself and then his brother.

"You," the man said, pointing. "Yasin. I need you to come with me."

"What for?"

"No questions. I need you to help."

Yasin looked anxiously at his brother. "I—"

The man glared at him. "I'm not asking, I'm telling. You know who I am?"

"No," Yasin said, already cowed.

"I'm in charge. The prisoners are my responsibility. You do what I tell you as long as you are assigned here. And I want you to come with me. Now."

"Give me a moment," Yasin said.

The man harrumphed, but turned his back on them and walked across the dusty yard to a pickup that had just pulled up.

Yasin took Aqil by the shoulders. "Don't worry," he said. "This will be fine. I'll get us out again. There'll be a way. I've read about people getting out. We just need to work out how to do it."

"I'm frightened, Yasin."

"I am, too." The older brother found a smile. "But we won't be here long. Do you trust me?"

"Yes."

Yasin drew Aqil closer and hugged him tight. "Do what they say. I won't be long. We can talk again when we're alone later."

Aqil's throat was tight and he felt tears in his eyes. Yasin gently disengaged their embrace and held Aqil so that he could look into his face. He reached up and gently wiped the tears away. "I love you, Aqil," he said. "I'm sorry about all of this. It's my fault. But we'll be fine. I promise."

Chapter Thirty-One

Isabella had been left in her cell. It was impossible to gauge the time in the pitch-black room, but the fact that she had been given two breakfasts and two dinners suggested that they had kept her there for two full days. She slept as much as she could, and when she was awake, she kept herself occupied as best she could. She put together a routine of exercises that she could do in the confined space, a series of push-ups and crunches that left her muscles burning and her skin covered in sweat. She would rest afterwards, close her eyes and try to recreate the big room outside the cell, the corridor, the doors and then the courtyard outside. She was allowed to use the toilet twice during what she took to be the first day, and she used the short trip to the hole in the floor at the end of the row of cells to fill in those parts of the immediate geography that she hadn't been able to recall.

The last trip to the toilet had been hours ago. Isabella banged her fist on the door.

"Hello?"

There was no response.

"I need to use the toilet."

Nothing.

"Excuse me!" she called again, louder this time. "Please? I need to use the bathroom."

She heard the sound of approaching feet and then the click as the key in the lock was turned. The door opened and bright light streamed inside. Isabella blinked until her eyes adjusted; when they had, she found that the young guard that she was looking at was not one that she had seen before.

"I'm sorry," the guard said. "I didn't hear you."

Isabella looked at him with a mixture of surprise and curiosity. None of the guards had ever apologised to her before, and this one spoke with a timidity that suggested that he was uncomfortable with what he had been asked to do. He had the usual AK-47, but he held it awkwardly in a way that suggested he was unfamiliar with the weapon. He wore it on a strap and his right hand was nowhere near the trigger; she could have disarmed him well before he would have been able to aim and fire, and for a moment, she considered it. She had bunched her right fist and was about to close the distance between them when she saw another guard in the gloom ahead of them. The man took a step forward, into a shaft of light, and she saw it was one of the older men, and one whom she had already identified as more proficient than the others. She relaxed her fist and let her arm fall loose at her side.

"This way," the new guard said.

That was the other thing about him: he was English.

She walked along the row toward the toilet. When they were a little farther away from the other guard, she turned her head to him. "What's your name?"

"Aqil."

"You're English?"

"Yes."

"From the north?"

"Manchester. Who are you?"

"Daisy."

They came to the end of the row. The toilet was in the final cell. There was no concrete floor in this one, and a hole had been dug in the floor. There was a drop beneath it that led either to a cesspit or a sewer. If there was no other option, and she was desperate, Isabella had already decided that she would jump into the hole in the hope that it was a sewer she could follow.

There was no door on the cell. The guard, Aqil, turned his back, and Isabella went inside and relieved herself. She paused there for a moment longer than she needed, her eyes closed as she ran through the possibilities that his obvious inexperience might present to her. He was still standing with his back turned; she could have broken his neck without his even knowing what had happened to him. That someone so obviously out of his depth had been brought in to guard her was encouraging, but this wasn't the right time to take advantage of it. She would wait.

"Thank you," she said.

He made no move to escort her back to the cell. "Where are you from?"

"London."

"What are you doing here?"

"I was kidnapped. They took me. I shouldn't be here."

Isabella watched his face. He was older than she was, although not by much, but his eyes bore doubt and uncertainty. His fingers trembled a little as he rested them on the weapon. She saw weakness in the boy, something that she could exploit.

"Where are we?" she asked.

"They didn't tell you?"

"Not much. We were in Turkey. We came in on a helicopter."

"This is al-Bab," he said.

"Where is that?"

"Twenty-five miles from the Turkish border."

He stood there, still unmoving. Maybe she could forge a relationship with him? "What are you doing here, Aqil?"

"I came to fight," he said.

"Did you?"

"Yes," he said tersely, perhaps sensing that she doubted him. "You think I can't?"

She had doubted him, and she was irritated with herself for letting him know it. "No." She put a little unrest into her own voice. "Not at all. I just . . . I just haven't had the chance to speak to anyone else from England."

Isabella saw the second guard approach and started back to the cell.

"Don't talk to them," the guard said in broken English. "You guard them only. If they talk, you tell me. I deal with them. Understand?"

"Yes," Aqil said.

The guard walked right up to Isabella and took her by the arm. "You hear me?" he said, digging his fingers into the soft flesh below her shoulder. "You don't talk. If you do, I put bullet in your head. Understand?"

"Y-yes," she pretended to stammer. "I've been in there so long, I just—"

He yanked her hard, propelling her into her cell before she could finish the sentence. He slammed the door shut and turned the key.

"No more toilet," he said, his voice muffled through the door. "You need to piss, you piss in there."

Chapter Thirty-Two

I sabella wasn't left alone in her cell for very long. The door was unlocked and opened, and she saw Aqil standing there again.

"Let's go," he said.

"Where?"

"Out."

Isabella stepped out of her cell. The other cell doors were all shut. She didn't know whether that meant the al-Khawaris were here or not.

"I'm sorry," she said.

"What for?"

"I didn't want to get you into trouble."

"I'm not," he said. His tone was brusque; he was overcompensating. "Put on your proper clothes."

Isabella collected the niqab, abaya, and gloves and put them on. They stepped outside. There was a minibus parked on the corner of the street, and Aqil indicated that they should make their way to it. A group of men stood next to the vehicle. They were all armed, two with AK-47s and the others with handguns. As they approached, the men nodded a greeting to Aqil. None of them looked at Isabella.

It was an unusual sensation, almost as if she didn't exist. She realised that there might be a benefit to the garments after all.

⌣

Aabidah was waiting for her in the hotel reception. She took Isabella by the arm and led her to the staircase that they had ascended yesterday. Aqil followed behind them.

"You like this hotel?" the woman said.

"It looks very nice."

"This is where the *al-muhajiroun* stay."

"The who?"

"Foreign fighters. Our foreign guests are treated very well, too. Your cell is not very pleasant, is it?"

"No," she said.

"You do not have to go back there. We have a room for you here. All you have to do is co-operate with Abu. Tell him what he wants to know. Answer his questions. It is very simple."

⌣

Abu was waiting for her behind the desk in the same room that she had been taken to before. There was a silver platter on the desk, with a pot and two china cups.

He smiled solicitously at her. "You can remove your veil," he said. "I am not offended."

She did as he suggested, relieved on the one hand by the cool air that circulated across her hot flesh, and worried, on the other, by the fact that she could no longer rely upon the veil to hide her expressions. She was going to have to concentrate harder to per-suade him that her answers were truthful.

"That's better. I can see you now."

171

She found that her attention was attracted by those small, perfectly white teeth and the manicured moustache, so black that it was surely dyed.

"Would you like a cup of coffee? It is flavoured with cardamom. Very strong."

"Yes, please."

Abu lifted the coffee pot and poured the coffee into the two cups. He pushed one of them across the desk and Isabella took it. Abu raised his cup in a little salute, smiling at the foolishness of it. Isabella put hers to her lips and sipped. It was thick and black.

He replaced his cup on the desk. "I have a few questions for you, Daisy. Do you mind answering them?"

He was unfailingly polite. Isabella wondered whether that was part of his strategy, to try to persuade her that he was a friend and that perhaps he might be able to help her in her predicament. It wouldn't hurt to play along with that charade. He might offer her an inducement if she could persuade him that she was being truthful. A room on her own, perhaps. One that would be easier for her to escape from.

"No," she said. "I'll tell you whatever you want. I just want to go home."

"Yes," he said. "I'm sure you do. This must be very frightening for you."

"Yes," she said. She didn't have to act too hard to persuade him that that was true.

"What is your name?"

"Daisy."

"And your surname?"

"McKee."

"Thank you, Daisy. I do have questions that I need to have answered. I need to understand why you are here. The al-Khawari family, that I can understand. But you are not like them. A young white girl—it makes no sense that you would be with them. Can you understand why I find that curious?"

"I suppose so."

"So tell me: how are you connected to Mr al-Khawari?"

"I'm not. I know his son, that's it."

"Khalil?"

"Yes. We go to the same school."

"I spoke to Khalil yesterday, Daisy. All afternoon. It was an interesting conversation."

The man paused, leaving a space that he evidently hoped that she would feel compelled to fill. It was a standard interrogation trick. Her mother had taught her that she should never volunteer information. And she had told her that the more you said, the more lies you told, the more the chance that you would say something that might trip you up. Far better to hold your tongue.

"Are you not curious what he had to say?"

She had to say something. "What did he say?"

"He says that you had only been at the school for a few days. He says that you made a special effort to get to know him. Is that true?"

"Which part?" She chastised herself as soon as the words left her mouth; she couldn't afford to give the impression that she was confident enough to give him attitude. She remembered how Daisy would feel: frightened, timorous. That was the role. She had to play it.

"Both parts."

She paused and made a show of biting her lip. "Well, yes. I had been there a few days. But it wasn't how he says at all. He made an effort to get to know me. I think he liked me. He bought me a watch."

"Ah, yes. This one?" The man reached into a pocket and took out the Rolex that Khalil had purchased for her when they had been together in Geneva. "It is a very expensive watch, I think?"

"Yes," she said. "He's very rich."

"His father is very rich indeed," the man agreed. He put the garish watch back into his pocket.

"Khalil invited me to his birthday party. I wasn't sure that I wanted to go."

"Ah yes, the party." Abu smiled at her. "He told us about that, too." He reached up with a finger and ran it across his moustache.

"I wish I'd never gone," Isabella said.

"I can imagine. You wouldn't be here if you had stayed away, would you? What happened? Mr al-Khawari and his son both say that you were found in a part of the house you should not have been in. Is that true?"

She frowned. "I got lost. I was looking for the bathroom."

"And you ended up in the study?"

"His house is enormous. I didn't know where he was."

"No doubt," the man said. "But what happened with Mrs al-Khawari?"

Isabella had known that the question would be coming. "She attacked me. She found me in the study and tried to drag me out."

"She says you attacked her."

"To defend myself."

He stroked his moustache again. "Why were you on the helicopter with the rest of the family?"

"Because they forced me to get onto it with them."

He shook his head, smiling, his mean little teeth showing between his thin lips. "I will be honest with you, Daisy, I am very uncomfortable with all of this. I like certainty, and at the moment, I cannot say that I am certain about anything. There are a lot of questions that need to be answered. Can you see that?"

"I'm just telling you the truth."

"I am sure that you are, Daisy. Never mind. We will speak again tomorrow. I will get to the bottom of it. I always do." He stood and smiled again. "You will wait here for me. I am going to speak to the al-Khawaris again. I will speak to you after that. I think I am getting to the bottom of things."

He gestured that she should stand, too, and she did.

"Don't forget your veil. You are not at home now."

She took the niqab and arranged it so that the double folds fell over her head, obscuring her face. The world closed in again, her field of vision reduced to what little she could see through the eye-slit. She allowed herself the luxury of relaxing her face, letting her expression go slack after the strain of her pretence.

"May I give you a little advice, Daisy?" Abu's voice seemed far away now. She didn't answer, and he continued. "You have a few hours to yourself now. You should use them profitably. Think about the situation you are in. This is not a safe place for a Western girl like you. My people are being bombed every day by your government and the governments of the West. My brothers and sisters, and the children of my brothers and sisters, are being killed. Every day, more die. If those people knew that you were here, they would want to make an example of you. You understand what I mean when I say that, don't you?"

She tensed, understanding precisely what he was saying, and gave a small tilt of her head.

"I can help you. I am the only person who can help you. The only thing that you need to do is to tell me the truth."

Isabella watched him as he got up, crossed the room and opened the door. Aabidah was waiting outside. The two of them had a quick conversation, too quiet for Isabella to overhear, and the woman came inside and took Isabella by the arm. She pulled her roughly.

"Come on," she said.

Isabella followed the woman out of the room. Abu was standing on the other side of the door. "Think carefully, Daisy," he said. "Think about what we talked about. I will see you shortly."

Chapter Thirty-Three

Aqil took Isabella to another room in the hotel. Aabidah came with them, and there was no chance for Isabella to try to engage him in conversation. The room was plain and simple, with a desk and a bed. Isabella went over to the window and looked out. They were several floors up, with a view that offered a vista of the city. She saw more buildings that had been flattened, pyres of smoke that issued into the dusky sky and, below her, vehicles running in both directions and the bus that they had arrived in, still parked at the side of the road.

Aabidah spoke to Aqil and left him alone with Isabella. They stood in awkward silence for ten minutes. Isabella took the opportunity to try the window. It was locked. It didn't matter; even if she had been able to open it, there would have been no way she could have escaped through it.

"Don't," Aqil said. His tone was nervous and uncertain.

Isabella turned to him. He was at the door, his body turned a quarter toward it as if his anxiety was split between the prospect of Aabidah's return to find him talking to Isabella, and of Isabella herself.

"Come on," she said. "Help me."

"Please, Daisy. Don't."

"You need to get me out of here," she insisted.

"I can't," he said. "What can I do?"

"Give me that"—she pointed at the AK—"and get out of my way."

He shook his head and laughed nervously at her suggestion. "Don't be crazy. They'd kill me. And how far would you get? You're in the middle of the city. Did you look out the window?"

"Come with me, then," she said. "Help me."

She saw the confusion on the young man's face. She could see that her snap impression of him had been accurate: he didn't want to be here any more than she did. It was the first real reason for optimism that she had found since she had been brought here.

She was about to persevere with him when the door was pushed open and the veiled Aabidah returned.

"What are you doing?" she said.

"I was just about to . . ." Aqil started, the words trailing away as the woman bustled by him and came right up to Isabella.

"Put your niqab back on."

Aabidah was just inches away from her. The woman was a similar height to Isabella, but that was all that she could say with certainty. What she looked like, her build, most of her body language—they were all hidden by the concealing garments.

Isabella paused, balanced on the fulcrum of a decision: make her move now, or wait for something better. The fact that the woman was so close to Isabella gave her confidence. Her Krav Maga instructor had taught her several techniques that would have served her purpose; the fighting style was driven by the tactic of disabling one's opponent as quickly as possible, and a straight-fingered jab into her throat or an elbow into her face would have done the job very well. Aqil was craven, and she didn't expect that he would put up any resistance either. She would be able to escape the room with an automatic assault rifle and fight her way out of the hotel. But Aqil was right. Even assuming that she was able to exit the hotel, it was the start of the evening in the busy centre of a city that was unknown and hostile to her. She had no idea where she would go. They would chase her down before she could get a hundred yards.

She gritted her teeth in frustration. It wasn't the right time. She would have to wait.

"I'm sorry," Isabella said. She took the niqab from the back of the chair where she had lain it and put it back on again.

"Were you talking to him?" Aabidah said sternly.

"No," she said.

"You liar. I heard you. You don't talk. You don't take off the niqab, ever. You think Abu will protect you if you disobey us? He will not. You do not want to find out what would happen to you without his protection."

"I'm sorry . . ." she said, forcing herself not to do what she wanted to do most of all: show them that she was not the helpless little girl that they all thought she was.

Aabidah turned to Aqil. "And you," she said with a derisive flick of her gloved hand. "You guard her. You do not talk to her. What is it? You miss *keffir* girls?"

Aqil stiffened. "No," he said, taken aback by the woman's sudden vehemence and the realisation that, despite her gender, she held a position of influence that he would be well advised to respect. "I told her to put the niqab back on again. I told her not to talk."

"She is a prisoner, not a guest," Aabidah said. "She is not to be treated hospitably until she has explained what she is doing here." She turned to the door and waved at Aqil to stand aside. "He is ready to see her again now. Bring her."

Chapter Thirty-Four

Abu was waiting for her again. He was sitting in the chair behind the desk and he looked as friendly and welcoming as he had done before.

"Hello again, Daisy," he said. "How are you?"

"Scared."

"Yes, of course you are. Please, take off your niqab. I would like to see your face."

She did as she was told, removing the heavy veil and folding it on her lap.

"That's better. Did you think about what I said?"

"Yes."

"Good. I had a look at the accommodation I would like you to have. Not here—I decided that I can do much better than that. We have nice houses where our Western guests can stay. I have such a house for you. A very pleasant house—it used to belong to a doctor. She was posting things about us that were not very friendly. We found out, of course, as we always do, and she had to answer for her crimes. Her house is vacant now. I would like you to have it."

"Thank you," she said.

"But you need to persuade me that you should have it, Daisy. That you deserve it."

"I've answered all of your questions. I've told the truth. I don't know what else to say."

"You are standing by your answers? Everything that you said is the truth?"

"Yes," she said. She didn't know where Abu was taking the conversation, and it wasn't difficult to make her reaction one that suggested she was anxious. She *was* anxious.

"I spoke to the al-Khawaris just now. I told them what you told me. They say that you are lying and that you should not be trusted."

"I told you the truth, I swear."

"It is what you said about Jasmin al-Khawari that concerns me the most. She is very clear that you attacked her. She says you knocked her out and then you tied her up. Her husband and son have both confirmed this. I suppose it is possible that you struggled. Perhaps she fell and banged her head. Yes?"

"That's right," she said. "That's what happened."

"But then you tied her up. Why would you do such a thing?"

"I was frightened. She was crazy. I didn't know what she'd do. I was going to leave the house and I didn't want her coming after me."

"Really, Daisy? I hope you don't mind me saying that that sounds a little far-fetched."

"It's the truth. I swear it."

"Shall I tell you what Mr al-Khawari thinks?"

"What?"

"He thinks that you were involved with planting evidence for the British government."

"That's ridiculous."

"That's what I told him, Daisy. Ridiculous! How old are you?"

"Fifteen."

"Precisely. How would a fifteen-year-old girl be involved with British intelligence? But it puts me in an awkward position. I am a military man. Understanding the strategic picture is important to me. I like to understand everything about a situation before I make a decision, and I do not feel comfortable that I really understand the situation with you. Can you see my dilemma?"

"I'm telling you the truth," she repeated. "I don't know what else I can say."

"There is something else. Emails that the British government says came from Mr al-Khawari's computer have been provided to the media. These emails establish a connection between the caliphate and the attacks at Westminster and the Houses of Parliament. He says that they are fabricated. I doubt that you have seen these emails, have you, Daisy? Do you watch the news?"

"No," she said.

"No. You are young, of course. Why would you be interested in things like this?" He smiled, his white teeth glittering between dry lips. "I have reviewed the emails. Our intelligence specialists have reviewed them. They are undoubtedly fabricated. The ones that were sent to him from the caliphate, some of them come from people who were dead when they were supposed to have sent them. They are very good fakes. It would be impossible for them to be disproved without specialised knowledge. But they *are* fake. Apart from anything else, Mr al-Khawari has no connection with the caliphate. He never has. It seems obvious to me that he has been put forward as what you might call a stooge. Your government would like people to think that we were responsible for the attacks, but we were not. They have nothing to do with us."

"What does that have to do with me?"

"I don't know, Daisy. I was hoping you might be able to tell me. The emails were certainly on Mr al-Khawari's server. He tells me that his network was impregnable from the outside. He says that he paid many tens of thousands of pounds to ensure that his system could not be hacked. He says that the only way those emails could have been placed on his server is by someone who was inside his property." He put his elbows on the desk and leaned forward, fixing her in a cold and pitiless stare. The bonhomie and good manners disappeared as if at the pressing of a switch. "Someone like you, Daisy. How did you do it?"

"I didn't do anything!"

"Who were you working for?"

This was it. She knew that she had to be persuasive. "I don't know what you're talking about. I was there for Khalil's party. I got lost. That's it. This is all a horrible, horrible mistake." She forced herself not to blink, breathed more quickly, and then thought of her mother. The tears came, and she let them roll down her cheeks. "I just want to go home."

Abu was not moved by her demonstration. He did not ameliorate his stern expression, he did not smile, nor did the warmth return to his eyes. He allowed her to sob and she took the opportunity to look down and cover her face with her hands. It seemed like the natural thing to do, and it gave her a moment to compose herself. She was in a precarious position. If he disbelieved her, she knew that she was in the utmost danger. She knew what might happen to her. She had to persuade him that it was ludicrous to believe that a fifteen-year-old girl was involved in the scheme that he had sketched out.

"Stop crying," he said peremptorily. "It is pathetic."

She wiped the back of her hand across her eyes and sniffed.

"I am disappointed," he said. "I do not like being lied to, and I think you are lying to me. Salim's story is credible. The only thing that I find difficult to believe is that your government would enlist a girl like you to do its wishes. But then, on the other hand, maybe it is not so impossible to believe. They are desperate. Public opinion is against the course of action that they have determined to take. Perhaps they would do desperate things. Perhaps everything that has happened over the last week—the attacks, the use of Mr al-Khawari in this way—perhaps it is all for the furthering of their agenda."

"Please," Isabella said. "I don't know anything about any of this. I just want to go home."

He stood and straightened his uniform. "I'm afraid that won't be possible, Daisy. The hotel is impossible. The house—that is certainly impossible. You will go back to your cell. I want you to think about the situation you are in. Perhaps you underestimate how serious it is? Let me correct that for you: unless you tell me the truth, all of the truth, you will be executed. There are people in this building who would have killed you already, but I told them that we had to wait. Perhaps I was wrong. And there is value to our cause in executing a young Western girl like you. You know what will happen to you? You have seen our videos?"

"No," she lied; she had seen them.

"Perhaps I will have a guard show them to you. Do not make the mistake of thinking that this is a bluff. I do not bluff."

"I've told you the truth!"

"No, you have not. Think very carefully about what you've said. You will be brought back to me here tomorrow. Unless you are more forthcoming, we will have to try other ways to have you tell me the truth. Less pleasant ways than having a nice little conversation like we have had today. And if I still feel that you are lying, tomorrow night you will be taken to the main square and you will be executed."

He stalked across the room to the door, opened it and left without another word. Aabidah came inside and gestured with an irritated stab of her finger to the niqab in Isabella's lap. She put it

183

on and allowed the woman to take her by the wrist and pull her to her feet.

"You are lying," she said. "Silly little bitch. He is soft with you. If it was me, you would have been taken to the square and stoned. You would have been hanged or put on a cross. You better tell him what he wants to know, or that is what will happen to you."

The woman yanked her by the arm, impelling her to the door. Isabella looked around, her vision hampered by the niqab, searching for a weakness or an opportunity that she could exploit. There was nothing. Perhaps she could get away from Aabidah, but what then? Nothing had changed from earlier. She didn't know this building. She didn't know the locale, save that it was full of people who were not her friends. She had nowhere to go and no one to help her. She wasn't prepared to placidly accept her fate, but neither was she prepared to make a reckless attempt to escape.

Aqil was waiting for them outside. He followed behind them as they descended the stairs, crossed the reception and went to the minibus.

She would watch and wait. They thought that she was a helpless little girl, lost and alone. She would foster that. It was her biggest advantage. She would wait for the right opportunity, and when it presented itself, she would seize it.

Chapter Thirty-Five

Aqil took the seat behind the girl as the bus returned the prisoners to the jail. He stared at the back of her head, everything obscured by the veil. There was something about her that he found unsettling. She seemed to be calmer than she had any right to be in the circumstances in which she found herself. She had been confident enough to talk to him in the room while the woman was away. She had waited until they were alone, and then she had spoken. Why was that? Could she see that he was frightened out of his mind? He was trying to play the part, but it felt totally unconvincing and he knew that his doubts would show. He was almost crippled by fear. He had felt sick all day, and as the bus drew to a halt outside the half-wrecked building, he felt worse.

The doors opened and the passengers disembarked. Aqil stayed close to the girl, the muzzle of his AK just a few inches from her back. They reached the entrance to the prison. One of the guards was behind the little wooden hut that protected the front of the building. He saw them approach, pushed himself out of his chair and stepped outside.

He intercepted Aqil. "You are English?"

"Yes," Aqil said.

"Your brother, too?"

"Yes. His name is Yasin. He was here with me last night. What's happened?"

"Yasin," the man said, nodding. "We did not know his name."

"What do you mean you *didn't* know? What's happened?"

"Your brother was killed last night."

Aqil felt a sudden sickness and tasted acid vomit in the back of his throat. He swallowed it down, desperate not to show weakness in front of everyone.

"How?" he managed to say.

"An infidel drone. The convoy he was in was attacked. Seven brothers were killed, including him. But it is good. He has been martyred. He is in Paradise now, Allah be praised. It is what he wanted."

No, Aqil wanted to say, *it was not what he wanted.* Yasin knew that they had made a terrible, terrible mistake and all he had wanted to do was go home. Aqil felt hot tears in his eyes and couldn't stop them from spilling over his cheeks.

"Do not cry. It is joyous news."

"Can I see him?"

The man chuckled. "Have you seen what happens after a drone strike? There is nothing left to see. He is gone. His sacrifice will not be forgotten, but we must continue with the work of the caliphate."

"So what . . ." He stopped, the emotion clotting his throat. "So what do I do now?"

"What you were doing before. The prisoners must be guarded. You will remain here. After that, when we have no further use for them, they will be executed. You will help us do it."

Chapter Thirty-Six

I sabella was taken to the same cell as before and locked inside. The darkness was thick and impenetrable, with just the tiniest gradation of grey visible at the intersection of the roof and the wall. She sat down on the mattress and allowed her eyes to get used to the darkness again. She heard the sound of footsteps as the guard headed back to the front of the building, but nothing else, not even the whimpering from Jasmin next door. She had come to expect her sniffling as a part of the building's soundtrack.

Isabella had glanced around the cell again as she had been pushed inside, before the door was closed and the darkness descended. Everything was as it had been before. There was nothing that she could use as a weapon. No way to escape. She would have to wait until they came for her again, until they took her back to see Abu.

She wouldn't be able to wait for a better opportunity any longer than that. That would be her chance. Perhaps her chances would have been best when she had been left alone in the room with Aqil, but she had hoped that another, better chance would present itself. There would be no point in speculating or regretting what might have been. She would have to act. Her single advantage was that they had no idea who she was and would almost certainly underestimate her.

She would make that count.

———⌣———

She lost track of time. She didn't know when it was that she heard the sound of feet approaching the cell. Several hours later, for sure. She thought that it must have been one of the irregular patrols that the guards undertook, checking that everything was as it was supposed to be, but it quickly became apparent that it wasn't that after all. She heard the sound of the key to the cell door as it was inserted into the lock, and then the sound of it being turned.

Aqil?

Isabella had already decided she would attack him if he opened the door.

She hopped to her feet and closed her eyes a little so that she wouldn't be blinded by the light from outside.

The door opened, and she saw Aqil standing there.

She grabbed a double fistful of his jacket, pivoted on her right foot and hauled him into the cell. She tripped him, drove him onto the mattress, planted him there with her right knee in the middle of his sternum and drew back her fist to pummel him.

"No!" he said, raising his hands and holding them above his face. "I want to help."

Her fist was bunched so tightly that she could feel her nails pressing into her palms, and her bicep throbbed with adrenaline, but something told her to pause. Aqil's face was dimly lit in the light from the bulb outside, and enough of the glow was cast onto his face that she could see how terrified he was.

He wasn't here because he had been told to get her. This was something else.

She didn't strike him.

"Quickly," she said. "And keep your voice down."

"What you said last time—you asked why I was here."

"To fight. That's what you said."

"Yes," he said. He looked as if he was about to go on, but his face dissolved and he looked away.

"What is it?" she said.

He was crying. "I don't want to be here. It was a mistake. I should never have come."

"What are you saying, Aqil?"

"You asked me to help. I will. Let's go. I'll get you out of here. We can leave together."

Isabella thought as quickly as she could. Thoughts scampered through her head, difficult to pin down and weigh up. The dominant one was that this was her chance. She knew what her mother would have done: Beatrix would have knocked him out, locked him in the cell, taken his AK and gone. It was dark now. She would be able to hide in the shadows, use them to help her to get out of the city.

But she thought around it a little more. What was the alternative? She could go with him. There were all sorts of problems that he might be able to help her surmount. How would she get by the guards? How many were there? At least one, but maybe more. He could give her the information that she needed, and help her deal with the problem. There were other advantages of having him around, too. Women were not supposed to be on the street without a chaperone. If anyone saw her, out on her own after dark, she would be arrested. He could help her to avoid that, too.

And then doubts. He was frightened. What would he be like if they came under fire? Could she trust him?

"Please," he said. "I want to do the right thing. I'm going. Tonight. I can't leave you here. You're just a girl. How are you going to get away without me?"

It was so pitiful she almost chuckled at it. Here he was, pinned to her dirty mattress, half a second from being hit in the head, and with no idea at all who she was and what she was capable of doing. Perhaps he really did want to do the right thing. That was in his favour. But he thought she was helpless, a poor little lost girl whose only chance was if he helped her. But he had it the wrong way around: if he did want to get out of the city and the country, his only chance of making it was if *she* helped *him.*

"They're going to kill you," he added redundantly.

Isabella leaned back, removing her weight from his chest, reached down for his fatigues again and pulled him back to a sitting position.

"Get up," she said.

"What? I—"

"*Quickly.*"

Her decisiveness—and the fact that she had thrown him to the ground so easily—now seemed to register on Aqil. He stood.

"Where is your AK?"

"Outside," he said.

"How many guards are there?"

"One. In the guardhouse outside. We take shifts."

Two guards? Okay. That seemed reasonable when the prisoners were so securely locked up.

She went outside and he came behind her.

"The guard," she said. "He's in the guardhouse? The hut at the front of the building."

"Yes," Aqil said.

"What's the guard like?"

"What do you mean?"

"What do you think I mean? Is he thorough? Lazy? Is he likely to be asleep? What weapon does he have?"

"He's young," he said, stumbling over his words. "I think he's Syrian. He's scared of them, too. He won't be asleep."

"Weapon?"

He nodded at the AK that was standing against the wall. "The same as that."

"My niqab is in the cell," she said. "Get it for me."

He did as she asked. She turned, looking out into the gloom of the wide space and the shadowed hulks of its machinery, and started to work out what they would do.

But then she paused.

The al-Khawaris were still here.

She couldn't just leave them to be killed.

"Does your key open all the cells?" she asked him.

"Yes. The same one works on all of them. Why?"

"I can't leave them."

He shook his head. "No," he said. "They're not here. They didn't come back today."

"They're still at the hotel?"

"I don't know. No one tells me anything. I'm just a guard."

That changed things.

Bad luck for them, but there was no time to waste thinking about the al-Khawaris now. She would have let them out, once she was certain that they could not impede her, but she certainly wasn't going to go looking for them. Whatever was going to happen to them was going to happen.

"This is what we're going to do," Isabella said. "You're going to go and get the guard. Say that there's a problem. Tell him I'm ill. I'm having a fit. Bring him back here. I'll hide there"—she pointed to one of the larger pieces of machinery that they would have to pass to reach the cell block—"and I'll take him out. And then we'll run."

"How?"

"We steal a car."

He shook his head, his doubt suddenly overflowing. "This is stupid. We haven't got a chance."

"It isn't. We can do it, Aqil. Trust me."

"No, we can't. I'm too scared. And trust you? Come on, Daisy. You're, what, fifteen? Be real. What chance do we have?"

He had already forgotten how easily she had put him to the ground. Isabella decided he would benefit from another demonstration of what she could do. "Watch," she said.

Isabella knew all about AKs. It was important to be familiar with them, her mother had said, since the weapons were so ubiquitous. They had fired hundreds of rounds in the desert outside Marrakech, and Isabella had fired more in the months when she had continued her training alone. She reached down for the rifle, ejected the magazine and checked that it was unloaded. It was. She had performed the function check so many times that it was almost a muscle memory for her now, and she flew through it. She pulled the charging handle fully aft and released it, letting it fly forward, checking that it was fully in battery. It was. She moved the selector to safe and pulled the trigger to check that nothing happened. Nothing did. She moved the selector to fire and pulled the trigger to check that the hammer dropped. It did. She slapped the magazine back into the well and took the weapon in both hands, her finger through the guard and against the trigger.

Aqil watched her, his mouth agape.

She gave him a small smile.

"I'm not who they think I am," she said.

"So who are you?"

"It's better that you don't know. But I can get us both out of here. You just have to trust me."

Chapter Thirty-Seven

Isabella heard Aqil speaking as he led the second guard into the factory hall.

"She's ill," he said loudly. "Sick."

"What do you mean?" The second voice, that of the other guard, was uncertain and halting. It was obvious that English was not a language with which the man had much facility.

"I think she's epileptic or diabetic or something. She's fitting."

She heard the sound of footsteps. The light next to the cell block was illuminated, but the brightness was quickly swallowed up into the blackness that filled the big space.

The darkened shapes of two men went by. Isabella detached herself from the deeper blacks that clung to the machine and took two quick steps to close the distance between her and them. It was too dark to identify Aqil. She hoped that he had remembered to put himself on the other side of the guard and not on her side.

His fault if he hadn't.

She had turned the AK around so that the wooden buttstock was facing away from her. She raised the rifle so that it was level with her head, let out a low whistle and, as the man turned in her direction, drove the butt into his face.

The man folded in the middle and collapsed to the floor.

"Jesus."

"Aqil?"

"You nearly took his head off!"

Isabella turned the rifle around and aimed down at the man on the floor. She heard the sound of his breath whistling in and out through a mouthful of broken teeth, but he did not stir. He would be out for a while. There was no need to shoot him.

"Give me a hand," she said.

They took an arm each and dragged the man deeper into the shadows until there was no way he would be noticed until he awoke.

"Let's go," she said, leading the way.

Isabella opened the door and looked outside. She remembered it from before, but it looked different after dark. The skeletons of buildings that had been razed to the ground were on either side, and across the small parking area, a larger building had been torn apart by a bomb, leaving a large crater surrounded with blackened and charred struts scattered across it like matchsticks. There were huge chunks of rubble on the ground. The factory was bounded by a chain-link fence, and beyond that, Isabella could see the darkened shape of the skyline in the distance.

"Where are we?" she asked him.

"I'm not sure."

"Think, Aqil."

"The northern part of town."

"Do you have a map?"

He shook his head.

She was losing her patience with him already. "Fine. Which way did you come in?"

"We went across the border at Reyhanli." He paused, saw the irritation on Isabella's face and added, "It's to the southwest. It took us six hours to drive here. You want to go that way? It's miles. And we'd have to go around Aleppo."

"We're not going anywhere near Aleppo." She tried to remember her geography. Aleppo was in the north of the country, and they were north of that.

She pointed away from the city. "Turkey is that way. It can't be far to the border. We'll try to find a car. But until we do, we'll walk." She looked up at the sky. The moon was directly overhead. "What time is it?"

"Late."

"We need to move."

———

The factory was part of a wider complex of buildings. The streets were quiet, with no traffic. There were no lights visible; Aqil explained that it was because the electricity supply was intermittent and usually rationed for the daytime. They passed buildings that had been blown apart by explosions and others that had been allowed to burn to the ground. The road was littered with debris, and they frequently changed course to avoid large chunks of masonry that had been tossed into their way, or craters that had been gouged out of the asphalt.

Isabella was alert, pausing regularly so that she could reacclimatise herself to their changing surroundings. The guard she had knocked out would wake up eventually—assuming that she hadn't scrambled his brains—or if he did not, both his and Aqil's absence would be noticed when the shift changed. It was remotely possible that their absence would not be noticed until morning. If that was the case, maybe they had a chance. There were five or six hours until dawn, and they would be able to put several miles between them and the factory by then. She knew that she walked at between three and four miles an hour; fifteen miles did not seem unreasonable. That was a good head start.

Aqil walked silently alongside her.

"Back there," Isabella said. "You said 'we crossed the border.' Was that with your brother?"

He didn't answer at once, and when he did speak, his voice was low. "Yes. We were going to get away from here. And now . . ."

And now he was dead.

Isabella had never felt comfortable with expressing emotion. It was a hang-up from her unhappy childhood that had never been given a chance to heal. She knew that she should say something, so she managed a simple "Sorry."

They walked on, crossing the road to skirt the wreck of a car that had been left to burn down to blackened steel and ash.

Isabella glanced over at him. He was glum, his eyes downcast. "Why did you come out here?"

"It was the worst mistake I ever made."

"But why?"

He paused for a moment and just walked on silently. Isabella waited. She could see that he was trying to find the right way to answer the question. "I have—I *had*—a twin brother. Aamir. He was involved in the Westminster bombing. I don't know how, but he was there, in the station, when they blew up their bombs. But he didn't do it. He changed his mind, and he ran. But then he was shot and killed, and his body was dumped into the Thames. My older brother, Yasin, the one who came over the border with me, he thought the police murdered him. I let him persuade me."

Isabella could have mentioned that she had been there, at the station, when the bombs were detonated, but she did not. She didn't want to put an end to the conversation with her anger, so she walked on, quietly, while Aqil considered what to say next.

"My family were victimised. Racism. It never stopped. They'd done nothing wrong. My brother was dead. My mother is ill and my father has never done a thing wrong in his life. They love our country."

She repeated the question. "So why are you here?"

"Because I was angry. And because I didn't think. I let myself be persuaded to come when I should have told Yasin he was crazy. I don't want to be here. He didn't, not since we arrived. We both wanted to go home."

Isabella had other questions for him, but she put them aside for now. The boy was hopeless. Isabella could see that if they were going to get out alive, it was going to be because of her and despite him. But he seemed genuine. And he had taken a big risk to free her from the cell. He could have left without her, but he had not. It was fortunate for him that he had a conscience, because he wouldn't have lasted five minutes on his own. She had already given thought to leaving him and making for the border alone, but she decided that she wouldn't do that.

They were close to the desert now, and she could see the dunes and foothills in the gaps between the buildings. As they turned the corner, they saw that the road petered out and became a rough track. It ascended a gentle slope, crested the hill and disappeared to the north. There was a shack ahead, to the right of the road, and there was a car parked next to it.

Isabella put out a hand to stop Aqil. She waited, listening, and then, when she was confident they were alone, she crossed the road. The car had been parked next to the building. It was a Hyundai Lantra, an older model, and it was bearing its age gracelessly. It was dented, the front wing had been replaced with one in a different colour, and the window in the passenger-side door was missing its glass, the opening covered with a plastic sheet that had been taped to the frame.

Isabella tried the door of the car. It was open. It was open. She looked for the keys, running her hand beneath the seat and then pulling down the sun visor.

Aqil watched her. "Anything?"

"No."

"So how are we going to start it?"

"Don't worry about that," she said.

Beatrix had taught her many things in the year that they had spent together, and hot-wiring a car was one of them. The Lantra was old and lacked the security features of newer models. She found a sharp stone on the ground next to the car and used it to pry off the plastic cover on the steering column. She pulled out the three bundles of wires inside and picked out the wires that led straight up the column to the starter, battery and ignition. She found the red wires for the battery, stripped away the insulation and twisted them together. She stripped the starter wire, too, and sparked it against the battery wires.

The engine turned over and started.

Isabella couldn't help a smile.

"Where did you learn to do that?" Aqil asked, staring at her dumbfoundedly.

"Get in," she said. "We need to be as far away from here as we can."

Chapter Thirty-Eight

Isabella turned to Aqil. "Can you drive?"

"I passed my test in the summer," he said.

"So?"

"I'm all right."

His answer didn't fill her with confidence, and she wondered whether she should drive. She decided against it. Women were not supposed to drive, and even though it was dark and the streets in this part of town were deserted, it wasn't impossible that they would come across a patrol, and it made sense to avoid creating obvious problems for themselves. And, she reminded herself, she had the assault rifle. That was certainly going to remain her responsibility.

She opened the rear door and slipped into the cabin behind the driver's seat. Aqil settled down, rehearsing the procedure for pulling away with a deliberateness that suggested that he had overestimated his confidence behind the wheel.

"You'll be fine," Isabella said. "You've just got to drive carefully. We don't want to stand out."

"What if I stall it?"

"You won't."

"They have patrols. What if they see us?"

"We'll deal with that when it happens. Just relax. Let's go."

He put the Hyundai into gear and almost stalled the engine, depressing the clutch just in time. Stalling would be a problem, Isabella saw. She wondered afresh whether she should drive. Aqil cursed under his breath, released the handbrake and pressed down on the accelerator. The car started forward, the suspension creaking ominously as it bounced down from the raised kerb.

"That way," Isabella said, pointing down the street. There was a junction ahead that would allow them to turn to the north.

Aqil turned the wheel and the car rolled ahead.

They found their way to the main road that headed north out of al-Bab. It was a two-lane highway, in reasonably good condition compared to the bombed-out city that it served. Aqil drove carefully, seemingly gaining in confidence as they progressed. The buildings around them became sparser and the desert started to take hold of the landscape.

Isabella had started to believe that they were going to make it out of the city without incident.

"What's that?" Aqil said, squinting through the windshield.

Isabella had seen it, too. She saw the red taillights of a car that had stopped ahead of them, and then, as they drew nearer, the shape of buildings immediately to the left and right of the highway and an obstruction in the middle of the road.

"Slow down," she said.

They drew closer. Isabella peeked between the two front seats and looked ahead. It was a checkpoint. There were two cars ahead of them: a Peugeot 207 and an old Volkswagen Golf. The roadblock did not look particularly professional. There was a four-by-four and a Humvee that had been parked end to end, blocking the road, but the desert on either side of the road looked to be passable. It was flat and did not have any large rocks or other obstructions that would be a problem to traverse. There were two hastily erected wooden buildings on the left and the right, with light shining from small windows. The Golf's headlights shone ahead, and Isabella watched as the shape of a man was lit up as he passed through the beams.

"What do we do?" Aqil said.

Isabella took off the niqab. "We can't stop," she said. "You don't have any reason to be out here."

"No," he said.

"And they're probably looking for us already."

"So? What do we do?"

"We'll drive up to where the Peugeot is now."

"You want me to talk to them?"

"No," she said. "Let them come up to the car. When I tell you, drive off again and go around them. Go to the left, onto the desert. The ground is better on that side."

His voice was tight with tension. "But they'll shoot at us."

"They might."

"So what do we do then?"

"Leave that to me."

The insurgents finished with the Peugeot and waved it on. The Volkswagen rolled forward, the driver braking as the nearest sentry raised his hand. Isabella stayed low, behind the seat, but looked out the window for additional sentries.

"Edge forward a little," Isabella said.

Isabella watched as Aqil nervously clasped and unclasped his hands around the wheel. "Why don't we turn around?" he said. "There was another turning. We passed it—we could go that way, go around them."

"Too late. You think they won't come after us if we turn around? Don't be crazy. Our best chance is to run. We've got surprise on our side. Drive."

He did as she asked, the car jerking as he inexpertly put it into gear. Isabella wished that she was driving, but she knew that she would be more useful with the Kalashnikov. She stayed low, looking out from between the seats, the rifle held down low in both hands. The two insurgents were on either side of the Volkswagen. The man next to the driver was crouched down a little and leaning over so that he could speak to the occupants of the vehicle. His partner was walking around the car, inspecting it, looking—perhaps—for the prisoner who had escaped just a few hours earlier.

Isabella slid the index finger of her right hand into the trigger guard. She reached with her left and laid the barrel of the rifle in her palm. She closed her grip, holding it loosely.

The second guard had a torch and he shone the beam into the interior of the car.

"Ready?" Isabella said.

"No."

"Yes, you are. Wind down your window."

He did as she asked; the mechanism was rusty, and the handle squeaked as he turned it. She felt the coolness of the air on her face as it filtered into the stuffy cabin.

"It's going to be very noisy. Ignore it. You just need to drive us away from here. That's all you need to do. Okay?"

He didn't answer.

The sentry at the window of the Volkswagen had straightened up. The second man was walking back around the car, his back turned away from them.

"Aqil?"

"I'm frightened."

The Volkswagen pulled away, sliding around the four-by-four and then gathering speed as it headed north.

The first sentry waved at them to come forward.

"What do I do?" Aqil said.

"Take it easy," Isabella replied. "Drive on. Nice and slow."

Aqil released the handbrake and almost stalled the car again. He cursed, low and urgent, panicking, and Isabella knew then, for certain, that it wasn't going to go down the way she wanted. It wasn't going to be smooth. He put the car into first gear and jerked forward. Isabella stayed low, hidden behind his seat. She felt the trigger against the pad of her index finger.

Aqil braked and the car came to a stop.

The engine coughed; Isabella prayed that he wouldn't stall it.

She heard, over the spluttering of the engine, the sound of footsteps approaching.

She was down low now, holding the rifle vertically so that it was hidden behind the seat but ready to aim when she needed to. She couldn't see anything. She had to go on instinct.

The guard called out to Aqil. "Turn off the engine."

Isabella could almost feel Aqil freeze. "Don't," she hissed.

The voice was closer now. "Didn't you hear me? Turn off the engine."

Isabella straightened up, bringing the rifle down and pointing it so that the muzzle was between the edge of Aqil's seat and the frame of the window. She saw the guard. He was a metre away and his own Kalashnikov was pointed down at the ground. He saw Isabella. His eyes widened in shock and he started to bring his own rifle up, but it was always going to be too late for him.

Beatrix had trained Isabella how to shoot an AK. She gently squeezed the trigger and loosed off a burst of three rounds. The distance between her and the guard meant that it was almost impossible to miss, and she did not. All three rounds found their mark.

The insurgent stumbled back, tripped and fell beneath the line of the window, out of sight.

"Now!" she yelled. "Go!"

Aqil stamped down on the gas, but his foot was still on the clutch. The engine whined impotently.

The second guard had already started to turn at the distinctive bark of the AK. He was on the other side of the car, the wrong side for Isabella, and she couldn't aim at him through the open driver's window. She pulled the AK back, shoved it into the gap between the two front seats and took fresh aim. The man had raised his own AK and he fired before she did. The rounds blew out the windshield, shards of glass tumbling into the cabin. The passenger seat juddered on its fixings and a puff of upholstery blew out into the rear of the cabin. Isabella drew a bead on the man and fired off another three-round burst. The remnants of the windshield exploded, the shards blown out over the bonnet this time. The guard was hit and he fell to the ground.

Isabella saw a vehicle approaching from the other side of the barricade.

"Aqil!" Isabella shouted. She had no idea whether he had been struck.

The engine revved again, and still they did not move. At least he wasn't dead.

"The clutch."

"I can't . . . it won't . . ."

"Release the fucking clutch!"

It was too late now. The vehicle on the other side of the blockade was a pickup truck. It had stopped to disgorge four more regime soldiers. They were all armed, and they were fanning out around the four-by-four and the Humvee. They must have heard the sound of gunfire; maybe they had seen what had happened; maybe it was just bad luck.

"Aqil," she said as she reached for the door handle, "listen to me. We can't drive now. We've got to run. Back into the city."

The engine revved impotently again. He was panicking.

Isabella pulled down on the handle and flung the door open. "Come on, Aqil. *Run!*"

She stepped down, using the open door for concealment. She peeked around the frame so that she could position the four new arrivals in her mind's eye. They had split into two groups of two. The first two were behind the Humvee and the second pair were behind the four-by-four. The four-by-four was closest. The four of them were staying in cover; the two shot men on the ground provided a very compelling reason why it was in their best interests to be cautious. But there would only be a temporary stand-off. They would realise, very quickly, that there was only one enemy facing them, that she was a young girl and that she was very badly outnumbered. They would be able to flank her.

Isabella wouldn't give them the chance.

Aqil was still in the car. "Aqil, listen. We have to run. I'm going to go back into the city. If you stay here, you'll either be captured or killed. It's up to you, but I'm going on three."

Isabella was sheltering behind the rear door; she couldn't go forward to help him get out of the car without exposing herself to the enemy. Nevertheless, as she reached her left hand down to grasp the AK around its forestock, she heard the door open. She couldn't see whether Aqil had got out or not, but she couldn't wait any longer.

"One."

Isabella shuffled closer to the edge of the door.

"Two."

The abaya was impeding her. She undid the clasps and let it fall to the ground. She slid her finger into the trigger guard.

"Three."

She stood, aimed the rifle at the four-by-four, and opened fire. There was little prospect of hitting the men, but that wasn't necessary; she just wanted to give them a good reason to stay where they were. The rounds streaked across the medium range between Isabella and the blockade, pinging brightly off the vehicle's bodywork. The soldiers reeled back behind the bulk of the vehicle, and Isabella encouraged them to stay there with another well-aimed volley.

Now that she was standing, she could see that Aqil had got out of the car. He was sitting on the road, his back pressed against the open door, his knees hugged to his chest and his arms over his head. He was terrified, but there was nothing Isabella could do for him. He wasn't coming with her. She looked up again, switched aim and fired another three rounds at the Humvee.

Her volley rattled off the armoured hull as she turned away from the car—and Aqil—and ran.

Chapter Thirty-Nine

I sabella ran as fast as she could. She had run every day in Marrakech, miles and miles, and she knew that she had the endurance to run hard for forty or fifty minutes. She needed to put as much distance as she could between herself and the men at the blockade. She wouldn't be able to outrun them. They had their pickup, and it wouldn't take them long to round up Aqil and then come after her.

They had travelled north, to the residential district on the outskirts of the city. The road to the south led into a quarter that was dominated by five- and six-storey apartment blocks. There were two hundred metres between the checkpoint and the start of the blocks. Isabella sprinted, the AK clasped in her right hand. The weapon felt heavier with every stride, but she couldn't relinquish it. She pumped her arms and legs until her lungs were on fire, and then she kept running. She didn't look back, but as the road passed through a narrow grove of cedar trees, she heard the sound of incoming gunfire. It was a burst from an automatic weapon, the rounds passing harmlessly overhead.

Isabella gulped down as much air as she could in ragged gasps and ran harder.

She sprinted until she was within the curtilage of the first apartment block. There was no one else on the street—she wondered if the regime insisted upon a curfew—but there were lights in some of the windows in the flanks of the buildings on either side of her. The residents had been disturbed, perhaps, by the sound of gunfire. Isabella was sweating hard as she turned onto a side road, a narrow canyon formed by blocks that faced each other on opposite sides of the road. The district had evidently been subjected to some sort of bombardment, for the road between the two buildings was pregnant with the debris of an explosion. Huge bites had been taken from the buildings: some had suffered the indignity of having their balconies peeled away; none of the windows had been left with glass, and other buildings had been bestowed with blackened scars from where fires had been allowed to burn themselves out. The debris in the road was significant, with huge chunks of rubble and twisted metal girders that had been flung around like pick-up sticks. Isabella picked her way across the pile of rubble with care, knowing that to twist her ankle now would be disastrous. She knew, too, that this road would be impassable for any vehicle that might be in pursuit.

She had negotiated the first half of the obstruction when she heard the sound of an engine and then, immediately after that, the squeal of rubber biting on asphalt. She heard the sound of a door opening and then a man's voice, a word barked out in Arabic that she couldn't hear over the gasping of her breath. She clambered over a large mound of rubble and slid down the other side as she heard the ugly rattle of gunfire. There was enough debris to shield her, but that could only be temporary. The men from the blockade had dealt with Aqil and they were coming after her now.

She scrambled down the slope, the loose rubble skittering ahead of her, and, staying low, crept across so that she could see around the mound of debris to the road beyond. The jeep was there, with the figures of three men visible in the moonlight. She raised the AK and fired off another controlled burst. The men dropped, the rounds sailing overhead. It didn't matter; she just needed a few extra seconds.

Isabella turned and surveyed the way ahead. There was more rubble in the road, enough to slow her down. Now that her pursuers were on foot, too, the rubble would not serve quite the same advantage. They might be able to move more quickly, and if she had to slow down to negotiate it, she would be vulnerable to their rifles. No. She needed an alternative. There was a narrow alleyway to her right. Two apartment blocks shouldered up close together, a green, white and black Syrian flag painted on one wall and a large square of red paint on the other. There was just enough space between the walls of the buildings for a person to be able to pass through, provided the gap was negotiated in single file. The alley was dark, but she could see a glimmer of light at the end of it.

It was as good a way forward as any.

She vaulted a tangled nest of thick metal wires and ran hard again, sprinting until she was inside the alleyway. The temperature was two or three degrees colder in the darkness, but Isabella ignored it and ran. There were bags of trash that had been dumped here, and rats the size of small cats paused, indifferent, to regard her with sly languor as she rushed by. She heard the sound of a man's voice at the other end of the alleyway; it was an Arabic curse and then a clear instruction: "Follow her!"

Isabella emerged in a small market square. It, too, had been shelled. The buildings that formed it had been shattered; yet more debris spilling out in treacherous piles. A white pickup truck was on its side, the windshield ruined by a filigree of cracks, the glass now a milky opaque grey. Telegraph and electricity wires draped down from their poles, and bullet holes pocked the hood of the pickup and the walls beyond it. The square was presided over by the minaret of a mosque, with another in the middle distance behind it.

A man tripped and fell in the alley behind her. She heard his grunt of pain, his curse and the invective of another man who was stuck behind him. She turned, aimed the rifle and fired another three-round volley into the black maw. She thought she heard a yelp of pain and wondered, maybe, if she had been fortunate enough to score a hit. She saw muzzle flash, much closer than she had expected, and flinched as a track of impacts was scored across the stone cladding to her right. She felt the sting as razored chips scratched across her face. She turned and ran.

The piles of debris in the square were insurmountable, though a path had been cleared around the perimeter. She followed it, edging around the flatbed of the overturned pickup, and then, once the road was clear of debris, rushed toward the first mosque. The road continued for another hundred yards until it was crossed by another, and as Isabella ran on, she saw a large vehicle rumble across the junction. It was the Humvee, and it jerked to a sudden stop.

Not good.

The mosque had been flattened. The damage was more severe than would have been caused by a shell; it was as if a giant hand had slapped down on it, flattening it completely. Isabella had seen reports of barrel bombs that were dropped from regime helicopters, and she wondered whether something like that had happened here. The minaret was precarious, but somehow still standing, a lonely sentinel presiding over a huge mound of rubble. There was no way Isabella could scramble up the slope in time, but just as she was about to disregard that side of the road as a way of escape, she saw that the explosion had torn an opening in the building that had once abutted the mosque.

More shots. She flinched, the bullets chewing up a storm of fine dust as they landed short. She glanced back to the junction.

Two men had disembarked from the Humvee. She looked back to the overturned pickup and saw another pursuer emerging around the side of the vehicle.

Three men, at least. She had to get away from them. She scrambled ahead, leaping over the debris until she was at the opening. The wall had collapsed, offering access to the ground floor of the building. Isabella hopped down. It was dark, the scant moonlight absorbing into the gloom so that she couldn't see for more than six feet. There was a flight of stairs in the middle of the floor, and acting purely on instinct, Isabella crossed the floor and ascended. The building must have been declared unsafe, because it had been abandoned. Isabella climbed to the first floor, then the second, third and fourth. The stairs ended at a landing that, in turn, ended at a closed door. Isabella turned the handle; it was unlocked, and she opened it. The door offered access to the roof. She scampered outside, closed the door behind her and surveilled her new surroundings. The minaret was to the left, the perspective altered now that she was halfway to its top. The roofs of the buildings on the same side of the street stretched away to the south; some were a little higher, others a little lower, and the way forward was littered with satellite dishes, walls and sills, clotheslines and boxy air-conditioning units.

The satellite dishes were all pointing in the same direction, many of them hopelessly corroded, the assortment looking for all the world like a collection of oversized mushrooms. She picked a path to one of them, particularly large and blackened with rust, and hid behind it. She turned back to the door and knelt down. She brought the butt of the rifle to her shoulder, sitting down on her right foot and supporting the flat of her left arm, just above the elbow, on her bent left knee. Her mother had taught her the position, lecturing her when she tried to rest the point of her elbow on her knee; this, she said, was as unstable as a ball sitting atop a ball.

She cupped her left hand, giving the fore end of the rifle something to settle into, and then relaxed until she felt stable.

She aimed, peering down the iron sights just as the door flew open, crashing against the wall. One of the insurgents stood framed in the doorway. He must have been green, or perhaps he had underestimated her, because as he looked out and saw Isabella, he was practically already dead. She squeezed the trigger and fired off a single round. There were only twenty feet between them, she had a stable firing position and she had already taken aim; she knew that she would be able to hit him, and conservation of her ammunition was becoming a pressing concern. The round struck the insurgent in the breastbone, on the centre line of his body, where all of the vital organs were to be found. The sudden impact knocked him back a step, and his heel caught against the sill of the door. He overbalanced, toppled over and fell back into the gloomy landing.

Isabella knew that the others would be behind him, but they would have to be very careful now. Perhaps they would wait for reinforcements. It didn't matter. Isabella did not intend to wait for them to formulate their plan.

She turned and ran, crossing the roof of the building and vaulting a shallow sill that marked the beginning of its neighbour. She crossed that building, clambered atop a waist-high wall and then dropped down the six feet to the roof of the next building along. The skyline was dark, with only a few lights shining, but she could make out the spectral fingers of minarets, the bulk of a particularly large office block and electricity pylons that strode through the centre of town. The next building was taller than the one she had just crossed, so she tossed the AK-47 up before her, clambered atop an air-conditioning unit that was next to the wall, and leapt, her hands fastening around the lip of the roof so that she could haul herself up and over the edge.

She ran on, running out of roof as the block came to an end. She risked a glance down and saw the Humvee parked in the centre of the road, blocking it in both directions. It looked as if it had been abandoned so that all of the occupants could give chase, and for a moment, she contemplated the possibility of stealing it. She dismissed the idea as foolish: there was no easy way down to the street from her eyrie, she had never driven a Humvee before and it was a particularly conspicuous mode of transport. Better to make less noise.

She turned left, to the east, and hurried on. The block continued for another dozen buildings before it ended at another junction. The sixth building was interesting. The roof was taken up by a large cupola, and to the left, there was a flight of iron stairs that descended into a courtyard. She edged around the cupola, her feet just small enough to manage the meagre lip of concrete that was all that stood between her and a twelve-metre drop into the courtyard. She put her rifle in her right hand, held onto the guard rail with her left and started down the stairs. They were ancient and badly corroded, and the addition of her weight swung the top flight of stairs away from the wall. She clutched the guard rail, but the newel posts were loose, and the rail and several of the balusters detached from the structure and tumbled down into the courtyard. The metal parts landed with a deafening crash. Isabella thought she was going to be sent plunging down to the ground herself, but managed to adjust her balance so that she could launch herself, dropping down to the landing. It was more substantial than the stair and was able to absorb her impact.

She paused, the sound of the impact still ringing out, and cursed her misfortune. There were windows facing into the courtyard, and she saw a pale face in the one that was opposite her, and then another in the one adjacent to that. She was making too much noise. She was clumsy. Her mother would have been furious with her.

She heard the sound of running feet above her and settled back down into a kneeling position, aiming the AK back up at the roof.

She inhaled and exhaled, regulating her breath and trying to slow her racing heartbeat, just as her mother had instructed, and as she waited there, she saw the shape of a person silhouetted against the moonlight. It was a man, and she could see the top half of his body as he looked down into the courtyard. She slid the rifle to the right, sighted on the man and fired another single shot. The round found its mark and the man clutched his gut, taking a step forward into space and then toppling over the edge. His body flipped over as it raced by Isabella's vantage point, and bounced with a sickening thud against the courtyard's tiled floor.

Two down, but Isabella knew she needed to keep moving. She continued down the stairs, more carefully now, negotiating the remaining flights without further incident. She paused at the body of the insurgent. His right leg was bent back and pinned beneath his buttocks, and blood was running from the bullet wound, slowly filling the grooves between the tiles. Isabella spared a moment to frisk him. He was wearing green camouflage, black boots and a bandolier with ammunition pouches. There was a pistol in a holster that was clipped to his belt. She took it and then unbuckled the bandolier and slung it over her shoulder. It was heavy; that was good.

The courtyard was accessed through an open arch that led to a passage that ran beneath the building to the road beyond. It was comfortingly dark, but Isabella raised the stock of the AK and pressed it into her shoulder, taking an offhand aim; it was more difficult to keep the gun stable this way but by far the best for mobile, fast, urgent shooting. She proceeded into the darkness, gasping a little from her flight across the rooftops, but trying to keep her breath steady so as not to disturb her aim. She reached the mouth of the alleyway, paused to listen—there was no sound beyond the plaintive mewling of a hungry cat—and put her head out and checked left and right.

She saw the running lights of the Humvee and the scoops of light that were thrown against the facing wall by its headlamps. She couldn't see anyone. Where were they? In the first building, where she had shot the first insurgent? On the roof, following the second man? She was considering her next move when she heard the wail of a muezzin. It reminded her of being home, in Marrakech, and prompted her to look up to the sky. The first call was *fajr*, offered between the very beginning of dawn and the sunrise. She hadn't checked the time, but it must have been just after five. The sky was lightening; it was barely perceptible, but the darkness was a little less black when she looked between the buildings to the distant horizon. She had intended to flee the city, but now she reconsidered. It might be safer to wait until night.

She took a deep breath, and after checking once again that the way ahead was clear, she sprinted out of the alleyway and headed east toward another block of apartment buildings.

Chapter Forty

Isabella jogged down the street until she reached a crossroads. The four apartment buildings that were built around the intersection had all been badly damaged by another explosion. One of the buildings had received the worst damage, but its neighbours had all been wrecked, too. The road had been cleared, with piles of rubble pushed back by excavators so that they formed a slope up against the walls of the buildings. Huge concrete slabs had been dislodged from one of the buildings, looking now like the overlapping plates of an armadillo. A truck had been flattened by debris and was covered in dust. The fascia of another building had been stripped, revealing the skeleton of iron struts and girders beneath. The buildings had been abandoned. Isabella picked the one that had suffered the least significant damage and made for it.

The entire ground floor was open, and Isabella hurried into the deeper darkness inside. Most of the internal walls had been blown away, revealing a staircase that had been left at least partially intact. She ascended, climbing to the first and then the second floor. The damage was less severe here, and she followed a corridor that offered access to a dozen doors. The third door she reached had been left ajar. She listened carefully and, happy that the room beyond was quiet, took her AK and used the barrel to push the door all the way open.

She advanced, her finger on the trigger, and scouted the apartment. There was a gash in the wall at the other end of the first room, and it admitted enough of the dawn's light for Isabella to be able to make out the details. The place was small, just three rooms: a room with a bed and a sofa, a connecting kitchenette and a tiny bathroom. The windows had lost all of their glass and had been covered with sheets, and shafts of light arrowed inside through bullet holes that had been torn in the fabric. The sofa and bed were covered with fragments of rubble, and thick dust was everywhere. Isabella felt something shift beneath her feet, and as she reached down, she could feel the shapes of dozens of spent cartridges. This apartment must have been used by a sniper.

She went to the opening in the wall and looked out. She was directly over the junction, with good sight lines in three directions. The sun was rising, a spectrum of greys that were gradually smearing the black. She went back to the door and closed it, heaving the largest chunk of rubble that she could find and resting it against the door so that it wouldn't be able to be opened without disturbing her. Then, satisfied, Isabella rested the AK against the sofa, swept away the biggest pieces of debris and sat down. Dust puffed out around her as she leaned back into the cushion. She closed her eyes, finally allowing her body to rest.

Isabella woke to the amplified ululation of another muezzin calling the faithful to prayer. She opened her eyes to find that light was streaming into the apartment from the jagged gash in the wall. She collected the AK from the sofa and made her way to the opening. The sun had risen all the way now, almost to its apogee, and she guessed that the summons must be for *dhuhr*, the noontime call to prayer.

She went back to the sofa and laid out the equipment that she had stolen. She checked the AK first. She ejected the magazine, careful not to get grit into the mechanism, and checked the witness holes that had been machined into the side of the magazine tube. She looked for the lowest hole with brass showing and counted: she had just ten rounds left. She hooked the front of the magazine into the receiver and pulled it back so that it clipped home.

She checked the pistol next. It was a Glock 17, probably captured from the Syrian army or police. Isabella had practised with Glocks before and was comfortable with it as a side arm. She pressed the release button and collected the magazine from the grip. It felt satisfactorily weighty, and when she checked, she saw that it was fully loaded with 9×19mm Parabellum cartridges. Seventeen rounds. Twenty-seven rounds between the two weapons.

She examined the bandolier next. The ammo pouches contained an additional four magazines for the Glock, and as a bonus, the four grenade pouches were full with Russian-made RGD grenades. Isabella tore one of the pouches open and removed a grenade: it was an oval cylinder with no external ribbing except for a ridge where the two halves of the grenade joined. The surface had a few small dimples on it and was painted in olive drab. She hadn't used this kind of grenade before, but the principle of its operation was identical to the American-made variants that she had practised with, and she was confident that she would have no problems should the need to deploy them arise.

Isabella checked the kitchen. She turned the taps, but there was nothing; the water supply had been disconnected. There was a tiny fridge, and as she opened it, her nostrils were assailed by the pungent odour of rot. Food had been left inside, but with no power to maintain the temperature, it had become rancid. She checked the cupboard, but it was empty. It reminded her that she hadn't eaten since yesterday and she was hungry. She hadn't had anything to drink since she and Aqil had escaped, and with the temperature already hot and stuffy in the apartment, she knew that could quickly become a problem. She would have to find something to drink before she left the city tonight. She had a significant distance to cover before she reached the border, and she would need to be properly hydrated.

There was a flimsy wardrobe in the corner of the room between the bed and the sofa. Isabella went over to it and opened the doors. Whoever had lived in this flat had vacated it in a hurry, because they had left their clothes behind. Some of the clothes were for a child, with a cute pair of dungarees, vests with poppers that fastened between the legs, plus jeans and tops for an older child. Hanging among the children's garments were a woman's clothes. Isabella took them out of the cupboard and laid them out on the bed. There were loose-fitting trousers and blouses, plus an abaya, a niqab and gloves.

She went back to the opening in the wall and risked another glance outside. The road beneath her was busy with traffic, impatient drivers leaning on their horns as they were snarled in a slow-moving queue. Pedestrians went about their business, hurrying along in the gap between the traffic and the walls of the buildings, others crossing between the cars. The difference between now and the night before was stark. The road had been empty before, and it was busy and alive now.

She would have to wait it out.

⌣

Isabella stayed in the apartment throughout the afternoon. It became stuffier as the air grew warmer and warmer, but she knew that she was safe here. She planned on leaving as soon as it was dark.

She would find another vehicle and head north again. If there were roadblocks, she would abandon the car and skirt them on foot. Aqil had said it was only about twenty-five miles to the border.

Isabella thought that she heard something and went to the hole in the wall to check. She stayed there for a moment, far enough away from the opening that she would be cloaked by the gloom, and as she watched, a curious vehicle approached the junction. It was a van with a flatbed in the rear and, arranged there, a triangular hoarding that allowed for posters on the two longest sides. There was a poster fixed to the side of the van that Isabella could see. It had a picture of a life jacket on the left and a military vest on the right. The caption was in Arabic, but Isabella was able to translate it. It said 'What would you rather wear on Judgment Day?' and was, she guessed, a reference to the locals who were fleeing the country to risk their lives crossing the sea to Europe.

She heard the noise again. It was a man's voice, rendered tinny by an amplifier and played out through speakers that had been lashed to the cab of the van. The man was speaking in Arabic, his diction emotive and deliberate, each word invested with fervour.

The language was archaic and formal, but Isabella was able to translate.

"In the name of Allah, the All Merciful, tonight will mark the execution of emissaries of the Crusaders whom Allah, may blessings be upon Him, delivered unto the soldiers of the caliphate, and a traitor who wished to exchange the caliphate for the false sanctuary of Crusader lands. Their crucifixions will take place in the main square, following the Isha prayer, and the men and women of al-Bab shall come and observe so that they may bear witness to the consequences of those who choose to involve themselves in the Crusader campaign. This will be a warning to those who wish to learn. Allah is the greatest."

Isabella watched as the van proceeded to the crossroads and then passed out of view. The man began to recite the message again, as if by rote, but Isabella didn't need to hear it again to know what it meant.

A traitor who wished to exchange the caliphate for the false sanctuary of Crusader lands.

Aqil?

Chapter Forty-One

Isabella spent the next two hours in confused indecision. She knew that she was safest staying where she was. She could wait until it was dark and then leave the city. She would be better able to escape on her own, without Aqil to slow her down. She was confident that she would be able to do it, too. She was well equipped and she was well trained. Even if she was unable to find transport or was forced to abandon it, she had experience trekking across desert. Beatrix had taught her both orienteering and endurance, and as part of her training, she had taken her out to Lalla Takerkoust, thirty miles south of Marrakech, and instructed her to find her way home while her mother and Mohammed, their housekeeper, had tried to find her. Isabella had covered the distance in two days without being detected. This was no different.

But leaving now would mean abandoning Aqil. She couldn't know for sure that he was the 'traitor' whose execution had been announced, but it would have been an unusual coincidence given what had happened last night. And it almost didn't matter. Even if Aqil was not condemned to die tonight, it would be soon. And if it wasn't at the hands of the regime, it would be another way. A drone strike, like the one that had killed his brother. Or on the front line, as cannon fodder in the battle against the government. He was hopelessly out of his depth. He wouldn't last five minutes.

But despite all of that, he had risked his life to free her. Isabella found that hard to ignore. Her mother, she was sure, would have counselled her to abandon him and think of herself. But she was not her mother, and she didn't know that she would be able to do that.

The sun fell beneath the line of the neighbouring buildings. The Isha prayer was at dusk, and it couldn't be more than an hour away now. Isabella still did not know what she was going to do, but she decided that she had to do something. If she stayed here, she was condemning Aqil. The alternative was to go to the square and observe. It might be that there was nothing she could do; that would be a pity, but at least she would know that, and abandoning him would not be quite so callous.

Isabella wore the abaya over her clothes. The previous owner must have been a slight woman, because the robe was about the right size to fit her. It was made of heavy material, pulling down on her shoulders, and was cut to be very loose, just like the one that she had abandoned; that was fortunate because it meant that she was able to wear the bandolier with the ammunition and the grenades without the bulk being too obvious. She pulled the niqab over her head; it was double-veiled, in the Saudi style, and reduced her field of vision to no more than a narrow slit. That was not ideal, but the anonymity that it would confer was worth the compromise. She pulled on the gloves, and when she was done, there was not an inch of flesh that remained visible.

She turned and looked down at the AK-47. There was no way that she could bring the rifle, but it was difficult to leave it behind. She consoled herself with the knowledge that there were only ten rounds left in the magazine, that she still had the Glock and that it should be possible to find a replacement if an automatic was necessary.

She hiked up the abaya and shoved the pistol into the waistband of her jeans.

And then, with a tight little knot of fear in her gut, she left the safety of her hideaway and descended the stairs to the darkening street below.

PART THREE

The Syrian Desert

Chapter Forty-Two

P ope had been in the city for two days. He had found a blitzed neighbourhood that looked as if it might offer him a refuge and a base from which he could range out and scout more widely. The buildings had been flattened, most likely by barrel bombs, but he was able to find a narrow passageway between the wrecks of two buildings where he had been able to hide the armoured Ranger. The buildings were in no fit state to be habitable, but one of them offered him a room on the first floor that he decided would be satisfactory for his purposes. The rest of the building was empty, and there was no reason for anyone to visit it. It was eleven by the time he decided that the room was the best that he would be able to find. He had blocked the door with his backpack, called Bloom to update him and then slept.

He woke early the next day, left the Ranger behind and scouted the city on foot. He wanted to get an idea of his surroundings and the strength of the jihadi deployment there. The soldiers did not strike him as particularly experienced or efficient, but they were numerous enough for him to conclude that they had enough men to hold it against a determined assault. That aside, it had been a disappointing day. He had returned to his hiding place that night with no new information on Isabella's location. He called Bloom again and received the same confirmation: as far as British interests were concerned, Salim and Isabella were still in the city. They were being held in a prison, and efforts were being made to locate it.

He had risen early again this morning and had gone out once more to continue his search. He had walked for eight hours, stopping occasionally in groups where he was able to eavesdrop on conversations, but once again he had found nothing. There was one topic of conversation that he overheard on more than one occasion: a sandstorm was blowing in from the desert and was due to hit the city in the evening.

He kept walking, but with nothing to show for his efforts. It was late afternoon when Pope approached a building that he assumed must have served as some sort of municipal facility before the city fell to the Islamic State. It was a three-storey building with a stencilled inscription on the pediment that confirmed, in Arabic, that it had been the town hall.

There was a line of metal railings that separated the building from the street, and a series of notices had been attached to them. A group of people were gathered before the notices, and Pope drifted toward them. It was evidently a place where local declarations were displayed. Pope edged into the crowd until he was close enough to read the notices. Some of them announced new regulations: the clothes that women should wear, the length of a man's beard, a new *diktat* that forbade the use of the Internet. There was nothing useful. Pope was nudged to the right as a local man pressed forward, and he waited and watched as an official affixed a new notice to the railings. It had a series of grainy pictures beneath a single headline.

Pope's mouth fell open. The pictures were of Salim and Khalil al-Khawari and a young man whom he did not recognise. The headline read that they were to be executed in the town square that night after evening prayers.

Pope turned and shouldered his way through the crowd until he was clear.

What was going on? There was too much about the affair that he did not understand. The al-Khawaris had been headed to the Lebanon, not Syria. They had been brought here against their will. And now they were to be executed? None of it made any sense. And what about Isabella? Where was she? Was she alive?

Pope needed information. The town square was at the end of the road. He didn't know what he would find there, nor whether there would be anything that he could do, but he needed to know more.

He turned and retraced his steps back to the block where he had been hiding. He collected his backpack from the room and went down to the Ranger. He stowed his kit in the back, started the engine and drove back in the direction of the city centre. He passed a mosque, and the speakers that had been hung on the minaret crackled into life.

Pope heard the muezzin's call to prayer. Dusk was falling quickly.

Chapter Forty-Three

The storm blew in off the desert, heralded by a brisk breeze that promised to strengthen. Pope parked the Ranger in a side street. There were other similar vehicles there; it did not stand out. There was a satchel in the back of the vehicle. He undid his backpack and took out the claymore mine. He hid the backpack in the back of the Ranger, put the satchel over his shoulder and set out.

The town square was formed by four rows of buildings that made a rectangle, with roads converging on it. The buildings were home to cafés and restaurants, and some had been decked out with banners and billboards that proclaimed the glory of the caliphate. Familiar black and white flags had been fixed to long wooden posts that had been fastened to the walls of the buildings, the pennants snapping in the sand-laden breeze. The centre of the square had been taken up by a raised platform. Three wooden constructions had been arranged there, propped up at an angle so that they were just high enough for Pope to see what they were.

They were crosses.

The storm was picking up in intensity, but the crowd was still large and growing as more and more people—mostly men—gathered at its edges. The atmosphere was frenzied. There was no alcohol here, at least not licitly, but there was an edge to the cheers and chants that sounded almost drunken.

Bloodlust.

Pope was glad of the sand that was sent whipping around the square by the wind. Most of the men had arranged their *keffiyehs* so that their faces were covered, and as he arranged his own scarf so that it covered everything save a narrow slit for his eyes, he did not feel as out of place as he might have otherwise. He walked farther into the square as a procession of cars, their horns sounding, turned on to the road from which he had entered and slowly nudged their way through the crowd to the middle of the square.

The light came from braziers that had been lit at the edges of the square and two spotlights that were aimed down from the top floors of two adjacent buildings. The farther away from the central area he stayed, the easier it was to stay within the pools of darkness. Pope was grateful for the dusk and for the wind. The fighters were identified by the uniforms that they were wearing: front-line soldiers in their green camouflage, black robes for the commanders, and black sweat-shirts and baggy trousers for those in the security office detail.

Vehicles had been parked around the edge of the square. There were four-by-fours, technicals with the flatbed-mounted machine guns and American Humvees. Pope made for one of the Humvees. It was in poor shape, with one flank crumpled inward as evidence of an explosion, and tracks of indentations where small-calibre rounds had dented the armour. It was parked a couple of feet away from the wall of a dilapidated building that was being used, Pope saw, as a café. The vehicle had produced a narrow passage between itself and the wall, and Pope paused before it for a moment so that he could take the satchel off his shoulder.

There were men atop the Humvee, half a dozen of them in fighting dress, all of them staring at the spectacle in the centre of the square. Pope turned and followed their gazes and watched as the executioners appeared out of the cars that had pulled into the square. Pope had seen footage of men like them in ISIS propaganda, as had everyone else. There were three of them tonight, each dressed in sandy-coloured desert robes, with their faces covered in similarly coloured swaths of material.

The men went to one of the cars and opened the doors. Three figures were hauled out. They were hooded, with their hands tied behind their backs. They didn't struggle. Perhaps the hoods spared them the knowledge of what was about to happen, or perhaps they were resigned to their fates. It was moot: there wouldn't have been any point in struggling. They were at the centre of a baying, hungry crowd. Even if they had been able to free themselves, there would have been nowhere for them to go.

Pope watched as the men were lined up, one in front of each cross. One executioner stood behind each man and, on cue, they removed the hoods.

Pope recognised two of them immediately.

Salim al-Khawari.

Khalil al-Khawari.

The third was a young man, no older than twenty. Pope did not recognise him.

All three of them bore the signs of recent beatings. Salim's face, usually so haughty, was disfigured by contusions that closed his right eye and plugs of dried blood in his nostrils. His son's face bore similar marks, and as he opened his mouth to gasp for air, Pope saw that he was missing one of his front teeth. The third man did not look up, but Pope could see that his ear was swollen and that there was a track of dried blood on his right temple.

The crowd was staring at the three men. No one was watching Pope as he stepped between the Humvee and the wall. He moved quickly, opening the satchel and taking out the claymore.

He activated the detonator and pushed the mine beneath the vehicle, as close to the fuel tank as he could, and then he went back out into the square. He had the remote control in his pocket, and he reached down and felt for the thumb-shaped depression that he would need to press in order to detonate the mine.

Chapter Forty-Four

Isabella had found her way to the central square. The truck with the amplifier had headed in that direction, and as she drew nearer, a crowd started to form. It was mostly composed of men, but there were a few veiled women, too. She knew that she shouldn't be out without a chaperone, so she crossed the road so that she could follow a group of locals with two women within their number. No one noticed her, and as the road became more crowded, she was able to leave them behind and make her own way again.

The crowd emptied into the main square. She looked around at the buildings, at the spectators hanging out of the second-floor windows. The spotlights that had been installed on the roofs of two of the buildings swept over the crowd before settling on the platform where three crosses had been erected.

A car bulled its way through the crowd, the driver sounding the horn to clear a path. It parked next to the platform. Isabella watched as two hooded men were dragged out of the car. They were dragged up the steps of the platform and passed unceremoniously into the custody of the executioners. They were turned to face the crowd and their hoods were yanked away. Salim and Khalil al-Khawari blinked out into the baying mob before both of them looked to the ground. All of Salim's bluster was gone now; the enforced trip into Syria and now the very obvious fate that awaited him had transformed him from the supercilious, haughty titan of business that she had met in Geneva to a fretful, panicked, bloodied man who dared not raise his eyes from the ground. Khalil, by contrast, seemed to have found a reservoir of strength. It was only evident by comparison to his father, but he was putting up more of a struggle until one of his jailers backhanded him around the side of the face.

A third figure was removed from the car. He was slight, slimmer than Khalil, and he didn't resist as he was led up the stairs. Isabella knew that it was Aqil. He, too, was turned to face the crowd, and the hood was removed. He blinked into the glare of the spotlights; she could see the terror in his eyes, even from here.

Isabella reached into the robe and felt for the Glock. Her fingers settled around the grip, but she left it there. What was she going to do? How could she possibly help Aqil? She was alone, lost within the crowd, and the fact that she had a pistol was an irrelevance. She could shoot a few of them, maybe even reach Aqil and get him down from the platform, but what would they do then? How could she get them away? It was impossible.

She looked up. Aqil was looking out from the platform, squinting into the spotlight that glared down on him.

She was distracted, and by the time she saw the two women, it was too late. They had been hidden in the crowd, rendered anonymous by their veils, yet as the crowd parted for them, she saw that they were distinctive because of the fact that they were armed with AK-47s.

They were from the al-Khansaa brigade.

They had seen Isabella and were making their way toward her with purpose. The crowd eddied around her and she tried to put people between her and them, but they were not so easily dissuaded from their pursuit. One of them called out, her harsh Arabic freighted with what Isabella took to be a European accent: "Stop!"

The crowd was thick ahead of her, and it would be difficult for her to pass through it, especially if the women made more of a fuss. Worse than that, if she tried to run, she would have to bypass the clutch of armed insurgents who had gathered to watch the executions. She was caught between the women behind and the men ahead.

She couldn't run.

The two women reached her. Both women wore the same loose abayas that Isabella was wearing. They were both short, around the same height as she was, and the rifles looked oversized in their gloved hands.

One of them stepped ahead of the other. "Where is your chaperone?" she said.

"He is here. In the crowd."

"He should be with you."

"I know," Isabella said. "I'm sorry. I lost him."

She knew that although her Arabic was acceptable, her accent was as bad as her interrogator's. It would betray that it was not her native tongue.

"What is your name?"

"Aqsa," she said, using the name of the hairdresser in Marrakech that she had visited the last time she had had her hair cut.

"We need to talk to you. We need you to take off your niqab. I need to see your face. You will come with us."

"I can't leave," she protested. "My husband."

"He will answer to the Hisbah for abandoning you."

"I'm sorry."

"Your accent—where are you from?"

The woman reached out and grasped Isabella's left shoulder.

Isabella knew that she was beyond the point where she might be able to talk her way out of the mess she was in. She brought up her left hand in a circular motion, the sudden impact shucking the woman's hand from her shoulder. The woman reached out to snag the niqab. Isabella raised her right leg and thrust out her foot, catching the woman in the groin. The woman dropped to her knees, but she did not relinquish her grip on the niqab. It was torn away as she fell.

Isabella felt the rush of hot air and the sting of sand on her face. She turned and started to run.

"Help!" the woman cried out.

Isabella reached for the Glock and pulled it out. The crowd had thickened and she had to shoulder her way through clutches of people who were arranged around the square. There were groups of insurgents, marked out by their uniforms. She barged into them and saw that there was an open space just ahead. If she could get there, maybe she could lose them in the streets and alleys.

She felt strong arms wrap around her torso. She struggled, but her arms were pinned to her sides. She was lifted from her feet and pulled down to the dirt, the arms still clasped around her body. She crashed down, the impact loosening her grip on the pistol. She dropped it, and as dirt and grit from the cobbles scraped across her face, she saw it six feet away from her. She struggled, but the arms encircling her were too strong and she couldn't wriggle free.

"Enough," came a shout into her ear. "Lie still."

Isabella was on her side, with the man who was restraining her lying behind her and clasping her to his chest. She brought up her knees and then jabbed her feet at his legs, trying to scrape down his shin. She found at least partial contact, and the man cursed in pain.

Her captor grunted with the effort as he squeezed her tighter.

Isabella fixed her eyes on the pistol, bucking and kicking in an attempt to break free so that she could collect it. She was looking right at it when she saw a man's feet approach it. The man was wearing Nikes, and she saw his legs and torso as he crouched down to collect it from the ground. He stood, stepped right up to where she was being held and pressed the muzzle of the pistol against her forehead.

"Stop struggling," he said, "or I will shoot you now."

She did as she was told.

"Get her up."

Isabella didn't resist as the man who had tackled her got to his feet and hauled her upright. She raised her chin and looked up, right into the face of Abu.

"Hello, Daisy," he said.

Chapter Forty-Five

P ope was only ten metres away when the fracas broke out.
The sight of the two women with AK-47s was unusual
enough as it was, and he had followed them as they moved
around the periphery of the square. He knew about the al-Khansaa
Brigade, the women who were responsible for ensuring that local
women met with the moral standards that had been laid down
for them. His attention was on them as they had approached the
other woman similarly clad head-to-toe in niqab and abaya, and
he had watched as the woman had taken issue with something that
had been said and done, freeing herself of the hand on her shoulder
and then kicking one of them to the ground. He had watched as the
niqab had been torn from her head, and had watched, agog, as the
third woman had turned just enough for him to see that she was
white, and blonde. And then, as she had reached down into her
robe and produced a pistol, he knew that he recognised her.

Isabella.

She had run from the women but had not got very far before
one of the men had caught her and wrestled her to the ground. The
man was wearing the desert camouflage of the execution squads that
had become infamous from the caliphate's slick propaganda videos.

He must have outweighed Isabella by sixty pounds, but she struggled mightily and he was having difficulty in restraining her.

Pope had no idea what she was doing in the square, but he knew she couldn't hope to get away from it. Even if she could have freed herself, she couldn't have been in territory more hostile than this.

A second man collected Isabella's pistol, crossed the distance to her and pressed it against her head. He said something, and Isabella stopped struggling.

Pope reached into his pocket again, collected the remote trigger and put his thumb over the stippled depression.

———

The sandstorm was gathering strength. The wind in from the desert poured down the streets, meeting at the square. It blew in from all directions, and the black and white flags snapped this way and that as they were snagged by competing gusts. Isabella could feel the tiny motes of grit and sand as they were blasted against her cheeks and forehead. A storm was coming, but it was going to be too late. The executions might have been delayed if they had been scheduled for an hour or two later on; but now, just minutes away, there would be no stopping.

Isabella was picked up by two men on either side of her: the man who had tackled her to the ground and Abu. They each had her by an arm, and there was nothing that she could do to get away from them. Abu had put her pistol into his belt; she eyed it jealously—desperately—but knew that there was no way that she could get to it. Even if she had been able to arm herself, there would have been nothing that she could have done. Her anonymity was gone and she was among dozens of enemy soldiers. How could she have escaped? It was impossible.

She bitterly regretted her decision to come back to try to help Aqil. It was foolish. Idiotic. She should have run. She'd had the chance to get out of the city and make for the border. She could have done it. Her mother would never have been so weak. Beatrix would have been furious with her. Isabella clenched her fists in frustration. Had she forgotten everything that her mother had taught her? Had it all been for nothing?

Abu turned her around so that she was looking at the platform. "Watch," he said into her ear.

The wooden crosses on the platform were lowered to the ground, and the al-Khawaris and Aqil were lined up before them. One of the men collected a leather satchel, and from it he withdrew a hammer and a fistful of nails. He held them aloft, his expression masked by the scarf that protected his face from the storm. The crowd signalled their approval.

Abu leaned in close again. "You will be next," he said, speaking a little louder to make himself heard over the whine of the wind.

The explosion was deafening.

It came from behind Isabella, a gut-shaking boom that tore through the howl of the wind and the noise of the crowd. Isabella heard it a moment before a wave of pressure rolled out and slapped her down to the ground. The detonation reverberated around the square, bouncing back off the walls of the buildings, the crowd toppling like skittles. The men on either side of her were thrown down, too, the difference being that Isabella reacted faster than they did. Abu had been thrown down a pace or two ahead of her, and as he rolled onto his side and looked back toward the source of the explosion, the angle of his body opened up enough so that Isabella could see the Glock. It was there, shoved in his belt, within reach.

She stretched out her hand, snagged the butt of the pistol and yanked it away.

He protested, rolling onto hands and knees and scrabbling toward her.

She shot him point blank. The bullet struck him in the top of the head, blowback splattering across her face. His body slumped face down on the cobbles.

The other man who had secured her had also been knocked down by the explosion. He was on his back, and he tried to scramble his feet beneath him, his efforts given additional urgency by Isabella's display of ruthlessness. He crabbed away from her, but he never really had a chance to save himself. Isabella braced the gun in a tight two-handed grip with her left hand canted toward the ground and fired a single round. He jerked at the waist, his torso collapsing back until he was lying prone, staring up at the darkness.

Isabella turned, ready to run, but found herself looking into the barrel of an AK-47. It was one of the women who had accosted her earlier. Her abaya was covered in sand and dirt from head to toe, but she had regained her feet and her rifle. Isabella saw everything in tiny increments: the tiny black hole of the muzzle, the way the spotlights glinted against the metal of the barrel and the receiver, the gloved finger curled around the trigger. She knew that she was about to be shot, that this was the end, but that, at least, she had taken two of them out with her.

She heard the sound of gunfire, but as she stood there with her eyes squeezed shut, she didn't feel anything.

Was this what it was like?

She heard something heavy falling to the ground.

"*Isabella.*"

She opened her eyes and turned.

"It's me."

The man was wearing a scarf, and realising that she couldn't see his face, he pulled it down. It took her a moment to recognise him; the delay was because it was incongruous. He had no business being here.

"Mr Pope?"

He was dressed like one of them, all in black, with a backpack slung across one shoulder. He was holding a Beretta M9 in his left hand. Isabella jerked her head around and saw that the woman was on the ground, her AK lying across her chest.

"Quickly," Pope said. His right hand was extended toward her. She allowed him to take her by the hand.

The onlookers were still recovering from the shock of the blast. Those who had regained their feet looked at the burning hulk of the Humvee and then up at the sky, searching for the aircraft that must have been responsible. Salim, Khalil and Aqil were hustled off the platform and back down to the car.

It was chaotic, and in the chaos no one noticed them as they ran. Pope led the way toward one of the roads that fed into the square. They passed the burning Humvee. It had been raised up and then dumped down onto its side, hungry flames dancing over it and spilling a column of jet-black smoke that was ripped apart by the wind. The crowd diluted as the bystanders started to panic. They spilled away from the square, fearing another attack. Pope gripped Isabella's hand more tightly and dragged her with him.

Chapter Forty-Six

Isabella held onto Pope's hand as he led the way through the square. The men and women were scattering into the streets that fed into the square like the spokes of a wheel. The crowd bulged as they approached the first junction, and as Isabella glanced through the throng of people, she saw two people on the ground. They had fallen, and now they were causing others to stumble and fall. Pope saw the congestion, too, and he changed course to avoid it. Isabella held on tightly to his hand as they skirted the scrum and ran hard for a quieter way out of the square.

Pope led the way, turning left and right until they reached a side street, then ran to a pickup truck that was parked in the mouth of an alley between two buildings. It was a technical, with a big machine gun fitted to the flatbed and plate armour welded to the front. He opened the passenger door for her and then ran around to the other side. Isabella got in.

"Get down," he said. "You've lost your veil. If they see you—"

"I know," she said.

She cranked the seat until it was back as far as it would go and then slid down into the space between it and the dash. The engine rumbled as Pope turned the ignition, pumping his foot on the gas until the engine started. The pickup jerked forward and then turned sharply to the right.

"Are you okay?" he said.

"I'm fine. Thanks to you."

"Don't thank me," he said. "I should never have got you involved in this."

He spun the wheel and hurled the pickup around a bend.

"Do you know where they kept al-Khawari?"

"The same place they kept me," she said. "There's an old factory on the north side of town."

"Could you find it?"

"I think so. Why?"

"That's probably where they'll take them."

"What does it matter?"

"I need to get al-Khawari out."

He swung the wheel again and the pickup swerved to the left. Isabella couldn't see anything. She looked up, around the edge of the dashboard and through the windscreen. The top floors of the buildings on either side of the road formed a canyon that they raced along. A ribbon of velvet sky ran between the shoulders of the buildings.

"You understand why I need to do that?"

"No," she said.

"Something is going on that I don't understand. He's central to it. I need to speak to him."

"You don't need to explain. Salim has been set up, hasn't he? We were used to set him up."

"How do you know that?"

"They questioned me. They told me. That's what they think."

"It's what I think, too," he said. "I will get you out. I promise. I just have to do this first."

Pope drove north, turning this way and that through a confusing mess of streets. On more than one occasion he turned onto a street that was impassable thanks to rubble from collapsed buildings, and had to reverse out and choose another way. He glanced in the mirrors frequently, concerned that they might have drawn attention to themselves, but there was no sign of pursuit. The explosion and the panic that it had created had terrified the men and women in the square and had seemingly sent the regime's soldiers into hiding. The streets were quiet. They had been able to slip away amid the confusion.

Isabella looked up at Pope. He was staring through the windshield intently, his jaw clenched. "Was that you?" she asked. "The explosion?"

"Yes," Pope said. "I had a mine."

They raced along a narrow street between rows of decrepit six-storey apartment blocks, only the upper storeys of the buildings visible to her. They sped out from between them and into a neighbourhood that was characterised by warehouses and factories, most of them burnt out.

"It's all right," Pope said. "You can get up. No one's around. Do you know where we are?"

She slithered back up and onto the seat and looked around. They were on the north side of town, the same area that she had passed through with Aqil as they made their ultimately futile attempt to escape. Many of the buildings had been flattened, the debris left where it had been strewn. Street lamps had been twisted and bent, others plucked out of the ground and tossed aside. Great piles of litter had been blown against the mounds of rubble. The wind continued to wail, eddies of dust and sand drawn up from the ground and tiny stones rattling against the truck's bodywork and chiming off the glass.

"This is the right area," she said. "The place they held us is around here."

"Do you know where?"

She gazed out at the wrecked buildings through the scrim of the storm. "I don't know," she said. "It's difficult to see anything. And they all look the same."

They were approaching a crossroads. Pope was about to reply, when he cursed and stomped down on the brake. The pickup shuddered to a halt, the back wheels sliding out until Pope steered into the skid and brought it back under control. Isabella looked to the left just as a convoy of vehicles raced across the crossroads. There were three vehicles: two technicals sandwiching a saloon car. There was a fighter in each of the flatbeds of the two trucks, scarves wrapped around their faces as they held onto the big machine guns for dear life. None of the vehicles was running with lights.

Isabella recognised the car in the middle. "That's the car from the square," she said. "The one Salim and the others were brought in."

Pope pressed down on the gas and the pickup jerked forward again. He swung the wheel, turning to the right onto the block that the convoy was already halfway along. The three vehicles were travelling fast, and Pope let them draw farther away from them. The roads were otherwise quiet, and even though they were running dark and the storm had reduced visibility to eighty or ninety metres, it was still simple enough to follow them.

They raced through the neighbourhood, the buildings flashing by on either side of them.

"Down," Pope said as he pressed down on the brake.

She saw that they had drawn in close to the last technical. The convoy had slowed, and the first pickup was turning off the road into the courtyard of a building that she recognised. The building was badly damaged, with huge chunks of rubble on the ground, naked pillars topped by iron girders but without roofs to support, and a wide parking area that was covered by earth and dirty sand.

"That's it," she said. "The prison. That's where they held us."

"Get down."

She did as she was told, sliding back down into the footwell again. Pope pulled around the technical at the rear of the convoy and drove on. Isabella looked up at him and saw that his eyes were on the rear-view mirror. "What do we do now?" she asked.

"Find somewhere safe to stop so we can work out what to do."

Chapter Forty-Seven

P ope drove for another minute before he slowed the pickup and turned off the road. Isabella climbed back into the seat as they bumped over a raised kerb and then traced a path between two metal fence posts, the mesh fence that would once have been suspended between them now flattened to the ground. The headlights of the truck reached out through the darkness into a courtyard that lay between two buildings. Both structures had been damaged: the one on the left was a lost cause, with just one wall left upright and the remains of the roof collected within the building's old curtilage. The building on the right was in better condition; the headlights revealed an ugly gash in the wall, but the structure was otherwise intact.

Pope drove carefully across the rubble, the pickup's old suspension creaking unhealthily, and rolled to a stop next to the second building. He reached around and down and collected a rifle from the footwell in front of the rear seats; then he opened the door and stepped outside. Isabella did the same; the wind whipped around her, snatching at the folds of the abaya and scouring her face with sand. She covered her eyes with her arm and hopped over the bricks and rubble, carefully making her way inside the building.

Pope had the rifle out in front of him; Isabella saw that it was an M4. A picatinny rail had been fitted to the front sight base of the rifle and he had taken a flashlight and slotted it into place. A beam of bright white light shone out to the left and right as he checked that the building was vacant. Isabella followed the beam as it stretched out into the large room: she saw overturned tables, hulks of industrial machinery and rows of racking. Isabella waited as he disappeared around a partially collapsed wall, and then saw the beam of the flashlight through a hole in the ceiling as he checked the floor above her.

He took his time and she went back to the opening in the wall and gazed out into the storm as she waited for him to return. She could see the dim shape of the building on the other side of the parking area, and the occasional glimmer of light from the town, but the storm had filled the air with a curtain of sand and grit. The road beyond the fence was empty.

She heard the crunch of Pope's footsteps and turned to see him approach, the rifle pointed down at the floor. "Clear," he said. "There's no one here. It's just us."

"Where are we?"

"A block away from where they pulled off the road. We'll be all right here. The storm helps. We're lucky—no one will be out tonight."

Pope went back to the pickup and returned with his backpack. There were large wooden pallets on the floor of the building. He took two of them and propped them up against the opening. The pallets were formed by slats of wood with gaps between them, and wind continued to blow inside, but they baffled the worst of it and reduced the amount of grit in the air.

Pope switched off the flashlight, rested the M4 against the wall, turned to her and put his hand on her shoulder. "Are you sure you're okay?"

"I'm fine."

"No injuries? They didn't hurt you?"

"No. I'm fine—really."

"So what happened?"

"When?"

"Everything. Start with Khalil's party."

It had been only five nights ago, yet it seemed like it was a lifetime away. She told him that she had planted the device, just as she had been instructed, but that she had been disturbed by Jasmin al-Khawari before she could leave. She told him about the fight and about how she had knocked the older woman unconscious and tied her up. She told him how she had been stopped by Salim and Khalil. "Something happened outside the house. They said it was a raid."

"They?" Pope said. "Who said that? Salim?"

"No. I was questioned here. A man called Abu. He said that the FBI raided the house."

"They did. I was watching. We didn't know that was going to happen. I still don't know what it was about."

Isabella continued. She told him how she had tried to escape, and how she had been overpowered and loaded onto the helicopter that had flown them to the airport. She told him about the flight aboard al-Khawari's private jet, the mechanical problem that had forced them to turn around and land in Turkey and then the trip through the country toward Syria.

She told him about the ambush.

"I know," Pope said. "I was there. I flew from Switzerland and got ahead of them. I was ready to stop the car and get you out, but the ambush happened before I could do anything about it. I followed instead. And then they brought the chopper in."

"That was you?" she said, remembering the assault that had almost freed her.

"Yes," he said. "I couldn't do anything else. The chopper . . . I was outgunned."

"How did you find me here, then?"

"We tracked the helicopter. I came over the border and followed it here. And then they were advertising the executions. They had pictures of Salim and Khalil. I didn't know you'd be there, but it was as good a place as any to start. How did you get away from them?"

"I had some help," she said. "One of the guards is English. He wants to get away. He let me out." She would get to that, to how she had escaped and to Aqil and to what she needed to do now, but first she needed Pope to tell her what was going on. "Will you be honest with me?" she asked him.

"Of course."

"Have you told me everything?"

"About?"

"You didn't know about the FBI. Salim was going to Beirut, not Syria. They were going to kill him tonight. And they told me things when they were questioning me. Things you need to know. But you need to explain what's happening first."

"I'll try."

"At the house," she started. "You said that it was to help break into Salim's server."

"Yes."

"And the device worked?"

"Yes," he said. "As far as I know, it worked perfectly."

"Are you sure it was meant to hack into his system? Did you tell me the truth about what it would do?"

"That's what I was told."

"I don't think that's what it did at all."

"What do you mean?"

"They questioned me twice. They asked me a lot of questions. They said the government released evidence that says al-Khawari and the people here were behind the bombings in London. That he put the money up, but it was their operation. But al-Khawari swears he had nothing to do with it. The man who questioned me said his organization didn't either. And, the more I think about it, the more I think he's telling the truth."

"I've had the same thought," Pope admitted. "ISIS ambushed him and brought him here. Why did they do that? They questioned him. They beat him. Maybe they got what they wanted, maybe they didn't, but they were done with him. They were going to kill him tonight."

It was a dense, confusing picture, and Isabella could draw only flashes of sense from it. "But how does that fit with what you told me?"

"It doesn't fit. If he was working with them, he would have gone straight to Raqqa, not Beirut, and they would have treated him like a hero, not tried to put him on a cross."

"Salim told them that there was no way that his servers could be hacked from outside. They know what I was there for. They know I was in Salim's house so that we could break the security. But he says it wasn't so that we could get the evidence that he was involved in the attacks. He says that it was so that the evidence could be planted. If that's right . . ."

Pope finished it for her. "Then the whole al-Khawari angle is a set-up. It means everything I was told was a lie."

Isabella listened as Pope told her about what had happened to him and Snow and Kelleher after the raid on al-Khawari's compound. He explained that they had been ambushed by a well-drilled and professional team, and that Snow and Kelleher had been killed. Pope had only escaped by stealing a boat and taking it into the middle of Lake Geneva. He had crossed to the opposite bank, stolen a car and travelled to Geneva Airport, where he had met Vivian Bloom. It was Bloom who had arranged for him to be flown to Turkey so that he could go after Isabella and the al-Khawaris. But Bloom had been very clear: they were running to Syria.

But they weren't.

"I think I've been very, very foolish." She thought that he was about to elaborate, but he stopped himself. "Never mind," he said instead. "We can talk about this later. The only way we'll work it out is if I can get to al-Khawari. I have to get him out of the country. He's the key to this."

"I'll help," Isabella said.

Pope shook his head. "No."

"You need help."

"Absolutely not. You've already been put in unacceptable danger."

"You don't have a choice," she said.

"Isabella—"

"You'll have to tie me up and leave me here. I won't stay and wait for you to come back." He began to protest, but she shut him down with a brusque, "Don't argue. I'm not a helpless girl. You know what I can do—you've seen. That's why you asked me to get involved with Khalil. How do you think I got away from them? I broke out of that building, stole a car and headed for the border."

"So what happened? Why are you still here?"

"The third man tonight? The third one they were going to kill?"

"He was young. Who is he?"

"His name is Aqil. He's from England. He let me out. We got as far as a checkpoint on the way out of the city. I shot two of them. We would've made it through, but Aqil lost his nerve. I headed back into the city, but I had to leave him. They came after me. I killed another two, found a place to hide and then waited it out. I was going to make another run for it, but then I found out what they were going to do to Aqil. I'm not going to run and leave him to be killed, Mr Pope."

"You're not responsible for him," Pope said. "He came here. You know what that makes him?"

"He didn't think it through—"

Pope interrupted, "It makes him a terrorist—"

"He's not a terrorist," Isabella replied, cutting him off in turn. "He's made a mistake and now he's out of his depth. And he wants to get out."

"I don't care what he wants. I can get *you* out, Isabella. And I'll get *Salim* out. But that's that. The more of us there are, the less chance we have of making it. I don't know anything about him, but don't make the mistake of thinking that he's your friend. This isn't a humanitarian mission. He chose to come here. He's as guilty as the others. If they kill him, it's his fault. It's nothing to do with us."

"I'm not leaving him." She stood. "It's up to you. You do what you have to do. But don't think you're responsible for me. I'm here because I agreed to help you. I could have stayed in Marrakech, but I didn't. I make my own decisions, and I'll live with the consequences. If you don't want to get him out, I'll just do it without you."

"No, Isabella."

She waved away his objection. "Like you say, it's just a block away. I'll take one of your weapons, or you can stop me and I'll go and find one. And it's not far to the border. I'll get him, get a car, and I won't stop this time."

Pope turned away from her. He reached up to scrub a hand against his scalp. When he turned back to her again, his expression was rueful. "Has anyone ever told you how alike you are to your bloody mother?" He shook his head. "All right. You win. We'll get them both."

"And Khalil and Jasmin?"

"You want them, too?"

"No," she said. "Not really, but they don't deserve to be left here."

"If they're there," Pope conceded.

"What do you want me to do?"

"You can help, but you do exactly as I say. Can you do that?"

Pope crossed the room to his backpack. He opened it, reached inside and withdrew a 9mm pistol. He held it up: it was a Beretta M9 semi-automatic.

"Did your mother show you how to use this?"

She took it from him, expertly ejected the magazine, checked it and pushed it back into the port. "What do you think?" she said.

Chapter Forty-Eight

Pope drove the pickup back down the road from which they had arrived, slowing as they approached the building where the prisoners were being held. They drove by, both of them straining their eyes as the storm obscured everything with windblown sand. Isabella could make out the three vehicles that they had seen, parked up against the wall of the prison block. There was a single light burning above the entrance to the facility, with a guard standing beneath it, partially sheltered from the storm behind the flimsy wooden guardhouse. The building looked almost unrecognisable from when Isabella and Aqil had fled from it; she had been concentrating on the way ahead, she supposed, and the storm was making everything look strange and alien.

He drove on for another hundred metres and then parked.

"I'll go back and scout it. Stay here."

"I know it," she said. "I'm coming."

Isabella opened her door. The wind was too loud for him to make himself heard without shouting, so he just paused, shaking his head and pointing back inside the cab.

Isabella ignored him and started back to the prison block.

Pope caught her up and put a hand on her shoulder.

"Do what I say," he said. His voice was muffled through his headscarf and almost inaudible through the wailing of the wind, but his irritation was obvious and unmistakeable.

She gave a nod to tell him that she had heard him and understood, and then, before he could say anything else, she set off for the block again. He gave up and followed.

There was no point in scouting the front of the facility. They had already seen it, and there was no realistic prospect of gaining access without being seen by the guard. The factory was surrounded by a concrete fence that was, in turn, topped by mesh and then coils of razor wire. It was too tall and too difficult to climb, but as they scouted along it, she saw something that gave her cause to stop.

Pope joined her. She pointed at a narrow gap at the foot of the concrete block. The ground fell away, leaving a hole that was fifty centimetres wide and perhaps forty centimetres deep.

"I can get through that," she said.

Pope looked down at the gap and shook his head. "I don't like it."

"Come on," she said. "What are you going to do? We can't go in the front without a firefight. We can't climb the fence without cutting ourselves to shreds. I can get under there with the Beretta, get around to the front and take the guard out. Wait at the gate. I'll let you in from the inside."

"I don't like it," he said again.

"Got a better idea?"

"You'd be on your own."

"Not really. You'd be here."

"On the other side of the fence," he said dubiously.

"Come on, Mr Pope. The storm's not going to last forever. You said it yourself: we have to take advantage of it. If you have another plan, let's have it."

He paused. His scarf was pulled tight around his face, his eyes barely visible through a narrow slit left. "I don't," he said.

"So?"

He was uncomfortable about it; she could see. "All right," he said.

Chapter Forty-Nine

Isabella lay on her back and slid beneath the concrete slab. She got her head and shoulders through without any problem and lay there for a moment, half on one side and half on the other, trying to listen for anything that might alert her to a risk that she might be observed. The wind was too loud; she couldn't hear anything. She wriggled ahead, the base of the slab pressing against her chest and then her hips. She reached down with her arms, levering herself upwards and then, by pressing with her feet and scrabbling with her hands, she was able to clamber out from the shallow trench. She rolled over, onto her hands and knees, and then raised herself up onto her haunches. She took the Beretta from the waistband of her trousers and scurried ahead. There was a margin of three feet between the concrete wall and the building, and as she pressed herself up against the bricks, she listened again. She still heard nothing.

She felt the adrenaline in her blood. Her fingers twitched, her right hand clasping and unclasping around the pistol, and she felt the jolt of energy in the muscles of her legs and shoulders. With her back squared against the wall, she shuffled toward the front of the building. The sand had gathered against the wall in little drifts, and her boots sank into it. The wind howled, seemingly louder and louder, and she had to squint when she turned her head into it.

She reached the corner of the building. The front of the prison block led away to her left, and she saw the wooden guard post. She waited there, crouched low, with the sharp corner of the building pressed into her back, and observed. The lightbulb in the hut swung to and fro in the wind, the cone of light lashing left and right. Isabella had seen the guard as they had driven by the front of the building, but now she was unsure whether he was still there. She gripped the butt of the pistol and was about to creep ahead when she saw a shadow detach from the deeper darkness inside the gatehouse; it was the guard, and he was coming toward her.

She slid back around the side of the building and positioned herself low to the ground so that she was resting on her toes, the brick against her back and with her weight pressing down on her quadriceps until they burned. She raised her left arm, her forearm pressed against the brick, and then aimed the gun at the edge of the wall. The guard appeared from around the side of the building, just ambling, perhaps something as mundane as stretching his legs. He stopped a metre from where Isabella was waiting and she took aim. He rearranged his headscarf, and as her finger began to tighten around the trigger, he turned and walked back toward the guard post.

Isabella came out from behind the wall and watched. The man kept going, walking to the other side of the building.

Isabella changed her mind. She hurried after him, the gun raised and ready to shoot, but rather than fire, she turned into the entrance to the building and tried the handle. It was unlocked; she opened the door and went inside.

She remembered the interior: the narrow corridor with two doors to the left and right and a set of double doors straight ahead.

The double doors opened out into the factory's main space, where the cells had been constructed.

She paused there for a moment and listened. Nothing, save the howling of the wind. Should she stop, go back and shoot the guard and let Pope inside? She decided against it. She would get Aqil first.

She stepped forward, stopping at the door to her right. She pushed it open with her left hand, the gun held out ready in her right. There was a small room with a screen down the centre that extended halfway across it. There was a latrine in the floor to the left of the screen and a sink to the right. The room was empty.

She let the door close, crossed the corridor and checked the other door. The room looked as if it was used as an office. There was a table and a chair, and three A4 ring binders stacked on the table next to a pile of papers. A black and white ISIS flag had been hung from the wall and, below that, there was a single hook. A bunch of keys had been left on the hook. Isabella collected them.

She went back to the corridor and, slowly and carefully, approached the double doors.

She pushed them apart and, the gun held out ahead of her, slipped between them and into the murkiness beyond. She remembered it: the cells that had been built against one wall of the old warehouse, the single light fixed to the middle of the wall, the gash in the ceiling through which particles of sand gently fell to the floor. Deep shadows filled the corners of the room, so dark as to be impenetrable, and as she paused to acclimatise herself, she thought she saw a blur of movement against the opposite wall. She aimed, the trigger against the pad of her index finger. She saw the smudge of movement again, but as she was about to fire, it moved through the light and she saw it for what it was: a mongrel, so thin that the corrugation of its ribcage was visible across the room, sheltering from the storm inside the building. It saw her, cocked its head and then shuffled away again into the gloom.

Isabella hurried to the cells. The first three, including her own, were empty, the doors left open. She looked inside and saw a mess of blankets, mattresses and discarded clothes on the floor of each of the narrow spaces.

The door of the fourth cell was locked. She slid back the peephole and looked inside.

She saw Salim al-Khawari.

He looked up at her.

"Be quiet," she said in a tight little whisper.

His face flashed through fear and confusion. "Who are you?"

She doubted that he would have been able to see her face in the gloom.

"I'm going to get you out," she said. "You need to wait there and be quiet. Understand? No noise."

He nodded.

"How many guards are here?"

"I do not know. I think—" he said. He paused, mid-sentence. "Daisy?"

"Answer the question," she said.

He stumbled. "I—I—there were two in the car with us. We were moved this morning before they—" He paused again, and she knew that he was talking about what had nearly happened to him and his son this evening. "They said the place was being closed down, but they brought us back here after the explosion. After the drone."

"There was no one else here?"

"It's just us. My son and me and the other one they were going to kill."

"Be quiet. I'll be back."

She continued along the line of cells. The next one was empty, the door open, but the following one was locked. She looked inside. Khalil was there, curled up on a mattress, his knees drawn up tight against his chest. He looked as if he was asleep, and she didn't disturb him.

The next cell was empty, but the one after that—the final one along the wall—was locked. She opened the peephole and looked straight into Aqil's face. He was standing close to the door and must, she guessed, have heard her whispered conversation with Salim.

"Daisy?"

"Yes," she said.

"What are you doing?"

She had no time to indulge him. She took the keys from her pocket, checked the lock and selected the one that looked most likely. It didn't fit. She picked another, and then another, and then another. She was beginning to think that the key that she needed wasn't on the ring, but as she tried the fifth key, the lock opened with a rusty click. She turned the handle and pushed the door open.

Aqil took a step forward and then paused in the doorway. He was frightened.

"I'm going to get you out," she said. "You and the other two from tonight. But I'm going to need your help. Is that okay?"

"To do what?" he said tremulously.

"Keep an eye on them. Warn me if they look like they are about to do something stupid. It's not for long—just until we get outside. There's help waiting."

"What help?"

"Later. Can you do that?"

"Yes."

She thought about not asking the second question but asked it anyway. "What about the woman they brought here? The wife?"

"I don't know," he said. "All the cells were empty when we came back. They must have taken her somewhere else."

Isabella nodded. Fair enough. She would have brought Jasmin out, too, but it appeared that she had been separated from the men. Shame. Bad luck for her.

"How are we going to get out?"

"I'm going to persuade the guard to let us out. We'll need to be quick. Now," she said, gesturing to the closed doors and handing the bunch of keys to Aqil, "let them out. And tell them to be quiet or I'll shoot them."

Aqil unlocked Khalil's door first, disappearing inside to wake him up. Aqil came out again and headed down the line to Salim's cell just as Khalil followed him outside. Isabella glared over at him, the gun held out in front of her so that he could see it. Khalil looked dazed, a mixture of fright and confusion running riot across his blandly good-looking face. Aqil opened Salim's cell and Khalil's father peeked out, his head turning to the left and then the right, his terror very evident.

Isabella went over to them.

"Daisy?" Khalil said, his confusion deepening.

"I'm going to get you out. But you have to do everything that I tell you. If you don't, I can't promise that I won't shoot you. All clear?"

"How are you going to do that?"

"We'll go out the front door."

"The guard?"

"I'll take care of him."

"How? You're just a girl."

She held up the pistol. "It's up to you, Salim. You can come with me or make a go of it yourself. I know what I'd rather do."

He looked dubious, and his lack of confidence lent additional edge to his fright. "And then?"

"We'll drive to the border."

Chapter Fifty

G etting out was easier than Isabella had expected. The guard was in the hut, looking out at the storm that was lashing the street. He didn't see her leave the building. He didn't see her as she approached the hut, pulled the door open and pressed the barrel of the Beretta against the back of his head.

"You're going to do exactly as I tell you," she said in Arabic. "Nod if you understand."

He nodded.

She told him that she wanted him to open the gate, and when he held up the key and nodded again that he understood, she led him at gunpoint out into the storm, past the concrete bollards and up to the mesh fence.

"Mr Pope," she called out.

He appeared out of the storm, his M4 cradled in his arms.

The guard unlocked the gate and dragged it open. Isabella indicated that he should lead the way outside, and he did.

"Who's this?"

"The guard," she said.

"Do we need him?"

"No," she said.

Pope reversed the M4 and drove the buttstock into the man's face. He crumpled to the ground.

Pope turned the gun around again and aimed at Salim, Khalil and Aqil as they came through the gate. All three men raised their hands.

"Mr al-Khawari," Pope said, "straight ahead, please."

Isabella led the way back to where they had parked the Ranger. Pope followed at the rear, covering Salim.

———

Pope arranged them so that Aqil was up front, with him, while Salim and Khalil were in the back with Isabella. She was sitting behind the passenger seat, with Khalil next to her in the middle of the bench and his father on the other side of the truck. She had the Beretta out, holding it across her chest so that it could be trained on them both.

Pope floored the pedal and the pickup surged ahead. The storm seemed to have grown even more ferocious in the time it had taken Isabella to free the three men, and the gusts were blowing with enough strength to buffet the truck as they headed to the north. Pope had switched on the headlamps, and she could see the storm of sand and grit in the glow that reached out ahead of them.

"You were supposed to let me in," he chided her.

"I changed the plan," she replied. "There was an opportunity and I took it."

"Never mind. The checkpoint—can you remember where it was?"

"The main road out of the city," she said. "We'll run into it. I don't think it's far from here."

"Can you describe it?"

"There were two cars blocking the road," she said. "And concrete blocks."

"Number of men?"

"Two."

Pope nodded.

"A checkpoint?" Salim exclaimed. "They'll shoot us."

"Not if we shoot them first," Pope said. "Isabella—can you drive?"

Salim was about to protest but stopped at the sound of her name. "Isabella? What?"

"That's my name," she said curtly.

"Not Daisy . . . ?"

She ignored him and turned to Pope. "Yes," she said. "I can drive."

"I'm going to pull over in a minute, and you and Aqil are going to change places. Mr al-Khawari—you and your son need to stay in the back. I'd like to get you out in one piece, but if I think you're going to be a nuisance, I'll put bullets in you both and leave you at the side of the road. Understand?"

"Yes," Salim said.

"What about you, Khalil? Is that going to be something you can do?"

The boy didn't answer.

"Don't worry about him," Salim said.

"Good," Pope said.

They turned through a maze of roads, and eventually Isabella realised that she knew where they were. She remembered the road from yesterday: the street became a slip road that fed into the main road that led out of the city.

"It's ahead," she said.

Pope slowed and pulled over at the side of the road. He collected his M4 and got out. So did Isabella. They met at the front of the truck.

He rapped his knuckles against the side of the pickup. "It's an automatic," he said over the wailing of the wind. "You driven one before?"

"Yes. That's fine."

"The steering is a little heavy. And it pulls to the right."

"It's fine. I've got it."

"Don't stop. You might have to go off-road to get around them, but don't stop. Not for anything. I'm going to be in the back with that," he said, gesturing up at the big .50-calibre machine gun behind its own armoured screen. "I'll knock on the roof when I'm ready."

She went around to the driver's side and got in. Pope slammed the door, nodded at her through the window, then went to the side of the truck. She watched in the mirror as he grabbed the lip of the flatbed and hauled himself up and over it. She heard the sound of his boots reverberating against the metal of the bed, and then she heard three taps against the roof.

She looked ahead, only just tall enough to see over the armoured panel that had been welded to the front of the truck.

She put the transmission into drive and pulled away.

Chapter Fifty-One

The checkpoint had been reinforced since Isabella's last visit to it. The same two vehicles were in place, blocking the way ahead, and additional concrete blocks had been placed on either side of them. There were two guards standing in front of the blocks, both armed, both wearing headscarves to protect their faces from the scouring sand. There was no other traffic out that night. The two sentries faced out, toward the city, their AKs hanging from straps that they wore around their shoulders.

Isabella didn't stop. She knew what Pope had in mind, and she knew that their best chance of success was to attack without giving the sentries a chance to realise the danger that they were in. She pressed down on the accelerator and the armoured pickup gathered pace. It bumped over the uneven surface of the road, bouncing through the potholes and then crashing over the small rocks that littered it. The suspension was already flattened almost to the ground by the additional weight of the sheet metal that cocooned the pickup like the plates of an armadillo, and it offered no give at all. She hoped that Pope had secured himself.

The engine roared, announcing their approach from half a mile away. The two insurgents on this side of the checkpoint couldn't help but notice them. They took shelter behind the concrete blocks, one aiming his AK around the side of the block to the left while the other rested his atop the one to the right. They started to fire when the pickup was a hundred metres away. They sprayed rounds in the general direction of the vehicle, most passing harmlessly overhead or to the side, a few clanging against the armoured plate, sparks flashing back onto the windscreen.

Isabella pushed the truck to fifty and kept the speed constant. She would have to slow before she swerved around the blocks, using the scrub on the side of the road to skirt them, but she would delay braking until it was absolutely necessary.

Two more men appeared from the other side of the barricade. One of them had an AK. The other was cradling a different weapon. It looked like an RPG. Isabella had never fired one, but her mother had explained how they worked in the event that one day she found herself in need of extra firepower. It was a shoulder-fired, single-shot smooth-bore recoilless launcher, the grenade loaded into the front and the backblast vented out of a nozzle at the rear. The Russians had popularised them, and now they were everywhere. There must have been thousands floating around in Syria. The insurgent lowered himself into a launch position, his right knee bent and his left knee flat to the ground.

Fifty metres.

There came a deafening roar as Pope opened up with the machine gun. A corona of fire flamed out right above the windshield and spent brass casings cascaded down onto the hood, bouncing away to either side of the onrushing pickup or gathering in the groove where the armoured panel met the hood.

Isabella tried to keep the wheel steady, fighting the unbalanced weight of the truck and the uneven surface of the road. She wanted to give Pope the best chance possible of disabling the threat ahead of them. Firing the big gun from the flatbed of a light pickup with a civilian suspension was not a recipe for outstanding accuracy, but perhaps accuracy was unnecessary here. What they needed was fear, the fear of God, enough to scatter the sentries for long enough that they were able to get through the checkpoint and away into the desert.

Twenty-five metres.

The gun roared and the roof shook. Isabella peered over the lip of the armoured plate just in time to see one of the vehicles that was parked behind the concrete blocks propelled into the air by the tremendous detonation that unfurled beneath it. The explosion lifted the vehicle up and then dropped it back down onto its side, tendrils of jet black smoke criss-crossing the sudden glare of red and orange light.

Isabella hit the brakes, slowing them down just enough before she swung the wheel to the left and directed the truck off the road. The front wheels crashed down into a shallow ditch and the springs groaned as the impact pushed the heavy armour down onto them. She heard the squeal as metal tore, and then a grinding crunch from the direction of the front axle. The rear wheels bounced out of the ditch and Isabella spun the wheel to the right, stamping down on the accelerator again so that the truck rushed by the checkpoint doing forty miles an hour.

The road was to their right, and ten metres to the left, the desert floor descended into a shallow channel. It was too dark to make out how deep the channel was, or whether there was any water running through it. One of the sentries fired as they flew past, his automatic volley jagging into the flimsy unarmoured wing and the door panel. Isabella looked down and saw ragged inward-facing petals where the rounds had punctured through the door; she didn't think that she had been struck, but she reflexively reached down and felt her torso and leg. Nothing.

"Khalil!"

She glanced up in the rear-view mirror. Salim was turned to one side, his arm reaching across his son.

"Khalil! He has been hit!"

There was certainly no time to stop, and Isabella cared very little for the spoiled brat in any case. She was more concerned with the fact that the machine gun on the roof had fallen silent. She didn't know whether the big gun could pivot so that it could be aimed to the side; if it couldn't, that might explain the silence. But she couldn't discount the possibility that Pope had been hit or thrown from the roof by the impact as they left the road.

She pressed down on the pedal. She had to keep going. She had to get them away from what was left of the checkpoint.

She glanced into the wing mirror. She saw the jagged line of bullet holes all the way down the rear door and the rear wing, the plume of sand that was being thrown into the air by the rear wheel and a sudden spurt of bright white light through the darkness of the storm.

They had fired the RPG.

Isabella yanked the wheel to the left, the wheels lifting for a moment before the huge weight of the pickup pushed them down again. The truck shot forward, launching off the raised lip of rock that preceded the drop into the channel and then arcing down into it. She glimpsed the streak of light as the grenade shot overhead, but her attention was focussed on the floor of the watercourse that was rushing up at her. The armour struck first with a tremendous crash. It detached from its mounts and crumpled back into the hood. The top edge slammed into the windshield, slicing through the glass and bisecting the left and right front window pillars. Isabella was thrown forward by the impact as the sharp edge of the welded iron sheet jutted out beyond the line of the dash. The seat belt bit and held her in her seat as the metal came to rest just a scant few inches from her face.

The pickup had landed at an angle of forty-five degrees, and now the back wheels fell back and pounded against the ground. More glass was detached from the windshield, falling into Isabella's lap.

She unclipped the seat belt, opened the door and stumbled out into the watercourse. There came a muffled crump from overhead and far away: the grenade had flown on and detonated against the ground.

Isabella looked around: the watercourse was dry, rocks strewn across the dusty riverbed. She grabbed the Beretta and scrambled to the sloping sides of the wadi, digging her hands and feet into the loose sand and earth and working her way back up to the top. She reached it, dug in her feet and anchored herself so that her head was just above the lip of the watercourse.

She looked back at the checkpoint.

The vehicle that had exploded was still burning, and as she watched, a secondary blast sent another spout of flame into the night sky. The blaze lit up the desert, bright enough to cast the figures who were approaching her in silhouette.

Two figures, both running toward her.

The first was ten metres in front of the second. It was a man. He was wearing a headscarf, the loose end bouncing up and down. She saw the shape of the long gun that he held out ahead of him, the muzzle swinging left and right with the cadence of his strides.

He saw her, slowed, and raised the rifle.

Isabella raised the Beretta and aimed.

She pulled the trigger. Nothing. She tried to rack the slide, but it was almost impossible and wouldn't go back without being forced. She had cleaned the gun after Pope had given it to her. It had been fine then, but the pistol had an exposed barrel and she must have got sand into it when she climbed out of the wadi. The obstruction was in the slide now, and the gun was jammed.

The first man aimed his long gun. She could identify it now: an AK-47.

The second man was five metres behind the first man. He stopped running.

The first man fired. The bullet landed short, spraying sand in her face. He was close, and it would have been easier to hit her. It was just a warning shot.

He barked out something in Arabic. The wind was too loud for Isabella to understand what he was saying.

She raised her hands, the Beretta in her right, and slowly and carefully tossed the pistol away.

The man approached. He jerked the rifle up. He wanted her to stand.

She put her hands on the rocks and pushed, bringing her knees up.

The man shouldered the rifle and aimed. She could see he was going to shoot her. She realised that she wasn't frightened. She was furious with herself for allowing her weapon to jam.

The man's body jerked as if someone had punched him, hard, behind his right shoulder. He took a step forward, and then another, and then his body jerked again, his arms flung out wide as the rifle fell to the desert floor. Isabella heard the report of the third shot a fraction of a moment before his body spasmed again; he stumbled for another step, tripped and fell face first into the sand.

Isabella got her feet beneath her, and fighting a wind that wanted to send her tumbling back down the slope, she stood. The second man was on his feet, too, and was approaching again. He held his weapon expertly, angled down at the ground. She couldn't see him through the swirl of sand in the air, but as he drew near, he raised his left hand, palm up, and called out.

The words were whipped away on the storm, but she didn't need to hear them. She recognised the chequered *keffiyeh*.

It was Pope.

He drew alongside and leaned down to put his mouth next to her ear.

"Are you all right?"

"Bumps and bruises," she called back. "What happened to you?"

"I jumped."

"What about the checkpoint?"

Pope pointed down at the dead jihadi. "All dead. He was the last one." He gestured down into the watercourse. "How are the others?"

"I don't know."

"What happened?"

"They fired an RPG."

"I didn't mean that—I saw." He nodded at the jihadi he had shot. "Why didn't you shoot him?"

She held up the Beretta. "Useless piece of shit jammed. The exposed barrel. It's all well and good giving the shell somewhere to go, but you're still fucked if you get sand into it."

Pope allowed himself an amused chuckle. "Take his AK. Much more reliable. And we might need the firepower."

Chapter Fifty-Two

They clambered down the slope together. It was obvious that the pickup wasn't going any farther. The armoured plate had broken away from its fixings completely, and had shattered the windshield and sheared through both window pillars. The grille had been crumpled and a cloud of steam was issuing from the radiator, quickly snatched by the wind. Even if they could have fixed the radiator, there was no way that they would have been able to make the pickup mobile again. Isabella remembered the ominous sounds coming from the axle. It was finished.

"Well," Pope said as they reached the bottom of the slope, "that's not going anywhere."

"What about the cars at the checkpoint?" she asked.

He shook his head. "One of them blew up. The other one is Swiss cheese. We're going to have to walk."

They saw that one of the pickup's rear doors had been opened, Salim's side of the car, on the opposite side to them. The wind dropped for a moment and they heard a sobbing in its place. Pope went first, switching on the flashlight that was attached to the barrel of his M4. She edged around the front of the car and saw Salim in the glow of the flashlight. He was leaning against the side of the pickup, bullet holes studding the panel on either side of him. Khalil was lying on his back, his head in his father's lap. Salim was stroking the boy's hair. Khalil wasn't moving, and the blood that stained the boy's shirt looked almost black in the flashlight's harsh glare.

Salim looked up, squinting into the sudden brightness. He mumbled something, too quiet for them to hear. He realised that they couldn't hear him, so he called out, louder, his voice cracked with sobs, "He's dead."

Pope swung the barrel of the rifle up and swept the light into the interior of the pickup. Aqil was slumped forward, held in place by the seat belt that was around his waist, his head pressed against the back of the seat in front of him.

Pope held the beam of the flashlight on him. "See if Aqil is alive," he said. "I'll speak to Salim."

Isabella went back around to the other side of the truck and tried to open the door. The impact had deformed the wing so that the door caught against the frame; Isabella gripped the handle and heaved. The door came free of the obstruction and opened. Aqil was still held in place by his seat belt. There was no obvious sign of serious injury, but there was a vivid bruise on his forehead and blood was running out of his nostrils and dripping into his lap. It looked as if he had been thrown forward by the impact, striking his head on the seat in front of him.

"Aqil," Isabella said, putting her hands on his shoulders and very gently squeezing them. Aqil blinked his eyes and tried to raise his head. He groaned. She reached down, unclipped the seat belt and then gently shook his shoulders. "Wake up, Aqil."

He blinked again, his eyes staying open this time. Isabella put her head inside the cabin and reached up for the courtesy light. She flicked it on, and it cast enough dim light for her to be able to see him without the need for Pope's flashlight. Aqil tried to speak, but the wind was rushing into the cabin and she couldn't make out the words. She leaned farther inside so that her ear was closer to his mouth.

"What happened?"

"We crashed. Are you hurt?"

"My head. I must have banged it."

"You did. Anything else?"

He closed his eyes again and then reached up with his hands and felt down his ribcage. "I don't think so. Bruises." He ran his fingers along the top of his thighs and groaned. He reversed them and looked down at his fingertips: the light fell on the blood that stained them.

"It's from your nose," Isabella said. "It's nothing. Come on—we need to get you out."

Isabella reached in, put her hands underneath his shoulders and very gently helped him slide around so that he could get his feet out and onto the hard rocky bed of the watercourse. She grabbed on and pulled him up, sliding around so that she could reach her arm beneath his shoulders and help him bear his weight. She helped him take a few steps away from the car until he was able to stand unaided. Isabella disengaged from him, staying close enough to intercede should he stumble.

He looked left and right into the darkness of the wadi that loomed on either side of them. "Where are we?"

"We got through the checkpoint, but we crashed. The truck is finished."

"How are we going to get away?"

"Unless we can find something else, we'll have to walk. You think you can do that?"

He nodded a little gingerly. "I think so. It's just my head. I've got a splitting headache."

Isabella joined Pope at the front of the pickup. Salim was on his feet to one side, standing over the body of his son. Aqil had slipped back inside the cabin to shelter from the sand.

"How's Aqil?" Pope asked her.

"He was knocked out. Says he has a headache."

"It might be a concussion. Walking through the desert in this"—he gestured around at the storm—"isn't going to be the best thing for him, but he can't stay here. There's no other choice."

"Salim?"

"He's coming. He knows he doesn't have any other choice. We'll have to leave the boy here. There's no time to bury him."

Pope took a small handheld device from a pocket and switched it on. Isabella recognised it: it was a Magellan GPS receiver. He studied the screen for a moment and then switched it off. "We're twenty-five miles from the border," he said.

"How long will it take to cover that?"

He closed his eyes in momentary thought. "We would normally be able to cover three miles in an hour, but the wind and cold won't help. Your friend might slow us down, and if there are dunes that we have to go around, or if the sand is soft, it'll take longer. I'd say ten hours to be on the safe side."

"We don't have eight hours before sunup."

"No," he said. "We don't. We'll see where we are at dawn. We'll either gamble and press on or find somewhere to hide."

"Could we find another car?"

"I'd rather stay off the road. They're looking for us. We'll walk unless someone can't go on. Then we'll reassess."

She nodded that she understood.

"Stay here with them for a moment," he said.

"Why? Where are you going?"

"Look at them. They need better clothes or they'll freeze to death. And we don't have enough water. I'll go back to the checkpoint and see what I can find." He put his hands on her shoulders and turned her to face him. "If you hear anything, or if I'm not back in fifteen minutes, you need to start walking. Head north." He pointed to one of the walls of the wadi. "Climb out and get going. Don't stop for anyone. If either of them slows you down too much, leave them and go."

She didn't answer.

Pope pointed to his backpack. "I'll leave that here. There's some rations, extra ammunition and a satphone. I'm coming back, Isabella, but if I don't, take what you can manage and go. You're resourceful; you can make it. I know you can."

Pope squeezed her shoulders, let go of her and climbed up to the desert floor. She saw his shadow as he paused at the top, but then he disappeared over the edge and was gone.

Chapter Fifty-Three

Isabella waited anxiously for ten minutes until she heard the sound of footsteps in loose sand and saw the same dark shadow as Pope scrambled down the loose slope and joined her next to the beached truck. His M4 was slung over his shoulder and he was carrying a bundle of clothing and two large half-gallon bottles of water. He dropped the bundle to the floor; it was composed of three padded jackets. He gave one to Aqil, one to Salim and the last one to Isabella. She pulled it on. It was baggy and too big for her, and when she zipped it up, the back of her hand ran over an opening in the fabric. She investigated with her fingers and found that the hole went all the way through the garment and was, she noted with mild distaste, still damp on the inside. It was blood. The jacket had been worn by one of the men that Pope had shot at the checkpoint. She didn't say anything. The other jackets were likely in the same condition, and she didn't want to draw any attention to it for fear of upsetting Salim or Aqil.

Pope handed one of the bottles to Salim and the other one to Isabella.

"You need to fill up on water," he said. "It doesn't matter that it's cold. You can be dehydrated in the cold just as easily as when it's hot."

Isabella remembered what her mother had told her: the vapour that she could see escaping from her mouth, the clouds that vanished into the wind, was moisture. It was precious, and it needed to be replaced. She unscrewed the bottle, took a long gulp, and then another. She took a third and final swig and handed the bottle to Aqil.

Pope reached into the pocket of his jacket and removed four chocolate bars. He handed them out. Isabella looked at hers. It was in a blue and white wrapper with a picture of a tropical beach on it, and the name—"Hum Hum"—was emblazoned across it in blue type. She didn't wait; she hadn't eaten for hours and she was hungry. She tore the wrapper and took out the two small bars inside. She stuffed the first bar into her mouth. It was milk chocolate with a coconut centre, and it tasted delicious. She finished it and then the second.

Salim and Aqil were both wearing their coats, and Salim had put on a woollen hat that he had found inside the pocket of his jacket. Isabella could see that he had been crying, and Pope had to gently move him away from his son's body.

The wadi ran east to west, and they needed to head north. Pope helped Salim clamber up the treacherous slope and then came back down to help Isabella with Aqil. The boy seemed to have found a little more steadiness on his feet, but he groaned as they dragged him up the slope with them, and Isabella wondered whether he might have been keeping quiet about another injury. She said nothing.

Pope arranged them: Aqil and Salim were in the lead, with Pope and Isabella bringing up the rear. Isabella could guess why he had chosen that formation. Pope didn't trust Salim and wanted him to be in front of him at all times. And it would allow them to keep an eye on Aqil. Their pace would be governed by the slowest member of the party, and it was likely to be him. Isabella had no intention of abandoning him, but she knew that Pope would not have the same qualms. She didn't know what she would do if it became clear that he couldn't go on. She would try to persuade Pope to find somewhere for them to shelter from the storm while he recovered his strength. But if he didn't agree? She would consider that when the time came.

They set off to the north. The sand was firm, and save the occasional rock that appeared from out of the darkness, the footing was secure. Isabella turned back after ten minutes. There was still a faint glow from the fire that had consumed the exploded car, just enough for the structure of the sentry house and the square blocks of concrete to be discernible through the debris that was being flung up by the wind. She narrowed her focus, but she couldn't see the pickup. The wadi was deep enough that it had been hidden from view. The desert was flat and featureless, and she was already unsure of where they had started. The orienteering that she had practised before had been much easier than this. Visibility was constantly changing. She was glad that Pope was with her.

The wind had brought clouds overhead and the cover was complete; there was no natural light at all. The wind rushed around them, stinging every exposed inch of Isabella's skin. She walked with her head bowed forward, the jacket zipped all the way up to her throat. It was quilted inside and provided decent protection from the worst of the wind. She put both hands into the pockets of the jacket and wore the AK on its strap. She would be able to get to the rifle quickly, should the need arise.

"Look," Pope said.

He was pointing back toward the city. She turned her head and looked. The checkpoint was a mile away from them. She saw the lights of two cars; one of the cars was already at the checkpoint, the twin beams picking out the concrete blocks and the hulk of the overturned vehicle. The other was approaching from the south, halfway between the first buildings of the town and the checkpoint.

They walked on, and when she turned back again, the second car had joined the first and she could make out the silhouettes of people milling around between the blocks.

"They'll come after us," Pope said. "We've been lucky. They won't be able to see the pickup from there. They won't know where to start looking. The storm will help, too. And we won't be hanging around."

Chapter Fifty-Four

They walked for two hours. The farther they walked, the colder Isabella became. The jacket kept her body reasonably warm, but the wind still found its way inside through the bullet hole, and she had to rearrange it so that the fabric could be folded over itself in an attempt to close the gash. It was her legs that were particularly cold; the jeans that she was wearing were made from thin denim, and her legs were quickly icy cold. She kept her hands in her pockets, but they soon chilled, too. There was a moment when Pope had paused, his hand on his weapon, and Isabella had instinctively removed her hands from the pockets and reached for the AK-47. Her fingers were so cold that it was an effort to bend the joints and uncurl her fists.

"What are we going to do when we get across the border?" she asked Pope.

"I'm not sure," he admitted. "I need to think. There's too much going on that I can't work out. I'm not sure who to trust."

"I don't care," she said. "I'm going home."

"No," he said firmly. "Not right away. You need to stay with me."

She turned her head to look at him. He was angling down, his head bent into the wind, and his face might as well have been carved from stone. "For how long?"

"Until I can work out what's going on."

"Why?"

"Because I can't say whether it's safe."

"No one knows where I live," she said.

"Don't be naive. I found you, didn't I? You think the Firm wouldn't be able to do the same if it wanted to? No. You need to stay with me."

They trudged on in silence.

Pope spoke again. "We'll go to Tuscany. I have an apartment in Montepulciano. It'll be safe. I spoke to my wife before this all happened. I knew something was wrong. I should've listened to myself. We can meet them there. Me and you."

"And Salim?"

"We get him over the border. Then I need to talk to him."

⌣

They crossed a narrow track. Pope had his GPS tracker, but he looked at it only sparingly. The ambient light from the display would risk revealing their location, and even with the additional cover of the storm, he did not want to take unnecessary risks. He had evidently remembered the features that they would pass, though, because he remarked with satisfaction that the road meant that they were on the right heading.

"What time is it?" she asked.

"Five. We're still twelve miles from the border. We need to think about somewhere to hide out. It'll be light soon."

They pressed on. Isabella looked back frequently, but she couldn't remember where the main road was and wasn't even sure that she would be able to see it. It was a surprise, then, when Pope issued a curt order to get down as the lights of a vehicle bounced across the desert three or four hundred metres to the right. The car didn't stop, but it did reveal the location of the road. Pope was tabbing close to it, using it as a reference point, but not so close as to risk their discovery should another car travel by.

They pressed on for another twenty minutes. Isabella found it more and more difficult to continue. Her body complained: the cold, the effort of traversing softer stretches of sand that made her calves burn with the effort of picking up her feet, the wind that scoured the moisture from her eyes and her mouth. Pope was not immune either: he walked with a steady stride, but his head was down and she could hear that he was breathing hard from the effort of hauling the heavy backpack that was loaded with his equipment. Salim was slumped forward, his hands in the pockets of his jacket, and he had fallen on three occasions, staying down until Pope had hauled him back to his feet again.

Of the four of them, though, it was Aqil who was struggling the most. He moved slowly, so much so that Isabella estimated that they were covering only half the ground that Pope had suggested might be possible. It was half an hour after they had seen the car when he finally collapsed. He had been stumbling for the last ten or fifteen metres, barely able to lift his shoes from the ground, but his toe caught against a rock that he hadn't seen or had been unable to avoid, and he staggered ahead for a further pace before he dropped to his knees.

Pope had moved ahead of them for a moment.

"Mr Pope," Isabella called, "wait."

Pope paused and turned his head. Salim must have been watching and waiting for an opportunity, and this, evidently, was it. As soon as Pope had turned away from him, he set off in a dead sprint. Pope was looking at Isabella and, upon seeing the surprise on her face, turned back as Salim put distance between them. The storm had abated for a moment, and visibility was a little better. The sky was lightening, too, and it was possible for them to see Salim as he struggled through the sand away from them.

Pope slipped his arms out of the backpack and let it fall to the ground. "If I don't come back, go north. You understand?"

Isabella shouted back that she did.

Pope turned away and sprinted after Salim.

Isabella went to Aqil. He looked dazed and confused, and as she was about to try to help him back to his feet, he doubled over and vomited on the sand. She grabbed onto him and tugged to stop him from falling over onto his side.

Concussion? Isabella had no idea, but she knew that there was no way he was going to be able to continue.

The wind picked up again. Isabella grabbed on to Aqil's shoulder and raised her head, looking for Pope, but she realised with alarm that she couldn't see him. The storm was easing, and visibility was better than it had been for hours, but there was still no sign of him. She knew in which direction Pope had set off, but that was it. She wondered whether she should shout. She decided that she had to risk it.

"Mr Pope!"

She strained her ears, but all she could hear was the wind.

"Pope!"

She closed her eyes, concentrating as hard as she could, but there was nothing. She opened her eyes again and looked down at Aqil. He looked as if he was asleep. She shook him, and then, when that failed to rouse him, she struck him with a light open-handed slap. His head lolled to the side, and his body, already a dead weight, slipped out of her grip and keeled over to the ground. Aqil wasn't concussed. She didn't know what it was, but it wasn't that.

"Mr Pope!" she called again. "Pope!"

Chapter Fifty-Five

Salim was faster than he looked, and Pope had to run hard to reel him in. The footing changed from hard sand to loose shale, and he had to concentrate on every step to avoid turning his ankle. He realised that he was climbing. He was tired, his reserves of energy almost depleted after his trek to al-Bab, but that was no excuse for his failing to see what lay ahead of him. He realised, too late, that he was climbing up to an escarpment. He reached the top, a narrow plateau that crumbled as he planted his boot in it, and then lost his balance and tumbled forward. He fell, landing flat on his face, the momentum enough to bring his legs up and over his head, flipping him so that now he was on his back. He started to roll, plunging down the suddenly steep incline with no way to stop himself. An avalanche of shale slid down with him, and sand got into his eyes and mouth and nostrils. He put up his hands to protect his head, felt a sharp pull as the sling that secured the M4 went taut and then an easing as it snapped and fell away. He rolled over and over, sideways now, his momentum gradually arrested as the incline levelled out. He rolled forward and bumped up against a shoulder of bedrock.

Salim must have fallen down the slope, too. He was ten metres away, but he wasn't moving. He was on his knees, his back to Pope, staring out into the desert at the single bright white light that was approaching them. The horizon was blurred, and it was difficult to distinguish between the ground and the quickly lightening sky, but as the light drew nearer, Pope heard the sound of an engine. It was a muffled whine, a purr rather than the usual roar of turboshaft engines, but he could see that it was a helicopter. It drew closer still, and he recognised it: an AgustaWestland AQ159 Wildcat.

Salim rushed ahead, waving his arms and yelling at the top of his lungs.

Pope instinctively brought his hand up, reaching for a rifle that was no longer there. He swivelled quickly, looking back up the slope of loose shale, and saw the M4 halfway up it. He was about to stand, but something told him that he shouldn't. Instead, he pressed himself up against the exposed bedrock so that he could hide behind it.

He peered over the top of the slip face. Salim was still waving his hands, and the pilot had evidently seen him, because the chopper was descending. The rotors kicked up a storm of wash, a vortex that propelled yet more sand into the air, and the Wildcat landed in the middle of it, the wheels sinking into the sand and shale as they touched down. The engine did not power down, the unusual muffled roar easier to hear now that it was close. The new day's sun sparkled on the black gloss of the fuselage.

Salim started to yell. He must have reached the obvious conclusion: the insurgency didn't fly smart new helicopters like this, so it must, therefore, be friendly. It was a reasonable supposition to draw, but still Pope stayed almost all the way down below the line of the bedrock. He watched as the door in the side of the fuselage was pulled all the way back and four men, dressed in desert camouflage, dropped down. They were all armed: two of them had FN Minimis and the other two had SA80 assault rifles.

Salim took a step towards them.

One of the men at the front of the group raised his rifle and aimed it at Salim.

Oh shit.

The bullets hit Salim before Pope heard the rattle of their discharge.

Salim fell back, landing flat on his back. The first man stepped up until he was standing over him, aimed down, and fired two more times.

And the second man looked out over the desert.

Toward the escarpment.

Right at Pope.

He had only been glimpsing over the top of the bedrock, with surely only very little of him visible, but now, as he pressed himself down on his belly, he found that he was holding his breath.

More gunfire.

Pope glanced up just as the top of the rocky shoulder exploded in a shower of fine stone chips.

He heard the reports from the rifle: *crack, crack, crack.*

Another impact, frighteningly close, and then another.

He was penned in. He looked up. It was three or four metres up the slope to the plateau from where he was, and the shale was soft and unstable. He could scale it, get up to the plateau and get out of range, but not quickly enough. And while he tried, he would be an easy target. The men who had just executed Salim would be able to aim and pick him off at their leisure.

He couldn't fight back either. His own rifle was stuck halfway up the slope. He could get to it a lot more quickly than he could get to the top, but he would still be vulnerable. He didn't think it would work, but he didn't have many other options. He certainly couldn't stay where he was. The folly of that particular course of action was reinforced as a round crashed into the shale behind his head, sending a little avalanche down onto him.

He crawled along the trench, changing positions, and then risked a look over the top of the rock.

Two of the men had advanced. Their faces were covered by scarves. One of them had a Minimi and the other had an SA80. The men saw Pope and fired again. Pope ducked beneath the lip of the rock as the rounds crashed all around him, a dozen little detonations of sand and stone cast into the air.

"Come out, Pope," a voice shouted up to him over the whine of the helicopter's engine.

"Come up here and get me."

"There's four of us. What are you going to do?"

Chapter Fifty-Six

I sabella saw the helicopter as it raced in from the horizon. It started as a small black speck, so low to the ground that it was almost indistinguishable. She heard the engines and the *whup-whup-whup* of the rotors, and she knew she had to see what it was. Aqil was unconscious now, and she didn't want to leave him, but she wouldn't be far away. She used Pope's backpack as a bolster, resting Aqil's head on it. She laid her hand on the receiver of the AK that was attached to the sling around her neck and jogged ahead.

She reached the lip of the plateau and realised why she had lost sight of Pope; he was at the bottom, sheltering behind an outcrop of rock that was before an undulating sea of sand dunes that gradually flattened out.

She saw Pope's rifle several metres away from him.

She saw Salim waving his arms as the chopper descended, losing him within the eddies of sand that were disturbed by the downdraft.

She looked down at the helicopter and she realised that they were going to be saved.

Pope must have called for the cavalry, and here they were.

She saw the door open and the men emerge from inside the helicopter.

Isabella was about to start down the slope herself when one of the men raised his weapon and shot Salim at close range. She dropped to her belly and backed away from the edge, staying just close enough to see over it as the man aimed downward and fired into Salim's body.

She glanced down at Pope pressed down on his belly. She bit her lip as one of the men raised his weapon, aimed and fired a volley that landed very close to where Pope was hiding. The other men followed his example and the desert rang with the sound of their gunfire.

None of them had seen her; she watched as one of the men turned back to the helicopter and held up a gloved fist: the signal that he wanted the helicopter to stay where it was.

Two of them advanced under the cover of the pair in the rear. They were closing the distance between themselves and Pope. She looked down and saw that Pope was on the move, too, crawling to his right. She looked across to his discarded rifle and realised that that must be what he was trying to reach.

Pope looked up again, and the advancing men sprayed him with another volley of automatic gunfire.

Isabella put both hands on the AK, sliding the strap over her head so that she could lay it flat. She rested her cheek against the receiver, closed her left eye and lined up the iron sights.

Pope flattened himself to his belly as the soldiers fired, a barrage that studded the slope behind him. It stirred up another fall of pebbles and he was quickly covered by them. He tried to slither back again, but he was frozen to the spot by another barrage.

"Come out, Pope."

"I don't think so," he called back. "Why don't you come up here? Let's talk about it."

"I'm going to count to five. And then I'm going to throw a grenade."

He heard the clatter of automatic gunfire again, but this time it was coming from above rather than from below him. He looked up to the top of the slope and saw muzzle flash.

Isabella.

He put his head up out of his fragile cover and saw the two men running back toward the helicopter. They were in the open and vulnerable, and although she hadn't hit either of them, she had bought him precious moments.

He had to take advantage of them.

He scrambled up the shale, his boots sliding as he clambered up to his M4. He grabbed the rifle, turned around onto his back, and started to slide back down the dune again. He dug his boots into the pebbles to slow his descent and aimed. The first three shots went high, but the soldiers heard them and ran harder.

The helicopter's engines grew louder and the rotors began to spin more and more quickly. It started to lift, the wheels emerging from the sand, a vortex of sand quickly obscuring it.

Isabella fired again.

The soldiers were sprinting now, running full pelt for the helicopter. Pope lowered his aim and fired again. This time, he was successful. A round hit the nearest soldier in the back. The man staggered ahead, dropped his Minimi, and fell onto his face.

The helicopter lifted up and into the air. The door was still open, and one of the men inside was reaching down. The second soldier dropped his rifle and leapt for the sill of the door. He grasped onto it and was pulled into the cabin.

Pope knew that they were still in terrible trouble. The Wildcat was equipped with a big Browning M3M, the .50-calibre machine gun mounted on a pintle in the open door. The pilot would simply ascend so that they had a few hundred feet of altitude, high enough to render Pope and Isabella's small-arms fire ineffective, and then the gunner would pick them off with the Browning.

He could only have a few seconds before they opened fire. He craned his neck and looked back; the helicopter was starting to turn.

"Isabella!" he yelled. "Get my pack."

He saw her head above the line of the sand. She was aiming her AK at the helicopter, and he saw the discharge from the muzzle as she loosed off a burst. There was too much noise—the sound of the helicopter, the report of her rifle—he didn't think that she had heard him.

"Get my pack!"

She stood and then stepped back, out of sight. Pope lost her.

Chapter Fifty-Seven

The helicopter ascended quickly and rotated through ninety degrees so that the port side was facing Isabella and Pope. She saw the big machine gun. One of the soldiers had fitted himself behind it and was taking aim. Isabella swung around as the gun opened fire, the big .50-calibre rounds detonating metre-high explosions of sand as they carved a track toward Pope.

She ran. She had no idea whether the rounds had hit Pope or not, and there was no time to check. Her elevated position had protected her before, but now the cover it had afforded had been negated. If Pope had been hit, then she would be next.

The AK-47 was useless to her now. She threw it to the ground and sprinted as hard as she could.

The sound of the helicopter grew louder and louder. It seemed to be directly overhead. She expected to hear the roar of the machine gun again, to feel the sting of sand as the rounds chewed up the desert floor.

She gasped for breath.

Faster.

Faster.

Aqil was still slumped against the backpack. She slid down to the sand next to him. She had seen the tube that was fastened to the side of the pack and thought that she recognised it.

It was an unguided disposable 66mm rocket.

It was a little over two feet long and, as Isabella unclipped the carabiners that attached it to the backpack, she realised she had no idea how it was fired. Her mother had discussed them with her, and she remembered that it consisted of one tube inside another one. The inner tube contained the rocket. The tubes were pulled apart and the rocket was armed.

She struggled with it, pulling and twisting it, but nothing happened.

She glanced up and saw the helicopter, nose down, off to her right, swooping in her direction. She saw the gunner as he adjusted the .50-calibre machine gun.

Come on!

She twisted and yanked and still nothing happened.

The helicopter was fifteen metres above the desert and thirty metres to Isabella's left.

"Isabella!"

Pope was running across the escarpment toward her.

"Give it to me!"

The pilot slowed to a hover.

She lobbed the launcher at him. He caught it, pressed down on a clip that she had missed and, with a loud click, the clasps that held the two tubes together were unfastened. The launcher extended and the sights popped up.

The gunner started to fire.

Pope swung the 66 around until it was resting on his right shoulder.

The fifty cal roared, louder than the engine and the rotors, and the desert floor exploded in a track of tiny impacts that aimed right for them both.

Pope pulled out the safety plug, put his eye to the rear peep sight, aimed and squeezed the rubberised trigger.

Whoof!

The round fired, the rocket launching it away on a fast upward diagonal track. It was too close for the fuse to arm, and instead of detonating, the missile punched a hole through the helicopter's side window, exited through the roof and ploughed through the rotors. The pilot lost control, the helicopter rotating sharply. The .50 kept firing, but the rounds swerved away from them at the last moment. The helicopter jerked downwards, quickly losing lift, and crunched down onto the desert floor. But the impact ruptured the fuel tanks and there came a huge detonation. The aircraft was ripped apart by an explosion that quickly expanded, a fireball of oranges and reds that tore it to bits.

Isabella slumped down onto her back and stared up into the morning sky.

PART FOUR

Montepulciano

Chapter Fifty-Eight

Aqil was dead. Pope had examined him, but it was obvious that there was nothing to be done. He said it was probably a subarachnoid haemorrhage, internal bleeding that would have been caused when he banged his head during the crash. It would have explained his symptoms and his sudden collapse. He told her that there was nothing that they could have done for him out there in the desert; he would have needed surgery, and that would have been impossible.

Pope left her with the boy's body as he went to frisk the dead men.

Isabella knew that Pope was right, but it didn't make her feel any better about it.

There was no time to bury Aqil, and as they hurried north, away from the crashed helicopter, Isabella turned back to the south to see a wake of buzzards circling on the thermals high above.

They had left a feast for them down below.

———

The terrain became more mountainous as bedrock and shale replaced the sand.

Pope paused for a moment. "Hold on."

He removed a satellite phone from his pocket and removed the rear cover. He took out the battery and a tiny circuit board.

Isabella watched him. "What are you doing?"

"I don't trust my orders or the man who has been giving them to me. There's too much going on here that contradicts what I've been told."

"What do you mean?"

"I think Salim was set up. I was sent here to kill him. Well," he corrected himself, "I came here to get you, but I had orders to kill him. The phone has a GPS receiver in it. I have a bad feeling that that helicopter found us because they used the tracker to find me. We got lucky. I don't really want to encourage a visit from a drone."

"Why would Salim be set up?"

"I have a few ideas about that," Pope said without elaborating. He put the pieces of the phone into his pocket and zipped it up. "Come on. We need to get out of sight."

⌣

They took shelter in a cave that Pope had spotted. There was a north–south road within a mile of their hiding place, and Isabella took Pope's binoculars and watched vehicles passing along it. The helicopter was too far to the south to be visible to her, but it was obvious that the crash site was the focus of the attention. She was watching the comings and goings just as a series of concussive detonations rumbled across the bleak landscape, preceding a bright explosion that stained the horizon. She looked up and saw a black speck high in the sky. She found the speck with the binoculars: it was an ugly aircraft with big air intakes and wings that bristled with ordnance, flying high and fast.

"What is that?" she asked Pope.

He took the binoculars and looked up into the sky. "That's an A-10 Warthog," he said. "They're clearing up the mess."

A pillar of black smoke reached up into the bright blue sky. Isabella put the binoculars down, retreated deeper into the cave and laid out to sleep.

——⌣——

They pressed onward that night, moving much more quickly now that they were unencumbered by Aqil or Salim, and they reached the border at two in the morning. Pope checked their position on his GPS and told her that they were five hundred metres to the south of Ar Ra'i. There were five miles between them and the larger town of Elbeyli.

The demarcation point was a barbed-wire fence suspended on concrete fence posts; Pope took a pair of pliers from his pack and snipped the wire to open up a hole big enough for them to slip through. There was nothing else to denote that they had crossed from one country into another, and although Pope warned her that they were far from safe, the psychological effect of crossing the border was marked. Isabella had flashed back to everything that she had been subjected to over the course of the last five days—the ambush, the helicopter ride, the interrogation and then the escape—and allowed herself a moment of relief that the worst of it all was behind her. The relief was followed quickly by pride. She had done it. She had taken the training that her mother had given her, the repetitive exercises that she had followed day after day after day both before and after her death, and she had deployed them to powerful effect.

She knew that she had grown up in the last few days.

And she knew, too, that she had begun to earn her legacy.

——⌣——

They left their rifles and the majority of their ammunition in a culvert just outside Elbeyli. Pope still had his Beretta and enough ammunition for most eventualities.

They stole a car and headed northwest, negotiating the whole of Turkey until they crossed the border into Bulgaria near Budakdoganca. They had no passports or any other travel documentation, but the border was open and they were able to drive across. They drove on through Bulgaria and made their way to a refugee processing centre on the border with Serbia that Pope said he had visited before. They abandoned the car and, obscured within a body of several dozen migrants from Syria and Iraq, were able to cross the border without having their documents checked.

Isabella insisted that they take a train from Pirot to Belgrade. She could see that Pope would have found another car and driven on without stopping, and she had noticed, with mounting alarm, that he had started to have difficulty keeping his eyes open, regardless of the cups of strong coffee that he bought whenever they passed a roadside vendor. The train was basic, with firm seats and a lack of ventilation, but Pope had fallen asleep almost as soon as they had pulled out of the station. He had slept throughout the journey and, as the train finally pulled into Belgrade's main station on Savska Street, Isabella gently shook him awake. He still looked tired, but the black pouches that had bulged beneath his eyes had receded.

They found a public telephone, and Isabella waited patiently while Pope made a call. He had lost a little of the worry in his eyes by the time he emerged five minutes later.

"Is everything okay?" she asked him.

"Yes," he said.

"Was that your wife?"

He nodded. "They're okay. But I'll feel better when we get there."

Pope said that they would be able to continue by train through the rest of Serbia and then into Croatia and Slovenia. The train stopped at the border, but the checks were rudimentary. Pope led the way to the toilet and they hid there. They heard the official as he made his way along the train, but they had left the toilet door ajar to give the impression that it was unoccupied, and he did not check.

They disembarked at Zagreb and continued into Slovenia by bus. The border checks were even less rigorous there: the bus stopped at the border post, the driver answered the questions of a bored-looking official who did not even board the vehicle and then they were waved through. They stole their second car, a Citroen Saxo, from a quiet public car park in Ljubljana and continued once again. They bent to the south and followed the E61 until they reached the Italian border at Sempeter pri Gorici. They abandoned the car, followed the border to the north, clambered over a six-foot-high wire fence and crossed the border into Italy on foot.

The town of Montepulciano was three hundred miles to the south.

Chapter Fifty-Nine

Montepulciano was a medieval town set atop a six-
hundred-metre-high limestone ridge that overlooked
the rolling vineyards that dominated this part of the
province of Siena. The *comune* was eighty miles southeast of Florence
and one hundred and twenty miles to the north of Rome.

Pope drove their latest stolen car, a Peugeot, through the narrow, winding streets until they reached a car park. They left the car
there and walked along the Corso, the main street that led into the
Piazza Grande. It was a beautiful space, a wide cobbled square that
was overlooked by the Duomo, the Palazzo Comunale, the Palazzo
Tarugi and the Palazzo Contucci. Pope gazed across the square to
a large stone building that looked as if it might have been adapted
to accommodate apartments. His bearing, which had been a mix of
anticipation and nervousness, now became pensive. They walked on
and his face darkened with worry.

"What is it?" Isabella said.

He didn't answer. Instead, he led the way to an outdoor café
next to a fountain with an ornamental lion and griffin. Pope led
the way to an empty table in the shade of an awning and held out
a chair for Isabella.

"What's wrong?"

"I need you to stay here," he said.

"Why?"

"Something's not right."

"Mr Pope—tell me."

"The shutters are closed."

"So?"

"It's midday, Isabella. The apartment looks out onto the piazza. It's beautiful. Rachel would never leave them closed this late."

"Let me come with you," she said.

He shook his head. "Just stay here," he said.

"Mr Pope—"

"Isabella," he snapped, "first of all, stop calling me Mr Pope. It's Pope. Or Michael. Second of all, just do as you're told for once."

She frowned at him.

"Please," he said. "Don't argue with me. I'll come and get you."

Pope reached the door to the building. It was self-locking, but something had happened to the mechanism and it was ajar. That was strange, and it added another layer to Pope's underlying anxiety. He pushed the door open and went inside. The entrance was communal, leading to a flight of stone steps that offered access to the rest of the building. There were four flats that had been created within the building's six storeys, each one accessed from a wide stone landing. The flat that he and his wife had purchased fifteen years earlier was on the top three floors.

The reception was cool, the stone cold to the touch. Pope waited there for a minute and listened. He heard nothing. His pistol was pushed into the waistband of his trousers, the barrel pushed up against his coccyx and covered with the tails of his jacket.

He reached around and withdrew it, crossed to the start of the stairs and ascended.

He stopped on the landing that offered access to the two lower flats. It was open, with a parapet overlooking the square. He listened again: he heard the sound of conversation from the piazza below, the siren of a police car in the distance, but nothing out of the ordinary. The couple who lived in one of the flats had a sausage dog, and he heard its claws as it scrabbled at something behind the door. He stopped at the door to the other flat on this level and listened again, but he heard nothing. It sounded as if it was empty.

He climbed again until he reached the third floor. A corpulent pigeon was resting on the parapet, and it resentfully flapped away as he ascended the final stair.

The doors to both flats were closed.

He crossed to the door of the neighbouring flat and listened.

Nothing.

He went back across the landing until he was outside the door to their flat. The key was hidden inside a plant pot that they left on the parapet; lax security, but Pope had never felt that their security was something that he needed to be particularly concerned about here. No one knew that he owned the flat. His nonchalance bothered him now, though. He wished he had given the safeguarding of the apartment a little more care and attention. It suddenly felt very vulnerable.

He put the key into the lock, turned it and pushed the door open.

He went inside and shut the door behind him.

The Asset had been waiting in the square ever since Pope had made contact with his wife. They had known that he was coming, and Maia had been able to make her way south from London in plenty of time. The grounding of civil airliners in light of the downing of British Airways Flight 117 had lasted for two days, but commercial pressures had been impossible to resist, and a limited service had been resumed. Maia had flown from Southampton because it was a smaller airport and security was less rigorous. The short flight to Orly took an hour and a half; she continued to Rome aboard an Air France Airbus A320 and touched down two hours later. From there, she hired a car and drove north.

Maia was dressed as a tourist, with a pair of jeans, a tight black polo neck jumper, and a leather satchel around her shoulder. She knew that she was as anonymous as she could be as she made her way across the busy square. She had forced the door when she had visited the apartment the previous evening, and it had not been fixed yet. She pushed it open and slipped inside.

She had a camera around her neck, but she took it off and left it on the wooden table that the owners of the apartments used as a repository for their uncollected post. She paused to take out a pair of latex gloves and overshoes from her pocket. She carefully pulled the gloves onto her hands and unrolled the overshoes over her boots. She would leave no trace of herself after her work was done—no fingerprints, no footprints—just as she had left no trace when the snatch team had visited before. There would be nothing that could be followed back to her. Her caution might not even have mattered. Maia's fingerprints had never been taken and her unusual DNA was not in any database. She had no friends. The list of people who might recognise her likeness was very limited. But her training had instilled in her an almost constitutional aversion to even the slightest possibility of detection.

She removed a shoulder holster from the satchel and put it on, pulled out her pistol and started to ascend the stairs.

Isabella exhaled in frustration, but she did as Pope had instructed. She settled back against the wooden chair and watched as Pope crossed the piazza. He was cautious, making a slow approach and stopping several times to ensure that he wasn't followed or observed. But it would have been almost impossible to be certain of that. The square was busy with tourists and locals going about their business. Isabella watched as Pope approached the building's studded wooden door, opened it and went inside.

"*Signorina?*"

Isabella looked up. A waiter was standing by her table, a notebook in one hand and a pen in the other.

"*Cosa vorresti?*"

Isabella did not speak Italian. "Excuse me?"

"What do you want, Miss?"

The waiter was standing at the side of the table between her and Pope's building. He was blocking her view. She thought that she saw movement behind the waiter. Someone was at the door to the building. She craned her neck to look around the waiter, but there was no one there.

"Miss? You can't just sit here. You must order."

"Coffee," she said.

The waiter muttered something in Italian but scribbled down her order and moved out of the way as Isabella leaned back in her chair to look around him to the other side. She had been sure she had seen someone—a woman, she thought it was a woman—but there was no one there now.

She looked out across the piazza. There was nothing that stood out. Tourists milled around, taking photographs of the Duomo. A small delivery van was parked next to a delicatessen as the driver unloaded produce from the back. Nothing out of the ordinary.

She had promised Pope that she would wait for him at the café, but she knew better than to doubt her instincts. There had been someone there.

She got up.

Chapter Sixty

The apartment was set out across three generous storeys that provided a thousand square feet of accommodation. The first level, equipped with a pellet stove and a fireplace, included a large living area, a large eat-in kitchen, a bathroom and a storeroom. Pope moved from room to room. The shutters were all closed. Rachel would never have left them like that during the day; one of the things she loved about the apartment was the way that the sunlight streamed inside. He paused in the living room. He gazed around at the familiar Tuscan decor: exposed wood beams, Cotto d'Este floors, brick and Cotto frames, wood thresholds and ancient exposed stones in the walls. The place was the same, yet the warmth and comfort that he had always associated with the place was missing now. He saw things that he recognised from home: a jacket that his elder daughter, Flora, had left over the back of a chair; the iPad that his younger daughter, Clementine, had asked for last Christmas; the book that Rachel had been meaning to read, left splayed spine up on the arm of one of the comfortable chairs. Pope picked the book up and riffled through the pages. He realised that his nervousness had mutated into something much worse. Pope was terrified.

He climbed the stairs to the next floor. It was composed of two adjacent bedrooms, a bathroom and another storage room. He went into the bedroom he shared with Rachel and saw the old details that had charmed her when she had taken a week off work to view the selection of apartments that the realtor had chosen for them. He looked down at the beautiful herringbone parquet flooring and then up at the wood ceiling in their bedroom. He stopped, his stomach falling. The bedside lamp that he had chosen from one of the boutiques on the Corso was missing. He went over to the empty table, got down onto his knees and ran his hand beneath the bed. Something sharp abraded his fingertips. He lifted the valance and saw a scattering of small fragments. He took the largest piece and held it up. It was a piece of cream ceramic, the same colour and the same material as the lamp that had once stood there. It had been knocked off.

He went outside to the landing again. He felt sick. There was a telephone handset on the small table that was pushed up against the wall. He put his Beretta on the table, picked up the handset and put it to his ear. There was no dialling tone. Someone had cut the line.

When he turned back to the stairs, he saw that he wasn't alone.

There was a woman standing at the other end of the landing. She was taller than average, perhaps five nine or five ten. She was slender, with long dark hair that had been weaved into a French braid. She was wearing jeans, desert boots and a tight black polo neck top that clung to her curves. She was wearing a brown leather shoulder rig with a double holster.

The holsters were empty.

The woman was pointing a Sig Sauer P226 at Pope's stomach.

They looked at each other for a moment. She was attractive, her face given additional character by a slight roundness and a flattened nose. Her eyes were brown and distracting; not because they had any particular distinctiveness, save the complete absence of life. They were soulless. It was like looking into a black mirror.

She spoke first. "Step away from the gun."

Pope paused a moment just to gauge her reaction; she raised her aim a little, aiming just below his throat, and he saw her finger start to tighten around the trigger. She wasn't kidding around.

Pope slowly raised both hands and took three steps away from the table. The woman advanced as he retreated, until she was next to the table. She took his pistol with her left hand and shoved it into the holster beneath her right shoulder.

"Downstairs," she said, inclining her head towards them.

"Where is my family?"

She angled her head again. "Do you want to see them again?"

"Of course I do."

"Then do exactly as I say."

She spoke with the faintest trace of an American accent; other than that, Pope couldn't place it. It was neutral and almost without inflection. In its own way, it was as disconcerting as her dead eyes.

Pope stood his ground. He looked over at his confiscated gun in her holster and felt stupid and hopelessly vulnerable. He had been careful inside the apartment, stopping to listen at regular intervals, yet this woman had been able to approach without giving herself away.

Pope was at the end of the landing that was farthest from the stairs. The woman was halfway along it, next to the table, her back to the stairs. She was looking at Pope, her attention focussed on him, so she didn't see Isabella as she ascended the stairs.

Isabella was clutching a kitchen knife in her right fist.

Pope played for time. "Tell me what's happened to them and I'll go wherever you want me to go."

The woman kept her eyes on Pope and took a backward step that brought her closer to the stairs, and closer to Isabella.

Isabella closed her fist around the knife and raised it.

She was silent and obscured by the dim light in the stairwell, but Pope saw the woman's eyes flick across to the freestanding mirror in the bedroom. It was angled so that it reflected the door and, beyond that, the archway that opened onto the stairs. The woman saw Isabella as she lunged out of the darkness, and at the last possible moment, she angled herself away from her.

Instead of landing between her shoulder blades, the point of the knife sliced into the woman's right shoulder. It was sharp, piercing the black fabric of her polo neck, the downward swipe cutting into the top of the deltoid and scoring a line all the way down the triceps.

The woman didn't flinch or exclaim or give any indication that the knifing had caused her an ounce of discomfort. It was as if it was a minor inconvenience. Instead, she took a quarter step so that she was parallel with the wall, pivoted at the waist so that her trunk was facing away from Isabella, and lashed out with an upward kick. She led with the ball of the foot, striking Isabella flush in the sternum. Isabella was knocked off her feet, the back of her head cracking against the tiles as she slid across the floor.

Isabella had bought Pope a moment and he took advantage of it. He surged ahead, closing the three steps to the woman, encircling her with both arms and locking the fingers of his right hand around his left wrist. He hauled her off her feet, ready to throw her into the wall, but she stretched out her right foot and locked it around the back of his right knee. She was slender, but he found, to his shock, that she was prodigiously strong. Pope outweighed her by at least sixty pounds, yet he couldn't throw her. Instead, she flexed her shoulders and broke his grip as if he were no more than a child.

Pope managed to latch the fingers of his right hand underneath the shoulder holster and yanked her back toward him, but she hopped up on her left leg and lashed the flat of her right foot against his chin. He felt as if he had been struck by a trip hammer. He managed to retain his grip on the leather strap; it was only by hanging onto it that he was able to prevent himself from falling to his knees.

He reacted on instinct: he put his shoulder down and bull-rushed her. He thumped into her midriff and drove backwards, wrapping his arms around her waist and hoisting her off the floor. They stumbled through the arch together, crashed through the wooden balustrade that guarded the drop onto the stairs and fell into space. They slammed down onto the stairs together, the impact expelling all the air from Pope's lungs. He bounced down the last few treads until he was sprawled out across the living room floor.

Pope was dazed, his head thick as if jammed full of sawdust, and there was a buzzing whine in his ears. He was on his back, covered with pieces of debris from the balusters and the handrail. He raised his head, sending the whine up by an octave, and looked for the woman.

She was on her feet, one of the broken balusters in her hand. She reached him and swung the baluster down at his head. He rolled to the side as the wooden shaft struck the tile and splintered. She raised what was left of it and swung it down again; Pope rolled out of the way for a second time, managing to get to his hands and knees as she swung the baluster for a third time. He ducked his head and raised his arm and the shaft crashed against his shoulder. A starburst of pain blasted out across the right side of his body as he scrambled to his feet.

She dropped the broken baluster and stepped up to him. He had a longer reach than she did, and he was able to fire out two stiff jabs as she came on. The first blow landed on her cheekbone and the second on her mouth, but neither stopped her. The second jab pressed her lips against her teeth and drew blood, but she let it run down to her chin without any concern. He backed away, noting one small mercy: his pistol had been jarred loose from her holster during her fall. The polo neck had been slashed open by Isabella's knife, the rent torn even wider during their struggle, and Pope could see the blood that was welling in the long, jagged wound. She came on, and before he could think about looking for where his pistol might have fallen, she fired out a left-handed jab that landed square on the point of his jaw. Pope assumed that she was right-handed but, even so, her left still carried some weight. It was a stinging blow and he took a clumsy step back, instinctively raising his guard.

She followed Pope across the room, moving easily on the balls of her feet. He backed against the edge of the table and held up his guard as she kicked up at him, her right shin thudding into his upper arm, and then, with an easy distribution of weight that did not disturb her balance, she kicked out with her left, aiming lower, into his unprotected ribs. He gasped, a mixture of surprise and pain, automatically dropping his left arm to cover his torso. She kept her balance on her right foot, drew back her left foot again and aimed higher. The top of her foot pounded into the side of his head and he staggered away. A deep and welcoming darkness swirled around him, and for a moment, all he wanted to do was throw himself into it.

He resisted, stumbling away from the woman until he was in the small kitchen. The woman stalked him. There was a knife block on the island; one of the knives was missing—Isabella had taken it—but there were three others. The woman reached out for one of them and closed in on him again.

Chapter Sixty-One

I t took Isabella a moment to work out where she was. She was staring up at a ceiling, laid out flat on a cool tiled floor. Her head was ringing and there was a tight ball of pain right in the centre of her chest. Her arms were at her sides, and when she pressed down so that she could raise herself up onto her elbows, the pain burst across her chest. She remembered: the woman had struck her there, right on her sternum. She pressed her fingers against it and was rewarded with a fizz of pain that scorched up to her brain. Broken ribs?

She heard a crash from the landing at the end of the corridor and gingerly sat up. There was the sound of two heavy impacts, one immediately after the other, and then the clatter of debris. She put her hand down on the floor and pressed down, getting her leg beneath her and pushing until she was back on her feet. Her head throbbed with pain, and she had to put a hand out against the wall until she was a little less dizzy.

There was another crash from downstairs, the sound of splintering wood and then another crash.

Isabella went to the landing. The balustrade had been destroyed, with several balusters and the handrail no longer there.

She saw the wreckage on the stairs below and realised what had happened.

Pope's Beretta M9 was on a tread halfway down the stairs.

There came the sound of a meaty impact and a gasp of breath.

Isabella descended the stairs, her balance affected by the blow to her head and the lack of a handrail to help her. She managed it, knelt down and picked up the pistol.

Pope and the woman were behind her in the kitchen area. The woman was facing Pope, her back to Isabella. She had a knife in her left hand. Her polo neck was ripped on the right shoulder and down the arm, with a livid wound visible beneath. Pope, his face bloodied and unsteady on his feet, was trying to maintain the distance between them. His focus was on the knife, but as Isabella raised the pistol and aimed, he was unable to stop the quicksilver flash of the blade that ended in his right triceps. The blade cut into his flesh; Pope punched with his left hand and the woman danced back, leaving the blade stuck there.

"Get away from him," Isabella called out.

The woman turned to face her.

Isabella felt another buffeting well of giddiness. She steadied herself on the table with her left hand and aimed with her right.

Pope put out his left hand, braced it on a kitchen chair, and clambered to his feet.

The woman backed up to the open doors to the balcony.

"Mr Pope?" Isabella said, her eyes staying on the woman.

"I'm all right."

The woman was at the door now. "Stay where you are," Isabella warned.

The woman glanced over her shoulder to the balcony and the drop on the other side of the parapet. Isabella knew they were on the fourth floor of the building. It was around twelve metres to the cobbles of the piazza. Much too far to jump.

"Where are my family?" Pope said.

The woman must have been able to see how high up they were, yet she took another step toward the open door.

"Stop," Isabella warned her again. "I'll shoot."

The woman stepped back again, still facing Pope but reaching out with her left hand and pushing the door so that it opened all the way. She turned to Isabella. "I'm sorry about your mother," she said.

The wooziness swelled and she tried to blink it away. "What?"

"She was an impressive woman."

Before Pope could say anything else, and before Isabella could shoot her, the woman took two quick sideways steps through the door and onto the balcony. She launched herself up and over the parapet, clearing it easily, and fell out of sight.

Isabella lurched across to the balcony and looked down. She expected to see the woman laid out on the cobbles below, but she wasn't there. There was an elderly pair of tourists facing toward the Duomo. Isabella looked that way, too, and saw the woman. She was limping, her right leg dragging, but she was still moving quickly. She reached the corner of the building and disappeared around it.

The elderly couple looked up at the balcony with incredulous expressions on their faces; Isabella pulled back so that she was out of sight.

⌣

"Isabella," Pope said. His voice was tight with pain.

The knife was still stuck in his arm.

"We have to get out of here," he said.

She looked down at his arm. "We need to sort that out first. Is there a first aid cabinet?"

He shook his head. "We'll have to improvise."

He told her what they would need: a tube of superglue and a roll of duct tape from a DIY kit. Isabella went upstairs to the storeroom and collected them.

Pope sat down and rested his arm on the arm of the chair so that Isabella could see it.

"What does it look like?"

The wound was unpleasant: the knife was embedded almost halfway to the hilt with perhaps three inches of the blade still inside his arm. The blade had been dragged down to tear open a gash that was two inches wide from top to bottom. "Quite deep. It's bleeding a bit."

"Okay. Wash your hands."

"There wasn't any disinfectant."

"Soap is fine."

There was a bottle of hand wash behind the kitchen sink. She poured out a little of the liquid and scrubbed her fingers until they were clean.

"Good," Pope said. "You're going to have to pull the knife out, clean the wound and then dress it."

"How do I clean it?"

He angled his head back to the kitchen. "There's some salt in the cupboard. Mix a tablespoon in a cup of warm water and use that."

She found the salt, prepared the solution and brought it back to the table.

"Take the knife out. Do it slowly. If it's nicked an artery, there's going to be a lot of blood. If there is, you'll need to get me to a doctor."

She took a breath, took a firm hold of the handle and slowly pulled the knife out of his arm. Pope shut his eyes and gritted his teeth.

"Sorry," she said.

"You're doing fine."

323

The last inch came free and more blood bubbled up to the surface. She inspected it. "Not too much," she said.

"I might've got lucky. Might just have gone into the muscle." He lifted his arm up above his heart, grunting with the pain, and the flow of blood slowed. "All right. Clean it out."

Isabella poured the solution into the wound, rinsing the blood away and revealing the clean edges of the incision. Pope grimaced with discomfort.

"Well done. You need to close it now. I'm going to apply pressure around it, hold it together, and I think the bleeding will stop. Put a layer of glue over the top. That should hold it closed. Then we can dress it."

He reached across with his left hand and pinched his arm so that the edges of the incision pressed together. Isabella took the tube of superglue and emptied it, squeezing it and then spreading out the glue so that it covered the wound in a thin layer. Pope checked it, nodded that it was satisfactory, and held his hand in place until the glue had cured. Then, at his direction, Isabella folded a clean tea towel around his arm and secured it with duct tape.

Isabella looked at her handiwork: it was a haphazard job, but Pope seemed content with it.

"We've been here too long already," Pope said. "We need to hurry."

He told Isabella to go upstairs and collect the other things that they would need: a small suitcase and fresh clothes for them both. She found the case underneath the bed in the main bedroom and two changes of clothes for Pope from the wardrobe. He told her that she should go into the bedroom that was being used by his older daughter and pick out fresh clothes for herself from the wardrobe. She selected a pair of jeans and two shirts, holding them up against her body and concluding that she was of similar height and build to Pope's girl. She put them in the case, too, and dragged it down the stairs.

Pope took one of the clean shirts and put it on, carefully sliding his injured arm into the sleeve. Then he went to a drawer in the kitchen, collected two passports and laid them on the table. Isabella took them and shuffled from one to the other: the first was of Pope, although the name on the detail page was Edward Hughes; the second was for Pope's elder daughter. Isabella looked at the photograph. They both had blonde hair, although the girl's was longer than Isabella's was. They both had blue eyes and they were both of a similar age.

"Immigration never checks them properly," Pope said. "You'll be with me. They'll glance at it and assume you're my daughter. It'll be fine."

"So what are we doing?"

"We can't stay here. Whoever that was will come back with reinforcements."

"Where are we going?"

"We need somewhere to hide out. I need to think."

"Italy?"

"No. Farther than that. Come on."

Pope stopped at the door and went back into the living room. There was a framed photograph on the table of him, his wife and his two girls. He took it, opened the suitcase and pushed it inside. He tried to lift the case, but the effort caused him to wince in pain. Isabella took the handle from him and they left the apartment, descended to the piazza and set off.

PART FIVE

Palolem

Chapter Sixty-Two

Isabella stopped at the local store and bought the things that she had come into town to get. She paid the woman behind the till with a one-hundred-rupee note and took the change. The woman had looked at Isabella with suspicion as she rang up the goods on Isabella's first few visits, but those occasions were a week ago and now she greeted her warmly. Isabella had taught herself a few words of Konkani, the local dialect, and her initial butcherings of simple sentences about the weather or how delicious she found the old woman's rice were met with amused laughter, and then patient correction.

"How are you?" the woman said.

"I'm very good," she said, concentrating on her accent. "Thank you for these."

"My pleasure, Daisy." She paused, holding her finger up as if to say that she had remembered something, and then told her to wait. She went into the room behind the counter and came out again with a delicate white flower that was veined with purple. She held it up for Isabella to see. She recognised it as a Saint Anton flower, a sweet-scented bloom that appeared after the start of the monsoons in June. The woman beckoned with her fingers that

Isabella should lean forward. She did and ducked her head a little more so that the woman could slide the stem of the flower behind her ear.

"Beautiful," the woman said, beaming a grin so wide that her missing teeth were revealed.

Isabella nodded and smiled as she said goodbye and walked out of the store. It was the middle of the day and blisteringly hot. She crossed the road to her scooter. She had been in Palolem for eight days and had become fond of it. The town showed all the signs of rapid growth fuelled by the tourist industry. The old woman had patiently explained over several visits that the town had once been a small fishing village, and Isabella saw that the original shacks and huts were still visible in the older parts of town. The woman explained that it had become a popular destination for tourists thirty years ago when it had first been featured in Western guidebooks and brochures. It was an easy sell: an unspoiled tropical paradise, where no one wore shoes and fresh coconuts could be had from the daily spoil that fell from the trees. Isabella looked around now and saw the effects of that rapid growth: some of the local fishermen had given up their boats to rent out rooms to visitors who wanted to wake up to the sound of the ocean; ugly brick constructions, at odds with the traditional local architecture, had been built to accommodate restaurants with bland food and clubs that played music until the early hours of the morning. There were laundry *wallahs*, vendors in search of dupes who stalked unwary tourists, and massage parlours where a variety of services, not all of them legal, were available. Fishing skiffs were converted so that they could take travellers out to sea in the hope of seeing turtles and dolphins.

Isabella put the bag into the scooter's pannier, stepped astride it and started the engine. The main street was busy, with tuk-tuks buzzing to and fro, a bus delivering a fresh collection of tourists and private cars bulling their way through the pedestrians who strayed onto the dusty road.

She set off.

Chapter Sixty-Three

Isabella rode the scooter along the coast road and, after two miles, arrived at the steps that led down to the beach. She took the bag of provisions, put the scooter's keys in her pocket and climbed down. The surroundings were stunning. The sea was smooth, a mirror of deep blue that stretched as far as she could see. The seabed sloped down at a very gentle camber and the waters here did not have the riptides that could be found farther down the coast; it was ideal for swimming. The beach itself was a mile long and shaped like a sickle, and Isabella could see all of it from her vantage point. The two points of the sickle comprised rocky outcrops, clad with green and brown vegetation, that jutted out into the sea. The sand was so bleached by the sun that it was almost white, and the beach was unspoiled.

The nearest airport, Dabolim, was forty-three miles away, and the nearest railway station, at Canacona, was not convenient. The tourists who arrived in search of a Goan paradise tended to travel to other destinations. Those who came for the local hashish headed for the hippie haven of Arambol in the north of the country. Younger travellers, visiting for beach parties and lost weeks of hedonistic excess, went to Baga and Calangute. Those few travellers who travelled south to Palolem came for peace and quiet, a chance to lose themselves in the heart-stopping beauty of their surroundings, somewhere to step off the grid and switch off from the rigour of their day-to-day lives.

Local fishermen lived in the shacks and huts along the shore. It was more traditional here, with none of the new accommodation that sacrificed charm and authenticity for the speed with which it could be constructed. The little village had the laid-back, almost somnambulant atmosphere that must have been how things were fifty years earlier. The men and women still enjoyed a siesta when the sun was at its height; the doors to the houses opened wide again as the sun dipped down to the horizon. The men pushed traditional boats out into the shallows and paddled out to deeper water to fish while the women sat outside their huts and split raw mangoes into halves with cutters that they held between their toes.

A rough path divided the beach from the rows of old buildings that comprised the village. Isabella continued along it, passing boats that had been pulled up onto the sand. She skirted the ancient stone well that provided water to the village; she saw a child, whom she recognised as the youngest member of a neighbouring family, sitting on the edge while working on a juicy jackfruit. The path climbed a little and she was able to look out over the roofs of the huts to the fields that made up the interior, green paddies that were harvested for rice. There was a pen full of cows that were too addled to do anything other than stand around, swishing their tails to discourage the flies and the birds that swooped down to peck at them.

Their hut was at the far side of the village. She climbed down from the path, her sandalled feet slipping in the hot loose sand, and approached. The neighbouring dwelling was occupied by a young couple, a fisherman and his wife, and both of them were sheltering in the shade of a nearby cashew tree while they drank chai.

Isabella said hello as the woman pointed, with a smile, at the flower that was still in her hair.

Pope was lying on his bed. He had been asleep when Isabella had gone out, and the note that she had left to tell him where she was had not been disturbed. She stepped farther inside and closed the door. He was still asleep. She put the bag of groceries on the table, then put each item away, making as little noise as she could. He grunted once and then turned over, revealing the bandage that she had changed that morning.

Pope had been very ill. He had become weak during the flight from Rome to Mumbai, but things had taken a turn for the worse aboard the southbound Mandovi Express to Panjim. He had become delirious, and, when she examined the wound in the bathroom, she saw the pus that was draining from it and the red streaks that led away from the raw entry hole. She could see the wound had become infected.

She had decided that he needed urgent treatment. She had helped him to disembark at Kankavli and had taken him to a local hospital. They had been there for a week. The doctors had diagnosed sepsis, and had operated on the wound and then packed it with gauze and left it open to drain. A course of antibiotics lowered his fever, and the infection was eventually successfully treated. The doctors charged twelve thousand rupees per night for a bed; Isabella paid the bill with ten hundred-dollar bills that she found in Pope's bag.

She was going to cook fish recheado for them both that night. It was a Goan dish with a whole fish—in this case a mackerel—slit down the centre and then stuffed with a spicy red paste, after which it would be shallow fried. Isabella had prepared the recheado masala the previous night, grinding Kashmiri red chilies, garlic, cumin, peppercorns and tamarind into a smooth but thick paste using vinegar. The masala was versatile and could be used with other seafood dishes; she scraped the surplus into an airtight container, the vinegar in it acting as a preservative. She poured out enough water for the rice and set it to boil on the stove.

"Isabella."

She turned. Pope was awake. "How are you feeling?"

"Lazy."

"They said you needed to rest."

"No," he said. "I'm feeling better. It's not as sore as it has been."

"You can take as long as you need until you're better," she said. "It's not like we have anywhere to go." He winced, and she regretted what she had said at once. She hadn't meant anything by it, but given what had happened, it was insensitive. "Sorry," she said.

"Have you been into town?"

"Yes."

"And?"

She took out the printout that she had made at the Internet café. She gave it to Pope, helped him to sit and then left him to read it. She took a bottle of water from the small refrigerator and went outside. The sun was sinking beneath the horizon, a golden stripe reflecting across the dark, still water. Isabella hopped down to the sand and walked down to the water's edge. She let the warm water run over her toes, staring out at the uninhabited island three hundred metres out from the beach. She intended to swim out there when Pope was better.

She turned. Pope was sitting on the wall, wincing gingerly as he lowered himself down to the beach. She would have gone to help, but he was a proud man and she could see easily enough that he was already embarrassed to have had to rely on her. He dropped the last half metre and followed her footsteps to the water.

"Anything?" she asked. She had sent an email for him yesterday and the printout was the reply.

"My wife and children are alive. He doesn't know where they are, but he said he's had it confirmed that they are being looked after."

Isabella was about to say that it was like what had happened to her when she had been abducted and used as leverage to stop Beatrix from going after Pope's predecessor as Control, but the symmetry was obvious and she let it pass. It hadn't worked out so well for the previous Control. It had ended with Isabella standing beside his hospital bed, a pistol held against his chest, a bullet fired into his heart.

"What about what she said? About my mother?"

Pope shook his head. "He doesn't know."

Pope rested his hand on her shoulder as they set off along the beach together.

"What do we do next?" she asked.

"We get some answers."

Epilogue
New York

Vivian Bloom took Virgin Flight III from London Heathrow to JFK. He travelled in the Upper Class cabin and took the opportunity during the eight-hour flight to read the classified report from Maia's ultimately unsuccessful operation to eliminate Michael Pope. It was not a particularly long document and had been written with the assistance of the scientist responsible for the Prometheus project. It was couched in defensive language, the man very patently aware that the asset, the spawn of a billion-dollar R&D program that he had helmed for fifteen years, had been made to look foolish by one man and a fifteen-year-old girl. He was right to be defensive. It was a farce.

Bloom put away his iPad and enjoyed the three-course lunch— Waldorf salad, chicken biryani and a caramel sponge, together with a glass of an excellent South African white—before indicating to the steward that he was ready for them to turn his seat into a bed.

He lay down and got some sleep.

⌣

They landed at a touch before four in the afternoon. Bloom used his diplomatic credentials to pass through immigration and was met by a luxury towncar for the drive into Manhattan. He stopped at his hotel at Madison Avenue and 42nd Street to drop off his bag and then continued on. He felt a strange mixture of emotion as they carved a route through the glass-and-steel canyons: frustration that it had been necessary for him to attend the meeting; anxiety that so many loose ends had been left untied; and a little trepidation, generated by the reputations of the other attendees who had gathered in New York. Bloom was more used to inspiring disquiet in the people he summoned to meetings with him. He was not used to the shoe being on the other foot.

The meeting was being held uptown in a bland corporate building, a fifty-storey glass and steel skyscraper that thrust up into the sky between similar buildings that housed accountancy firms and legal practices. The blandness continued inside, with a sterile lobby and floor upon floor of identikit offices. The chrome sign on the front of the building referred to it as 'The Spire,' a proud boast rendered inaccurate by the fact that it was dwarfed by the taller buildings that shouldered upward on either side. It was owned by an unendingly complex series of off-shore companies and trusts, their own shareholdings obfuscated by labyrinthine arrangements that would have given most forensic taxation specialists migraines were they to try and untangle them. That was by design. There was no reason for the building, or its owners, to be investigated, but it was a useful blind should that ever become relevant.

As Bloom stood in the lift that sped him up to the fiftieth floor, he considered that the building was owned not so much by any particular corporate entity as by a purpose. It was the physical space—one of several around the world—that housed the conspiracy, a place in which the plans and stratagems that would mould the future of the west could be planned and executed.

"Vivian!"

Bloom stepped into the conference room and saw that he was the last to arrive.

He looked at his watch. "I thought we were starting at six?"

Jamie King gave him one of his million-dollar smiles. "We are. We haven't got going yet."

Bloom hated the idea that they might have begun without him, and he hated Jamie King, too. The man was the founding director of Manage Risk, the world's largest military private contractor. He was a former Navy SEAL and still had that overbearingly loud and clubby personality that characterised so many of the American military men that Bloom had met during his decades in intelligence. King was among the worst of them. The bleached smile, the hail-fellow-well-met attitude, the permanent tan, the unnecessarily firm handshake—it all epitomised the kind of snake oil salesman that Bloom despised. Bloom looked at King now, leaning back in his chair with his hands laced behind his head, and reminded himself that it was necessary to do business with men like him in order to serve the greater purpose that had drawn them all together. The ends justified the means, regardless of how unpleasant he found them.

There were just four of them in the room, a subcommittee of a much larger organisation that numbered several dozen men and women who were drawn from various military, industrial and political organisations. The larger body was a grand coalition that was derived from the United States, the United Kingdom and a handful of other European countries. There were representatives from national intelligence agencies and international finance, as well as political influencers. There were vested business interests, too, including, most prominently, emissaries from the defence industry.

'The larger body.' Bloom shook his head at his euphemism. He found that the more correct 'conspiracy' caught on his tongue, although he knew very well that that was precisely what he was involved in. A conspiracy of common interests that found perfect alignment in the pursuit of a particular agenda. A criminal conspiracy? Yes, when judged against the standards that regulated the norms of everyday behaviour. Murderous, brutal and immoral? Undoubtedly, and Bloom regretted that. Driven by greed and the advancement of an elite? Yes, for some of the participants, although Bloom was not motivated by those base desires. For Vivian Bloom, the conspiracy was justified. It had been founded by far-thinking individuals who foresaw that unless decisive action was taken, civilisation would be thrown back into a grubby dark age from which it might never emerge.

There was an empty chair next to King, and Bloom took it. Opposite him was Theodore L. Carington Jr. Bloom knew the man: he had been US defence secretary a decade previously, a hawkish presence in the government of George W. Bush and a key instigator in the involvement of US forces in the coalition to topple Saddam Hussein. He had served as Secretary General of NATO after his time in government, and after that, he had served as the US Ambassador to Afghanistan. Carington was chairing the meeting.

"Thanks for coming, Vivian."

Bloom nodded his acknowledgment.

"I'll start by saying that we are as frustrated as you by what happened in Syria."

"Frustration doesn't really cover it," Bloom said, as diplomatically as he could manage. "I was told that the assets were infallible. I recall that my agents were described as analogue, while they were digital."

"Yes," Carington said. "That was what we said."

"And yet—and please correct me if I'm wrong—it appears that one of my agents, together with a fifteen-year-old girl, was able to subdue Maia and escape. That does leave me rather exposed back home."

"Yes. I'm sure it does. And again, it was unfortunate."

Bloom turned to the fourth man in the room. He was tall and slender, with a shaven head and glasses that would not have looked out of place in the office of a Silicon Valley start-up. Bloom had met him only once, at a high-level conference in New York. His name was Dr Nikita Valeryevich Ivanosky, and he was one of the senior staff responsible for Prometheus. "Have you spoken to her?"

"To Maia? Yes, she has been debriefed. Your Mr Pope was resourceful, but Maia easily had his measure. The girl"—he looked down at his notes—"Isabella Rose, surprised her. The girl had a weapon and Maia was stabbed. Maia assessed the situation and decided that the best tactical decision was to retreat."

Carington chipped in, "The assessment was influenced by the fact that she had already secured Mr Pope's family. We don't feel that there is any reason to be overly concerned. His hands are tied. He isn't likely to do anything while they are at risk."

"Where are they?"

"We're moving them to one of our sites in Poland," Jamie King said. "We can decide where to take them after that."

"What about Pope and the girl?" Bloom pressed. "Do we know where they are?"

"They took a flight from Rome to Mumbai," Carington said. "We have footage of them at the airport, but we lost them soon after that. Our coverage is spotty down there, at best."

"Do you have agents on the ground?"

"Of course. We're looking now. But it's a big country with a lot of people in it. We might have to wait for him to surface."

"He will," Bloom said.

"And we will be ready."

Bloom sighed. Almost everything was contained. Mohammed was dead. Al-Khawari was dead. Everyone who could cause them difficulties had been removed. Everyone except Pope and the girl.

But they had successfully collected Pope's family. That much was true. Even if Pope could dig through the layers of sewage to the truth, it would end in stalemate. What would he be able to do?

"Pope and the girl are footnotes," King said. "Let's not be held up by them. The good news is that the operation is having the effect that we hoped. The Westminster attacks were an excellent start, but they have been underscored by the shoot-down of the jet."

Bloom allowed a nod. "Polling has shown a change in public opinion," he offered.

"Polling is very last century," Carington said. "We can do better. Our friends at the NSA have built data models based on search engine activity and reactions across social media, and we've seen a very striking shift. Before the Westminster attacks, the UK was indexing a strong negative attitude towards further activity in the Middle East."

"Once bitten, twice shy," Bloom suggested.

"Exactly," Carington allowed. "The index shifted to a slight favouring of action after Westminster, but it took a big swing after Flight 117 went down."

King leaned back in his chair, flicking a hand as if to dismiss the information as something he already knew. "That might be, but it's not at that level here. I was watching CNN in the hotel. They were saying that this is a European problem. Strictly European. Neither the Republicans nor the Democrats are interested in getting themselves tangled up with it."

"Intelligence is suggesting that the British are going to invoke Article Five," Carington said. "An attack against one NATO member is an attack against them all."

"Like that's going to fly. The president will shut that down quicker than the babysitter's boyfriend when Daddy's car pulls up. Daesh isn't an enemy state."

"Daesh might disagree with that."

"You think he'll give a fuck about what they say? He's running for a second term. He doesn't want America to be in another war that doesn't have anything to do with it."

"And we knew that was likely to be the position, didn't we?" Carington said patiently. "We're taking steps." He looked down at his tablet. "We're jumping ahead of ourselves, but we might as well touch upon it now, since you brought it up. Doctor—do you want to report?"

"I won't say too much," Ivanosky said. "We're running it out of Chicago Station. Mercury and Mithras are in the field."

"You're not using a cut-out?" Bloom asked.

"Like Mohammed?" King said. "No. He worked well for you, but we couldn't find anyone suitable. And we don't have time to keep looking. The moment is upon us. We need to act now. I don't think it's necessary to go into operational details, save to say that you'll know it when you see it."

"When?"

King looked at his expensive Rolex. "Forty-six hours. Multiple venues, multiple events. Public opinion here will be different by the time we meet again."

Bloom didn't press. He knew what King was referring to. They had discussed the options when they had planned the London operations.

"There is one other thing," he said instead.

"Yes, Vivian?"

"I have a vestigial vulnerability—"

"You have a what?" King interrupted.

"I still have a problem," Bloom clarified with extravagant patience.

"Then say you have a problem."

Bloom ignored him. "We need to remove all evidence of Captain Pope's old unit. Group Fifteen. The surviving agents all need to be found and eliminated. All of them who were active when we shut it down—there can be no trace of them or of it. I don't know what Pope told them, but they're going to wonder what's happened to their boss. And I can't rule out that he'll make contact with them, either. You said it yourself. Group Fifteen is a relic. It needs to be abolished." He turned to the doctor. "You've been waiting for a chance to demonstrate the effectiveness of Prometheus. I'm not convinced after the first demonstration. Here's a second chance."

"What are you proposing?"

"Lend me one of the assets."

"And then?"

"I point out the targets and let it do its work."

The doctor frowned. "Really, Bloom? 'It?'"

"I prefer not to humanise them."

"They are as human as you or I."

"I think we might have to agree to disagree about that."

"Stop it, Vivian," Carington said. "You're deliberately antagonising him."

Bloom held up his hands, palms facing outwards. "Fine. Just give me one of the assets. I'll find the targets. He, she, it—whatever word you prefer—it can eliminate all of them. One by one."

"Doctor?"

"Of course. Mithras is in Paris. We can activate him easily enough."

"Do it." Carington turned back to Bloom. "And once that's done?"

"We find Pope. We find the captain and the girl and we kill them too."

About the Author

Mark Dawson has worked in the London film industry and lives in Wiltshire with his family. His work includes four series: The John Milton series features a disgruntled assassin who aims to help people make amends for the things that he has done. The Beatrix Rose series features the headlong fight for justice of a wronged mother—who happens to be an assassin—against the six names on her Kill List. The Isabella Rose series is a high-octane action-thriller series featuring Beatrix's daughter, trained by her mother to follow in her footsteps and become a world-class assassin. Soho Noir is set in the West End of London between 1940 and 1970.